THE GREATEST BETRAYAL

A romantic thriller with a shocking twist

IAIN HENN

Published by The Book Folks

London, 2023

First published as 'Obsessive' in 2018.

ISBN 978-1-80462-065-6

www.thebookfolks.com

PROLOGUE

There is a bird that sounds like a woman screaming.

Liz Carter first heard that cry when she was ten years old and staying on her grandparents' rambling farm. She had imagined a lost soul wandering in the dark, and the thought chilled her. Now alone and on the other side of the world, she thought of the curlew's eerie wail as she crashed through the thick foliage of prehistoric-looking ferns. She sighted a very different bird, a vulture that was perched on a low-hanging branch just ahead. The bird of prey flapped its wings as it lifted off the branch and soared away among the towering pines.

From the dense woodland behind her, Liz heard the crunch of the pine needles that covered the forest floor as her pursuers closed in. Enraged, relentless, murderous.

She was short of breath, her pulse pounding in her temples as she pushed forward. The sloping ground was rough and uneven and when she fell, she fell hard, gouging her knee. Covered in scratches from the shrubs and clad only in underwear, she clutched a bloodied branch, her feet stinging from the spiky undergrowth.

The birds of prey that hunted her were armed and ready to kill. She was everything they despised, and her very existence was now the greatest threat to their way of life, to everything they had, and they would never allow her to bring them down.

She pushed herself back to her feet, adrenaline pumping and clouding the pain, and she ran, sweat running in rivulets into her eyes.

No matter how fast she ran, the crashing sounds behind her became closer, louder.

I can't outrun them.

She stumbled on a stone and her foot slipped out from beneath her. She hit the ground again, pain searing through her ankle. She thought of her baby son and the man she loved and the thought of never seeing them again was like a spear through her heart. Terror consumed her.

And then she caught a glimpse through the trees of dark shapes in the distance, revealed by the filtered shafts of dim light. Her executioners.

Just minutes away.

ONE

Two years earlier

Sheets of rain were driven across the tarmac of Kingsford Smith International by a brisk wind.

Sharing an umbrella as they dashed across the open ground were Liz Carter and Trans Pacific Air's new marketing manager, Martin de Courcey. Another hectic moment in a week that had been a whirlwind for Liz.

She'd had many discussions with senior managerial staff at TPA about their airline, the state of the aviation industry, and their future plans, always in the company of Martin.

With his own piloting days behind him, Martin had gravitated to the marketing role with ease. He was energetic, still passionate about aviation, more debonair now than he'd probably been in his youth, and his finger was always on the pulse of everything happening.

Liz liked Martin. He was a little frenetic and inclined towards the dramatic, but he certainly kept everyone's adrenaline flowing. He hadn't chosen the best day to take her on a tour of the airport's operations, but Martin de Courcey wasn't someone who changed his momentum to suit the weather. And this was the first operating day of her new agency, the first day TPA was officially her client.

The umbrella came down as they entered Hangar Number Five. It seemed to Liz a cast of thousands was buzzing around the metallic giant, catering to its every whim: maintenance men, technicians, flight engineers, servicing its mammoth appetite for safety, fuelling, checks and double checks.

Back in Martin's office later in the day, Liz savoured a hot cup of coffee and watched the rain beating against the window that normally afforded a grand view of the bustling, big city, Sydney airport.

'Your window on the world is temporarily out of order,' Liz said as she brushed a single strand of her blonde hair away from her face.

'Now there's a line with some pizzazz,' Martin said. 'You say we need an integrated PR and ad campaign with a central message.'

'Absolutely.'

'One big, single corporate idea, like the great ad campaigns of the seventies and eighties. That "window" thing, maybe that's it.'

'Maybe,' said Liz.

'I remember some of those campaigns. Those brands — airlines and cars and petrol companies — became iconic. Of course, that was all before your time, young lady.'

'All the more reason it's due for a comeback,' said Liz. 'The trick is to make your name synonymous with the product.'

'Just like McDonalds when you think of fast food.'

'Exactly.'

After leaving Martin's office, Liz waited for the elevator. When it arrived, a tall, dark-haired man in an airline captain's uniform came out impatiently, colliding with her.

'My apologies,' he said, a twinkle in his sky-blue eyes. 'Wasn't intentional.'

'So, sometimes you intentionally collide with young women?'

'Not when I'm on the job.' A wide, warm smile spread across his face. He offered his hand. 'My friends call me Mac.'

'And what does everyone else call you?'

'Mac.'

She returned the smile as she took his hand. 'Then I guess it's Mac.'

'I haven't seen you around here. New to the cause?'

'Visiting. I'll be helping with some promotion for the company.'

'Ah, that's why you're here. To see our salubrious marketing manager.'

'Yes,' said Liz. 'So, you *can* be observant.'

Mac laughed. 'I can.' He tipped his pilot's cap as he headed towards Martin's office.

The elevator had left without her, so Liz re-pressed the button and waited. She didn't look back at the airline pilot as he headed down the corridor, but his brilliant blue eyes, chiselled cheekbones, and wide, winning smile stayed firmly in her mind.

A handsome airline pilot named Mac.

The idea came to her in an instant.

Captain Mac of TPA.

Personality, charm, and worldwide travel. Harking back to the glamorous twentieth-century era of America's Pan Am.

His window is your window on the world.

* * *

Liz drove out of the parking station and onto the busy main thoroughfare that ran in a loop around the front of the airport.

The traffic was almost at a standstill, inching forward at a snail's pace. The rain had eased back but was still constant. The window wipers swished back and forth, someone tooted a horn and Liz's attention was drawn to the opposite side of the road, just a few car lengths ahead. A car was stopped in the middle of the road, its front doors open. Beside it, a man and a woman were in a heated discussion, the woman's hand clasping that of a small child who couldn't have been more than two years old. The child was crying.

Suddenly, in one swift, vicious move, the man pushed the woman over with one hand while using his other to grab hold of the child. He pushed the child into the passenger seat, slammed the door closed and within seconds was behind the wheel, screeching away, the road on his side clear of the heavy traffic.

The woman got back on her feet, screaming.

Looking back on it later, Liz didn't recall what her thought process might've been. She'd simply reacted.

Instinctively she spun the wheel, pulling her car out onto the opposite side of the road, and making a U-turn, narrowly avoiding an oncoming vehicle that screeched to a stop with little room to spare.

What on earth am I doing?

Her eyes fixed on the kidnapper's vehicle, she followed.

TWO

How could anyone snatch a child like that? In plain sight, out in the open. Terrifying the helpless child. And the impact on a mother; unbelievable fear. What kind of person…?

Liz's mind whirled.

The car in front sped up, driving recklessly.

Liz wanted to scream out, "There's a child on board, you moron. The streets are slippery. There's traffic everywhere."

She pressed on the accelerator, keeping pace.

With one hand on the steering wheel, she took hold of her phone with the other and called the emergency number, then she pressed "Speaker" and placed the phone on the seat beside her.

She listened to the ringtone.

Answer, damn it.

The car in front weaved in and out of traffic and Liz could imagine the child in the passenger seat, crying. There hadn't even been time to strap on the child's seat belt.

She pulled out in front of another car, desperate to keep the fleeing vehicle within sight. Horns blared.

A woman's voice came on the line. 'What is your emergency?'

Liz blurted out what she'd witnessed, and how she was trying the keep the other car in sight.

'Do you know where you are now?' asked the operator.

Liz knew the area well enough to give an accurate description. It was one of the main roads in the inner-city suburb of Alexandria.

'I think he's heading for the freeway,' Liz said.

'Stay on the line,' the operator said.

Liz's hands were shaking. She gripped the steering wheel tighter in an effort to steady them.

Focus, girl.

She wasn't certain how long it had been – it seemed like forever and they were on the multi-lane highway now – when the first of the police cars, its siren blaring, came up in the lane alongside her. And then, as it came adjacent to the fleeing vehicle in front, she heard the police vehicle's loudspeaker ordering the driver to pull over.

Another police patrol car flashed by alongside her and she pulled back on her speed, allowing that car to take up a position directly behind the kidnapper.

Thank God, they're here.

Liz didn't need to stay there now, she'd kept track of the abductor's position until the police had intercepted him. But she couldn't leave. For her own peace of mind, she had to know the child was safe. Another vehicle came flashing by, this one was a Channel 0 news van. Liz was reminded of that famous chase on a US highway, over twenty years before, when police cars and news crews had followed OJ Simpson and the riveting scenes had been broadcast live.

That chase had gone on for hours.

She slowed as she saw the car ahead pull over to the side of the freeway. The police surrounded it and the man stepped from the vehicle, hands in the air. Liz pulled over and got out of the car. She was worried about the little boy but before she moved forward, she saw a policewoman open the passenger-side door and take the child in her arms.

Liz breathed a sigh of relief.

Poor kid.

Before she could get back in her car there was a newsman and a cameraman in her face.

'Are you the lady who called emergency while giving chase?' the newsman asked.

THREE

Later, when she entered her apartment, Liz stood for a moment and gazed at the photo of herself, aged eight, with her mother and her father. It was moments like this she realised how much she missed them, and how much of a good, decent, loving man her father had been.

She switched on the TV and the late-night news carried the story. Scenes of the car chase and the police apprehending the vehicle; the reporter on-air relaying the events; and a snippet of Liz herself, being interviewed at the scene.

'What was going through your mind when you gave chase?' the reporter asked.

'I didn't really think about it,' Liz said. 'I just reacted. It seemed like the right action to take.'

'And it was a very heroic action,' the newsman said.

Liz smiled. 'Oh, I don't think so, anyone would have done the same thing.'

'Most people probably wouldn't have,' the reporter said.

She learned from the report the kidnapper had been the boy's father. The mother had court-awarded custody and the father was angry at the decision. The woman and her son had just arrived back in Sydney after visiting her family in Melbourne. She hadn't expected her estranged husband to be at the airport. He'd intended to take off to somewhere unknown with the boy.

Liz's phone rang. She glanced at the caller ID and saw it was Martin de Courcey.

'Liz, I just saw you interviewed on the news. Are you okay?'

'I'm fine. I didn't exactly get my full fifteen minutes though, did I?'

'One hell of a first day in your new business venture,' Martin said.

'That's putting it mildly.'

'Make sure you look after yourself.'

'I will.'

'An experience like that is nerve-wracking even if you're not feeling it right now. I know you're just getting your agency started but taking one day to rest up won't affect anything–'

'Not a chance,' said Liz. 'Too much to do. And, Martin?'

'Yes?'

'I ran into a tall, dark, handsome stranger leaving your office today.'

'And who was that?'

'An airline pilot friend of yours.'

'Oh. Callan McKenzie.'

'Why don't you arrange a meeting?'

'You're interested in him? Can't say I blame you.'

'Nothing like that. This is business.'

'Business?'

'I've got an idea I'd like to run by you.'

'If you insist on working tomorrow then drop by and tell me about it. Then we can arrange this meeting with Mac. Maybe a dinner at my place?'

'Okay, you're the boss.'

Martin laughed. 'No. I may be the client but you're well and truly the boss. I think today's events showed that quite clearly.'

FOUR

The campaign broke on a Sunday, with full-page ads in the weekend newspapers and banner ads across the major news websites. There were radio spots, and sixty-second prime-time TV commercials with a specially composed James Bond-style theme. The objective was to present a glamorous, youthful, trendsetting image of Trans Pacific Air and its staff, with affordability and a diverse range of destinations as key selling points. But mostly, it was about Captain Mac.

In a PR coup, Liz had arranged several articles and interviews with Mac in the main media, positioned to capture Mac's down-to-earth charm, his aspirations, his love of travel, his boy-next-door accessibility.

The campaign's launch party kicked off on a Sunday evening at the Mercury International Hotel, in the Rocks district alongside Sydney Harbour. As he arrived at the party, Mac wondered how he'd allowed himself to be talked into this whole damn thing. He knew the answer, of course, and her name was Liz Carter.

Mac had initially been dubious about the whole idea when Martin raised it at the dinner Mac had attended with Martin and Liz.

'How would you feel about being the face of a national promotional campaign for TPA?' Martin said to Mac.

'I hardly think I'm your man.'

Liz launched into her pitch. 'We want the public to think of TPA before they think of any other airline, and people do just that when they relate that airline to its staff. We need one very relatable face.'

'And you think that's me?'

'Yes,' Liz and Martin said in unison.

Mac wasn't the slightest bit interested in being the media face of the company, but he was more than interested in listening to Liz and spending more time in her company. She wasn't the hyper, motor-mouthed type he'd been expecting. She was calm and refined, with strawberry blonde hair and a cute grin that was, if anything, disarming. Being part of her campaign was a sure-fire way of getting to know her better.

* * *

From the moment Mac stepped into the launch event at the Mercury International, he was confronted by a whirlwind of introductions, handshakes, and photo ops. Cameras flashed. And, when the CEO of TPA, followed by Martin, addressed the crowd, they ushered him on stage. More photos. Thank God he didn't have to give a speech or answer any questions.

He'd been handling the attention and the networking okay, but he was drained.

When he found himself again in company that included Liz, he whispered in her ear, 'I think you owe me a quiet nightcap at the nearest cafe, *big time*.'

'Give it another twenty, the night will start winding down, and I know just the place.'

'How do we get out of here without an entourage?'

'There's a side exit, past the restrooms,' Liz said. 'Perfect escape.'

'I'll be there.'

* * *

Mac felt the strain ebb away the moment he sat down in the cafe, further along the harbour foreshore. The Rocks district, which had been the city's first village in colonial times, was a mixture of cosmopolitan cafes and restaurants with quaint pubs and heritage-listed stone buildings.

'I can see the tension flowing out of you,' Liz said, taking her seat.

A waiter hovered, and they ordered coffee. Mac glanced at the skyline. It afforded a view of just part of the coat-hanger-shaped span of the Sydney Harbour Bridge.

'If that's life in the limelight, then the celebs can have it.'

'It's a bit much if you're not used to it,' Liz said. 'Sorry. Tonight was far more over the top than I anticipated.'

'Even for you?'

'I don't do as many functions like that one as you might think. And yes, they drain me too. And I'm not the one on show.'

'But you're the key behind the scenes.'

'Sure am.'

'Martin told me you're a country girl.'

'It didn't show?'

'No.'

'Grew up in Fisherman's Inlet, way down the south coast. Came to Sydney five years ago. Sometimes I think I've still got my city training wheels on.'

'Hardly. You're what… twenty-five, twenty-six…?'

'Twenty-seven.'

'Twenty-seven, and you've got your own advertising and PR firm.'

'More a boutique. Just me and a couple of assistants.'

'And clients like TPA. And quite a reputation, Martin tells me, in the industry.'

'That's thanks to Brian.'

'Brian Hartwell?'

'Yeah. His ad agency had the TPA account for fifteen years and he's close with Martin. Old friends. When Brian retired, his associates took over the firm. Brian encouraged me to set up on my own. I'd been working on the account, of course, and Martin had just moved into the marketing role from piloting.'

'It all came together.'

'Certainly did. I can't complain.'

'Brian and Martin wouldn't have backed you if you didn't have such a stellar track record.'

'I was incredibly lucky to have been mentored by the two of them. And what about you?'

'Similar in some ways,' Mac said. 'Though I'm hardly a country boy.'

'Mr City Slick.'

He laughed. 'Not too slick, I hope.'

'You're doing fine, so far.' She flashed her lopsided grin.

Mac responded with a grin of his own. *She gets me every time with that smile.* 'Martin was like an uncle to me while I was growing up. And a mentor. He's the reason I'm a pilot.'

* * *

Later, Mac walked Liz back to her car. 'Just keep your head down so you won't be recognised,' she said. 'You never know where those paparazzi are camping out.'

'You're full of good advice.'

'Seriously though, I hope that coffee went some way towards calming the stage fright.'

'You're the calming influence,' Mac said. 'And I could use plenty of calming while all this campaign hoopla is going on. Dinner, tomorrow night?'

'On a Monday night?'

'Fewer paparazzi about.'

'Touché.' She grinned. Looking into his eyes she had the unmistakable sense he was about to lean in for a kiss. Behind him, moonlight touched the waters of the harbour.

There was just a moment of hesitation, an unspoken communication passing between them, and... *yes*, he leant in.

It was a long time since Liz had kissed a man. *Really* kissed a man. She'd only launched her business two months previous. She had needed to focus on that, more than she'd focused on anything before. She couldn't afford distractions, and she certainly wasn't looking for romance. But this man, this Captain Callan "Mac" McKenzie was so damn irresistible.

To hell with it.

She returned the kiss the moment his lips met hers and it felt perfectly right, perfectly natural, and it ignited feelings of excitement and exhilaration she'd suppressed for far too long.

FIVE

Mac wasn't expecting the call he received at nine in the morning following the campaign launch. A producer from Channel 0's *The Morning Show*, asking if Mac would appear on the program that week.

Mac had hoped for a quiet day after all the glitz and glam of the day before. 'How did you get this number?'

'Came up in our research,' came the mile-a-minute reply. Then the producer was off with their spiel, one buzz phrase after another. Mac wasn't listening.

'You need to speak with the agency.' He ended the call.

After three more calls, from TV and radio stations, Mac switched off his phone. He wanted to call Liz and ask what the hell was going on, but he bit his lip. He didn't want to cause any friction ahead of their dinner. If Liz started receiving those calls and she tried to get through to him, then she wouldn't be able to. And that was probably for the best. For now.

He'd booked a terrace restaurant, overlooking the water, in the city's Darling Harbour – the extensive leisure and entertainment district, vibrant with its aquarium, maritime museum, Madame Tussauds, and its boardwalks, cafes, and restaurants.

Any tension Mac might have felt disappeared the moment Liz walked in. She was stylish as always, in a navy-blue, off-the-shoulder blouse, skirt, and knee-length black boots. A peck on the cheek and they were ushered to their table. Mac had no intention of raising the media interest. Maybe later. He just wanted to know more about this young woman.

'So, tell me all about this Fisherman's Inlet place,' he said. 'Quaint name.'

'Quaint town,' said Liz. 'My dad owned the local instant print and graphic design shop. I grew up around the presses and the art department. We knew just about everyone in town and probably the whole region.'

'Wow.'

'Small town, the only instant print place in the wider area, so not so wow. But it was a great place to grow up and I had the best dad – ever.'

'And your mum?'

'She died when I was nine. Brain tumour. She was so young, so vibrant one minute, then…' Liz felt the old familiar mist drift across her eyes. 'The illness happened quickly.'

'Oh, Liz, I'm so sorry. That must have been so hard on you and your dad.'

'They were so close. Soulmates. Dad never really got over Mum and he never ever let me forget her, or what a great mum she was. Every night, for years after, he used to get out a photo album, just for a short while, show me a picture of Mum and tell me the story behind the photo – maybe it was a day we spent at the beach as a family, maybe it was a shot of Mum at her school graduation, maybe it was a picture of Mum and Dad on an early date. There was always a story, and always something humorous.'

'It kept your memories of her much stronger.'

'Yeah.'

'What a good dad.'

'He was the best. A great man.'

And that's what I'm looking for, Liz thought.

'When Dad died,' Liz said, 'I was twenty-two. Everyone thought I'd take over running the print shop. But I wanted bigger and better things, wanted to spread my wings… bright lights, big city, and all that.'

'As in Sydney.'

'Yeah.'

'I'm guessing it wasn't the same there in the old town, and at the print business, with your dad gone.'

'I really just didn't want to be there any more after he passed,' she said. 'My dad and I used to spend our annual holiday on my grandparents' farm, way up north, near Cairns. After Dad died, I spent a little time there.'

'Reminded you of some good times?'

'Yeah. My grandfather was a real birdwatcher. He had an aviary on the property, kept a whole wide range of species. I never got tired of listening to them.'

'Are your grandparents still around?'

'No, they've passed.'

Mac's hand reached across the table and enclosed hers. 'I, for one, am glad you came to the bright lights, big city.'

'Speaking of bright lights,' Liz said, 'I had a number of calls today–'

'So did I. It's the reason I switched off my phone.'

'I'm so sorry. I know Martin and I assured you there'd be no great disruption to everyday life. Just a little bit of attention, mostly from passengers who recognise you from the campaign.'

'Does that mean I can sue?'

She laughed. 'Normally we have to beg, borrow, and steal to get any media attention for an ad campaign. I was doing well to get that little bit of press on Sunday when we launched. I certainly didn't expect every breakfast radio and TV show to want you on for a chat. Anyone would think you'd been chosen to be in the next series of *The Bachelor.*'

'No thanks.'

'Anyway, it *will* die down.'

'I'm much happier piloting 747s. The world makes more sense from up there.'

'I've probably got the hide of a bull elephant suggesting this,' Liz said, 'but if you did just a couple of those shows, maybe one radio spot, one TV, then it would be a great boost for the TPA campaign, the kind of publicity and corporate goodwill you just can't buy.'

'Won't that just invite more invasion of privacy?' Mac said, taking a more serious tone.

'Maybe for a day or two. But trust me, by next week you'll well and truly be yesterday's news. The moment the Kardashians or the royals do something, *anything*, you'll be forgotten by the hordes in a flash.'

'Cruel.'

'But true. Fifteen minutes and all that.'

Against his better judgement, Mac agreed.

Those damn eyes, I can't resist anything she asks.

SIX

When Liz first saw Raffaello Vetrani, he struck her as being like a golden-era Hollywood matinee idol but with the attitude, swagger, and the bad-boy charm of a twenty-first-century rapper. She wasn't sure she liked him though he had a commanding presence that was hard to ignore. His brother, Bruno, was good-looking in a different way, softer, more laid-back, projecting an affable rather than an arrogant nature.

They were seated in front of Martin's desk. When Liz entered the office, Martin, Raffaello, and Bruno all rose and Martin introduced them.

When he introduced Raffaello, the young northern Italian said, 'But please, Liz, call me Raf. Everyone does.'

'He wouldn't recognise the name if you called him Raffaello,' Bruno said.

'Whereas my little brother looks, sounds, and acts like a Bruno.' Raf wrapped his arm around his brother's shoulders. 'Isn't that right, little bro?'

Bruno smiled.

Liz couldn't help but notice the smile was both half-hearted and short-lived.

Sibling rivalry?

'The Vetranis own the catering firm that supplies TPA,' Martin told Liz. 'I've known these lads for… what? Three years…?'

'Closer to four,' Bruno said. 'Martin's been like an uncle and a mentor to us.'

'They asked for an introduction to you,' said Martin.

'We also own a number of other businesses,' Raf said. 'One of those is the Big Bear chain of petrol and convenience outlets.'

'We've been blown away by the ad campaign you've been running for TPA the past week,' Bruno said.

'It's had incredible cut-through,' Martin said.

'Not to mention your incredible act of bravery a little while back,' Raf said.

Liz waved the comment away. 'The sooner everyone forgets about that the better. I only want media attention on my clients and their products.'

Bruno nodded. 'Good to hear.'

'Cutting to the chase, Liz,' Raf said, 'we'd love it if we could sign up your firm to give us plenty of that media attention for Big Bear. We're budgeting for a big spend, and quite simply, we want to blow all the other P & Cs out of the water.'

'Nothing too ambitious, then,' said Liz.

Raf roared with laughter. 'No, we're quite timid that way.' He elbowed his brother. 'Aren't we, Bruno?'

'My brother is such an introvert,' Bruno said in a deadpan manner. 'But if he doesn't get his own way, he calls in his army.'

'Oh, I can vouch for that,' Martin said, exchanging a smile with Raf.

'If blowing the other P & Cs out of the water is what you want,' said Liz, 'then that is exactly what we're going to do.'

Raf lifted his right eyebrow, his expression one of satisfaction. 'And that is exactly what I wanted to hear,' he said.

SEVEN

'Talk about a whirlwind of a week,' Mac said, as Martin de Courcey placed the beers on the table. Both men pulled up bar stools. 'I feel like I've become this fictional Captain Mac character.'

'Nothing fictional about you.' Martin raised his glass. 'Cheers.'

'Cheers,' said Mac. 'But I really need to get back in the cockpit.'

'Your schedule's back to normal after the weekend,' Martin said. He'd had the airline rearrange the pilot schedules, so they could take advantage of the media interest in their campaign star. 'Those TV and radio appearances have given the first week of the campaign a mega-boost beyond anything Liz or I would ever have dreamed.'

'So I'm finally off the hook?'

'If Liz says you are.'

'She says I am.'

'Then you are.'

Both men laughed.

'The ad campaign will continue, of course,' Martin said. 'And yes, the public will go on associating Captain Mac with the airline – in a good way – but there's no reason why you can't get back to your regular life.'

'Good to know.'

'You've come a long way, Mac, since...' Martin shrugged. 'Well, you know–'

'Indonesia,' said Mac.

'I remember you once told me that time might heal some sorrows but not yours.'

'Low point.'

'Yes.'

'I'm glad to say "time" did its job after all.'

'And you and Liz?'

'She's fantastic.'

A couple of gorgeous young women appeared at their side, seemingly out of nowhere. 'Excuse me,' said the taller of the two, 'but we were over by the window, and we couldn't help but notice. You're... are *you* Captain Mac?'

Mac's smile was one of embarrassment. 'Well... yes...'

The women giggled. 'Could we get your autograph?' they said, almost in unison.

Mac shrugged. 'Ah... yes, of course.'

He reached into his pocket for a pen, catching Martin's eyes as he did. The TPA marketing man winked, as if to say "Relax, it's all a bit of fun but it *will* get back to normal."

* * *

After his end-of-week drink with Martin, Mac headed home.

Liz had a late function with another client, so Mac was opting for a quiet, early night. He reflected on the past week. Three TV interviews, half a dozen radio and magazine sessions, photo shoots – but most importantly, three evening dinner dates with Liz Carter.

They'd clicked, and he already felt as though he'd known her a lot longer.

Like forever.

He slept well, woke early, poured a coffee, sat on his balcony, and fired up his laptop. He clicked on *The Daily Chronicle* website and settled in to read the news.

His eyes couldn't help but be drawn immediately to a special feature article.

> *MEDIA FAVOURITE "CAPTAIN MAC'S" TRAGIC ROMANCE*
>
> *The face of TPA's national promotional campaign, Captain Callan "Mac" McKenzie, seems to be as popular with the press as a reality TV star, even if he doesn't have a reality series behind him. McKenzie may be wining and dining his PR lady Liz Carter, the woman who recently thwarted a child kidnap, and he may have the nation's females swooning over his dashing looks.*
>
> *However, "Captain Mac" also has a very real, very tragic romantic past with the daughter of an Indonesian family, the Sanjayas — a family with known links to crime and terrorism.*

Mac's heartbeat drummed in his ears as he read. The story was over-sensationalised, its slant on events totally misleading. He felt his anger rise. His mouth was dry, and his fury rose even further as his eyes focused on the name of the journalist whose byline was on the article.

EIGHT

It wasn't long before Mac's smartphone started ringing and didn't stop. He didn't answer. Nor did he switch the phone off. He wanted to see how long it would take for the pack of media vultures to stop swooping.

They didn't.

There wasn't more than a minute or two between some of the calls. However, most of the time as one ring ceased, another cut in immediately. By midday, Mac was over it and he switched it off.

There was a knock on the door of his apartment within minutes.

Liz.

She looked distraught. 'Mac, I'm so sorry, I had no idea–'

'You couldn't have known,' Mac said. 'I never told you about Sari Sanjaya, or that time in Jakarta. I've tried to forget. One day I would've–'

'You needed to be ready to talk about it.'

'Yes.'

'This journalist…'

'Carl Vickerson.'

'He was there?'

'Yeah.'

'And you had no idea he was going to write this article?'

'God, no. I haven't seen or spoken with Vickerson in years. He's obviously seen the campaign, the media attention, and decided to cash in on it for himself.'

'He had no right…'

'Not that I'm a film celeb, but does the media have the right to invade the privacy of film celebs the way it does?'

'Morally? No…'

'But there's nothing to stop them.'

'You could sue.'

'And invite even more attention and scrutiny…'

Liz's shoulders sagged. 'I've brought all this on you.'

Mac led her to his lounge. 'Take a load off,' he said, motioning for her to sit. 'And, please, don't blame yourself. You could never have known there was an issue like this or that someone like Vickerson would exploit it. I never even considered it myself. Why would I?'

'I know it's no consolation now,' Liz said, 'but this will soon blow over. Those gossip rags are the queens of the short attention span. They have a big new celeb exposé every five minutes.'

He shrugged. 'I know. Martin would say just take deep breaths. Ride it out.'

'Anything else this Vickerson can use to keep his story going?'

'That's what worries me. There isn't. But, Liz, most of the stuff in his article is pure invention.'

'It implies you knew Sari and her dad were involved with local rebel outfits.'

'Liz, his article implies I helped them. It's Vickerson *himself* who had involvements.'

'What kind?'

'Gunrunning.'

'*Guns*. Is there… proof of that?'

'No. But it became clear to me, the last night I was there, Vickerson used his cover as a foreign correspondent for other activities. And he was well-connected to an underground network when it came to spiriting people out of the country.'

'I spoke briefly with Martin before I came over,' Liz said. 'He says he's always felt responsible for introducing you to—'

'Everyone needs to stop feeling so responsible. I went to Indonesia under my own steam.'

'And this woman?'

'Sari.'

'What happened, Mac?'

Mac allowed his mind to be drawn back to that previous time in his life. 'Indonesia is a place of ongoing religious and political unrest that's completely at odds with the wonderful people there. Back then, Martin had a mild heart attack, so you'd hardly think Indonesia the place to go and rest up. But Martin loved the country, visited it often and was very good friends with Benny Sanjaya, a local businessman who lived on a boat on the harbour in Makassar.'

'And this was Sari's father?'

'Yes.' Mac had never forgotten his first view of the Indonesian islands, when he'd first gone there to visit his "honorary" uncle, Martin. Peering through the window of the descending plane, he'd been in awe of the islands, spread out all the way to the horizon like stepping stones. The chain of thirteen thousand tiny islands lined the equator, covering most of the East Indies. It was a mind-blowing thought. And he'd found the beauty of the whole region breathtaking.

'Martin had described Benny to me as having a boar-like appetite, a sumo wrestler's strength and a grin that could light up the heavens.' Mac allowed himself a brief smile at the memory. 'I remember thinking, the first time I met him, he fitted the description perfectly.'

'He was quite the character, then?'

'Oh yeah,' said Mac. 'And his daughter, Sari, ran the business side of things for him. Her father had been holding back on certain cargo runs until a recent surge in uprisings had passed, but Sari was frustrated by this, didn't think they should be allowing local troubles to affect the cargo runs.'

'She sounds headstrong.'

'You wouldn't have known it to look at her,' Mac said. 'Cute, petite… but oh yes, headstrong. Stubborn. And I would've told you about Sari at some point or other, Liz. First great love of my life, I guess, or something like that. Took me a while to get over her. But it was three years ago. A different life.'

'And this journo Vickerson was a friend of Benny's?'

'Yes.'

'And you're worried he'll keep his articles going with more lies and innuendo about you and the Sanjayas?' Liz said.

'To be honest, I have no idea what that man is capable of.'

'Then we speak to the lawyers,' said Liz. 'We see if we can take out an injunction against any more stories about you that are slanderous.'

'I'll do better than that,' Mac said.

'What do you mean?'

'I'm going to see Vickerson myself.'

NINE

Mac spent the day with Liz. They walked around the boulevards at Darling Harbour, ate lunch by the water, and Mac told her about Sari and those early days in Indonesia.

It brought the memories and the emotions flooding back, stronger than he'd anticipated.

'That's totally normal,' Liz said. 'It was a very emotional time in your life. It had a profound effect on you.'

'Now you're a counsellor,' he said.

'Pop psychology 101,' she said with a grin. 'I read it in a Sunday magazine.'

That night Mac lay awake in bed, his mind still going at a million miles an hour. The memories, now switched back on, wouldn't stop, flashing by at super-speed, and he found himself reliving that earlier time on fast forward.

Benny had been recovering from a serious bout of hepatitis, and Martin had stayed on there, flying the cargo plane until Benny was able to step back in.

Mac remembered Makassar as a racial melting pot, teeming with noise and colour, many of its streets and buildings steeped in history from another era. He recalled being met at Makassar Airport by Martin who then took him to Benny Sanjaya's home.

"Home" was not a house or a bungalow or an apartment but a two-masted *pinisi* sailing boat moored on Paotere Harbour.

* * *

'My father and I are always pleased to meet friends of Martin's,' Sari had said when she and Mac were introduced.

'And the best way to do that is to sit down to a meal together,' Benny said.

'Best way to approach everything here is to eat,' Martin quipped.

'Suits me,' said Mac, 'I'm famished.'

That first evening with the Sanjayas had been one of delicious food, laughter and good conversation.

Sari had accompanied Mac and Martin on a flight to Surakarta the following day where she had taken Mac to some friends of hers that bred Java ponies. These were light-bodied, short-necked, robust horses, popular with farmers, a breed of pony that had a long history on the islands, descending from the Mongolian wild horses of a previous era.

Sari told Mac what she knew of the ponies when she took him riding in the nearby rainforest.

A dirt road cut a winding path through dense green undergrowth. Magnificent, one-hundred-foot trees cast an emerald canopy above them. They stopped at a clearing and allowed the horses to drink from a stream. Leaning against a tree, Mac watched as Sari stretched out on a level patch of grass. He could not take his eyes away from her as the filtered sun caught different angles of her face. Her hair was ebony. Long and straight, it cascaded like silk over her slender shoulders.

'I can hardly believe how peaceful it is here,' Mac said.

'That's why I wanted to show you this place,' Sari said. 'Indonesia is not all noise.' She had only a light accent but she purposely accentuated it now, imitating some of the older women from the street markets whose English was less fluent than hers. 'It's not all busy, busy, busy.' She giggled.

They sat together by the stream and Sari asked him about his life back in Sydney. They hadn't been seated long when, on an impulse, Mac leaned in and kissed her. It wasn't an act he'd pre-planned or in fact considered at all, but his heart leapt as Sari returned the kiss, her mouth covering his, her fingers clasping the hair at the nape of his neck.

This wasn't turning into remotely anything like the visit Mac had expected.

The days turned into weeks and Mac didn't want to leave the world he'd discovered anew in Indonesia. There was an election looming and as a result, in some parts of the country, there was religious and political unrest, and rebel uprisings. They didn't concern him. They seemed a world away from the *pinisi* in the harbour where he and Sari made love in the early evenings while Benny was at the local tavern.

Steeped in his country's traditional culture, Benny wouldn't have approved of premarital lovemaking between his daughter and Mac. Sari was always discreet. She was a member of the more liberal-minded generation growing up in Indonesia, influenced by the Western world and less tied to the traditions of their parents.

'I don't know if I want to go back,' Mac said to Martin one lazy Sunday afternoon as they lounged about on the deck. Sari was away at the markets.

'You have to go back,' Martin said with a note of concern. 'You have a career, and what's more, a bright future ahead at TPA. Besides, would you be happy staying forever in a place like this? Sure, it's a novelty now, but in a few years you'll wonder what the hell you were thinking.'

'The way I feel about Sari is no novelty.'

'I can see that. But the two of you would be better off in your world – our world, Mac – than here. That's my take, anyway, though that's up to you and Sari and her dad. Have you spoken to her about any of this?'

'Of course not. I've been here less than a month.'

'Speak to her, Mac.'

* * *

Mac was thankful his occupation helped their long-distance love affair. He chopped and changed rosters with the other pilots as much as possible to get as many flights either flying to or via Indonesia. The other pilots jokingly referred to him as the "Eastern connection".

It was twelve months later when he took his four weeks' annual leave and again headed to Makassar. As always, Sari picked him up from the airport and they drove across the city to the harbour.

Later, they leaned on the railing of the deck and looked out on the sunset – the sun was a glowing red globe sinking into the watery horizon.

'Four weeks together… so good,' Sari said.

'I love these times here with you, your father, and Martin,' Mac said. 'But we also need to talk about the future.'

'You want to know when I can come with you to Sydney.'

'We have a month here together now,' Mac said. 'But after that? It's a while now since your father recovered from hepatitis and Martin will be heading back home soon.'

'I know.' She looked down, wringing her hands. 'I want to start our new life together. I love you very much, *selama saya hidup*.'

'You're still worried about leaving your dad?'

'Yes. He's much better flying the plane again now…' Her voice trailed off.

'There's something else on your mind?'

There was a long silence as they stood, soaking in the atmosphere of the twilight, just a sliver of sun left, a faint glow in the distance.

'There's something I haven't told you,' Sari said presently. 'Something you cannot talk about…'

'I'm listening.'

'My father's been getting involved with a group.'

'What kind of group?'

'An underground group. He says they're not rebels. They protest against terrorists who come from extremist religious movements.'

'He needs to leave that to the government.'

'He doesn't trust parts of the government. And the government's been keeping a watch on this group that he's in.'

'Watching them for what?'

'The government suspects them of the same violence as the terrorists. Of taking the law into their own hands.'

'Like vigilantes?'

'That what the government *thinks*. But that's not the case.'

'Your dad has always steered clear of those kinds of things.'

'Maybe… but he's always had strong beliefs. He's changed since he's been sick… he's more outspoken now.'

'I know you don't want him to know you've spoken to me, but, Sari, let me try to talk some sense–'

'Please no! He'll see it as a betrayal. And I know his intentions are good, always good.'

'But, Sari,' Mac said, 'does he realise he could be placing both of you in danger?'

* * *

Mac glanced at the bedside clock. 3 a.m.

You've got to be kidding.

He needed to switch off.

Why am I going back over all this now?

It annoyed him Vickerson's article had brought so many memories exploding back into his present life. He went through to the kitchen, fixed himself a Scotch, and hoped that would do the trick.

I need to sleep.

And I need to deal with Carl Vickerson.

TEN

Liz was in the office early the following morning.

So much to do.

At 10 a.m. she realised she'd achieved practically nothing. She couldn't get her mind off *that* news article and its impact on Mac. She was worried about his intention to track down and confront Vickerson.

Am I responsible for this?

It was her idea to make Mac the star of the ad campaign, and it was the campaign's success that had lured the journalist to write the feature.

How can I help?

She picked up the phone and called Martin de Courcey. No one else had the influence on Mac that Martin had.

'Hi, Martin—'

'I've already spoken with him this morning,' Martin said. 'I think he should leave it alone, as hard as that is.'

'Thank God, he'll listen to you.'

'Not on this, he won't.'

'He wouldn't do anything… stupid, would he?'

'Not the Mac we both know.' Martin's tone reassured her.

'Why is this journo suggesting Mac was involved with rebels and guns?'

'It got his article published, didn't it?'

'What's this guy like? You knew him.'

'I didn't know him particularly well. I thought he was an interesting character, very opinionated, driven, a little on the edge.'

'And he got on well with you and Mac?'

'Mac never liked him. But they got along well enough, I suppose.'

'So, why's he doing this?'

'I've just been doing a bit of research, to find out what Vickerson's been up to these past few years. He was a foreign correspondent when we met up with him in Indonesia, but a couple of years ago he lost his job, he's been freelancing, but work seems to have largely dried up for him. I don't know too much about journalism, but as you're no doubt aware there's a lot less of that work around since the downturn.'

'You think he's desperate?'

'Yes. But while it's one thing for a reporter to dig up any angle they can on a story, it's another thing altogether to fabricate lies about someone.'

'Martin, I'm worried–'

'Don't forget this is Mac you're talking about. He was his usual calm self when we spoke this morning. All he wants to do is ask Vickerson to lay off, as one old *'friend'* to another.'

After the call, Liz sat quietly. Her phone was ringing but she knew it was one of her clients and she couldn't talk business just now.

I should call Mac, see how he is, see if he's tracked down Vickerson's whereabouts.

As she reached for her phone, her assistant Sally strode into her office, a beautiful bouquet of roses in her arms. 'Special delivery for a special lady,' Sally said. 'And that's not me talking, that's what it says on the card.'

'They're gorgeous,' Liz said.

Sally placed them in a vase and Liz opened the card.

Liz
They said you were good but in the words of Tina
Turner, you're simply the best, better than all the rest.
The proposal you sent over is absolutely brilliant.
We are in your hands.
Let's proceed.
The brothers Vetrani

ELEVEN

The sleek, silver bird glided in and touched down. It taxied along the runway and there was an immediate hive of ground activity, men on foot and in small vehicles, galvanized into action. From the far side of the tarmac, Mac stood in the shade cast by the main building. Long, afternoon shadows fell across the vast expanse of concrete and glass of Kingsford Smith International.

Like all major airports it was a world unto itself, a miniature city with its own pulse, rising and falling, speeding and slowing. It was the backdrop to a thousand hellos and goodbyes, fleeting moments of happiness and sadness, smiles and tears as people came and went. It was a world Mac had fallen in love with from an early age, a world he felt he belonged to just as he felt he belonged when he was forty-thousand-feet high, in the cockpit. It didn't matter whether he was flying a small four-seater or one of the mighty birds of the TPA fleet – the exhilaration, the sense of belonging, was the same.

He turned and trudged along the road that passed the hangars, hands in pockets. He felt he'd been on a rollercoaster ride the past two months. There had been the sudden explosion of attention and hero-worship from the media and the public. And the ugly, unexpected appearance of the story about his love affair in Makassar and the disappearance of the woman he'd loved.

For a time, the memories and the hurt had flooded back, disorientating him from the present. Eventually, those feelings had faded again. The media interest had finally died down. Good riddance to the fifteen minutes he'd never wanted in the first place.

His attempts to find and face off against Carl Vickerson had come to nothing. Apparently, the journalist wasn't even in the country. No one seemed to know if he had a fixed address anywhere in Australia. His business was conducted via email and publishing portals. He was known to be on the move, from one city and one country after another, chasing and filing freelance stories, demand for his articles far greater now since the Captain Mac article.

What had crystallised in Mac's mind was his love for Liz Carter. No matter what else might be going on, he felt incredible whenever he was in her company. For the first time in a long time, he wanted to ask a woman to share the rest of her life with him.

So why is the rollercoaster starting again?

The question filled his mind.

The text message had been on his phone when he'd woken that morning.

Mac. Would like to talk. Are you able to visit? Sari

Even though it had been three years, he still had the same smartphone number. An address in Jakarta followed. Sari was still out there.

Why had she waited until now to make contact?

Why now?

Would like to talk.

It told him nothing. It posed a hundred questions without answering any of those left unanswered years before.

He hadn't told Liz or Martin about the text. He needed to think this through himself. He didn't need the past coming back to haunt him. Not now.

He knew Liz and Martin would have those same thoughts.

Can I turn my back on a message like this?

Mac then reminded himself Sari had turned her back on him. Had she seen the news article Vickerson had published a couple of months before? Was that what had prompted this contact?

He and Liz were about to head off for a week's holiday, just the two of them. Liz wanted to show him the area around Cairns where she'd often stayed with her grandparents when she'd been young. Her grandparents were gone now, and their farm had been sold, but Liz wanted to stay in a motel she knew on the beach, and to explore.

Mac held up the phone, reread the text message again. He resolved then and there that there was no going back. He deleted the message.

* * *

It wasn't hard, Mac thought, to believe you could be in another country when you were in Cairns. It was the mountains ringing the city; the harbour, the ocean, the tropical climate, and the lush green landscape.

It was on their second night there, sitting on the balcony of their apartment in the evening, that they heard the plaintive wail of the curlew.

'It sends a shiver down my spine every time I hear it,' Liz said.

'It's as though someone out there needs help,' Mac said, and the moment he said it he regretted his words, as the thought made him think of Sari.

'Or it's just another form of communication,' Liz said, 'that means something completely different to the birds.'

The following day they drove into the hinterland, did a tour of local art galleries displaying the works of indigenous artists, and stayed overnight in a quaint stone cottage in a glorious forest setting. That night the past couldn't have been further from Mac's thoughts, it was the here and now and these past two months with Liz that consumed him.

He kissed her deeply and it was as though his heart, his mind, his soul was joined with hers. They kissed for a long time, curled in each other's arms, and when he led her through to the bedroom he removed every item of her clothing, her blouse, her bra, her panties, slowly and teasingly. They whispered to each other about the little moments they'd been sharing on this holiday. Then he shed his own clothing and his body pressed against hers, the soft touch of her skin like a balm to his spirit. With each move, each light caress, the heat between them ignited further and far eclipsed the steamy heat of the night.

When they returned to Sydney, Mac knew he wanted to ask Liz to marry him. At the same time, he didn't want to rush the beautiful, natural pace of this relationship. And he wanted the proposal to be something special. He began to drop subtle hints and there was no doubt in his mind Liz was feeling the same way.

It was another two months later when he received the next text message from Sari.

Mac?

Nothing more.
The same address.
He deleted the message.

TWELVE

Another sleek, silver bird touched down and taxied along the runway. Watching these mighty, man-made creatures of flight always calmed Mac. The world in the air was like a retreat to him, not just a job.

Those endless skies around the planes were like a portal of infinite possibilities.

He wandered the edges of the tarmac, keeping close to the buildings, waving occasionally to other personnel.

These past six months with Liz had been something special.

Six months.

I'm an incredibly lucky man.

In his pocket was a small box with the engagement ring he'd bought to present to Liz. And in his right hand was the phone on which he'd received another text from Sari Sanjaya.

Just when he felt certain he'd lain the ghost of the previous messages to rest.

It's been at least two months since the last one, hasn't it?

Why was she sending these messages and why now?

The tone of this third message differed from the previous two.

> *Mac. I have no right to ask but I need your help. Would you come after all this time? If not, I understand. Sari*

This time he'd responded, sending a text and asking Sari to phone him. There was no call and no response to the text. Agitated, Mac phoned her number, only to find it had been deactivated.

What kind of trouble was Sari in?

He returned to Martin de Courcey's office. He'd left Martin and Liz there over half an hour before, when he'd gone out to walk. And to think.

Liz had raced over to the airport when Mac had phoned her about the message. Martin, of course, was the only other person he could turn to, and confide in, with a personal issue like this.

Liz and Martin were sitting in the visitor chairs along the side wall, talking softly, when he walked in.

'A lot to take in?' Martin said to him.

'Putting it mildly.'

'What are you thinking?' Martin asked.

Liz was quiet, but her eyes were awash with the same question.

Mac leaned, half-sitting, on the edge of Martin's desk. 'Even after all this time, I need some answers on exactly what happened over there. I didn't think I did, I believed it was ancient history, which of course it is, but there's a… desperation with this latest text. Something is wrong, and I guess I… need…' He searched his mind for the right word.

'Closure,' Liz said.

'How would you feel, Liz, if…' His words trailed away. He looked into her eyes, and seeing the understanding there, he sucked in a deep breath and found the words. 'If I went over there, found out what she's been doing, and helped her if I'm able to. But I won't stay long.'

'I'll go with you.'

'No, this is something I need to do on my own. Let me put it to rest in my own way.'

'You need to be careful. Don't get sucked into anything dangerous.'

'Martin?' Mac said.

'I understand you need some answers for your own peace of mind,' Martin said, 'especially after receiving more than one of these texts. But you need to forget all about Sari and stay put, Mac. Your life is here now.'

Mac pulled out his phone and held up the screen with the message. 'Martin, how can I find any peace with this in my head? And if she's in trouble, how can I turn my back on her?'

'And what exactly do you think you can do to help her?'

'Maybe nothing. But I can't really ever know without confronting her and hearing her story.'

Martin rose to his feet and placed his hand on Mac's shoulder. 'If I can't change your mind, if you *must* do this, then I can only repeat what Liz said. Be careful. Very careful. Fly in, see Sari, and fly out. Forty-eight hours, tops. You got it?'

'Forty-eight hours,' Mac said.

He flew out that evening. Liz and Martin were there to see him off.

Liz put her arms around him and squeezed tight. She didn't want to let go. 'I don't hold up well when we're apart for too long.'

'Fly in, fly out,' Martin said again.

Mac's response was to kiss Liz, then his lips brushed her cheek and he whispered in her ear. 'I'll be back before you know I'm gone.'

He pulled away, waving, stepping into the boarding tunnel.

Liz forced a smile. Deep inside, she was at war, fighting off a crushing wave of apprehension.

Be safe. Hurry back.

Forty-eight hours.

THIRTEEN

39

Déjà vu.

The sensation swept through him momentarily as he gazed out the window of the airliner.

Jakarta. The rhythm of its music, the smell of its markets, the cacophony of voices and dialects that swelled from its teeming streets. It reminded him of Makassar. So many memories, just from this bird's-eye view as the plane descended. So much hurt.

What do I think I'm going to prove by coming back?

It was a different Indonesia. The rebel activity had been pegged back. Whilst trouble spots and poor conditions still festered beneath the surface in several locations, the country was also prospering in trade and tourism. Two faces, that was hardly uncommon in this part of the world, or for that matter, thought Mac, in so many places on earth.

The sounds, the scents, the people – those were the same.

It was over four years since that first visit, when he'd met Sari.

They'd been together for twelve months, with him staying in Makassar every chance he got. It was during that final stay, on his four weeks annual leave from TPA, that he'd met Carl Vickerson.

The sight of the water below reminded him of Paotere Harbour and that night three years ago.

The night that changed everything.

* * *

When Benny had returned to the boat that evening he'd brought with him another Australian, a newspaper reporter named Carl Vickerson who was in the country on a special assignment.

'My paper and the government here think I'm writing about their trading arrangements,' Vickerson had said as he sat down to the evening meal with Mac, Martin, Benny, and Sari, 'which I am. However, I'm also preparing a series of articles on the whole damn mess being allowed to smoulder here. Benny and his contacts have been a great help to me.' He and Benny clinked their glasses together. 'Go, bro!'

Benny laughed out loud. 'Bro!' he said. It always amused Mac how much Benny enjoyed Western slang.

After having waited for an opportune moment, Mac saw that this unexpected guest and his exchange with Benny had given him the opening he'd been hoping for.

'Have you considered you could be placing both Benny and Sari in danger?' he said to the reporter.

Vickerson leaned back in his chair, giving careful thought to Mac's question.

Mac watched him closely. Vickerson, maybe in his late twenties, was young for a foreign correspondent, Mac thought. He was a lean, wiry type, sandy-haired, cocky, confident, articulate.

'There's no progress, no social justice achieved without some element of danger,' Vickerson said calmly. 'The local people, and the local businesses – like Benny's for example – are severely impacted by the religious tensions, by the terrorist uprisings, by the poverty, and the inequality. What does the government do apart from kowtowing to foreign powers? And don't get me started on the corruption. I know it affects *my* conscience, Mr International Airline Pilot' – he shot Mac a friendly but challenging grin – 'what about yours?'

Mac ignored the thinly veiled jibe. 'Of course it affects my conscience, but so does placing people I care for in danger… and contact with these kinds of people… well, are you telling me there's no danger to them?'

'Mac, your concern for us is always appreciated,' Benny said, 'but don't worry. We're careful in our dealings. And our story needs to be told. Carl is on our side.'

'I know there have always been tensions between the Christians and the Muslims,' Mac said. '*And* between the traditional and the extremist Muslims–'

'It's a powder keg,' Vickerson said.

'And the authorities have special police and military units dealing with it.'

'Not enough.' Vickerson's voice rose. 'Things might seem under control to the naive Western world, but beneath the surface it's escalating. And not everyone believes the special units are above reproach.'

'Then maybe it's time for Sari to join me in Sydney,' Mac said.

'You have my blessing for that,' Benny said. 'But only of course if you visit all the time!'

Mac relaxed and smiled. 'Wouldn't have it any other way, old friend.'

Martin had been thoughtfully quiet during the conversation. Now he took his glass and raised it towards the others. 'I'm glad to hear all that's settled,' he said. 'As you all know, I'm staying tonight at the hotel near the airport, and returning to Sydney on an early flight. So, let me propose a toast.' The others raised their glasses. 'To more peaceful times in this great country. To seeing you all again soon. And on a more personal note, to Sari and Mac.'

* * *

The following evening, after a much quieter onboard meal with Benny and Vickerson, Mac and Sari had walked arm in arm along the harbour promenade. The sea breeze was exhilarating. The reflection of the stars twinkled in the waters.

'It's hard for me to make the decision to move,' Sari said. 'But you're right. It's time.'

'Not if you aren't comfortable with it, Sari,' Mac said. 'Now your father's running the business again, perhaps just come for a holiday. See how you find it. Then we can make the decision together. If you really can't leave Makassar… then we'll come up with another plan.'

'Like what?'

'Like me moving here.'

She smiled and hugged him closer. 'Very noble. But no need. I want to be with you in Sydney.'

They were headed back towards the line of boats where the two-masted sailing craft was berthed when they heard the short, sharp, deafening cracks of gunfire split the silence. Up ahead they saw khaki-clad soldiers charging out of a military truck, figures illuminated by shards of moonlight and pools of neon glow.

Sari broke from Mac and raced forward. 'Father!'

Mac caught her by the arm and pulled her back. 'No, Sari, you could be hit.'

'They're firing at our boat.'

'You don't know that.'

'Look,' she shouted, 'they're surrounding it.'

Another burst of gunfire deafened them and this time there was no doubt the weapons were aimed at the boat.

* * *

Mac closed his eyes and willed the painful memory to pass.

Then a slight jolt as he felt the aircraft's wheels touching down on the runway and the powerful brakes took hold.

FOURTEEN

43

From the moment he stepped off the plane Mac wished he was back in Sydney.

He could still sense Liz's scent, still feel her arms embracing him.

Fly in, fly out.

Forty-eight hours.

He would book a room later. First, he needed to see Sari.

It was twilight when Mac arrived at the address sent in the text. It was a rundown apartment block in the older part of the city. Mac rapped several times on the door of Apartment 6E. The door opened to reveal a man in his mid-forties, in a singlet and sweatpants.

'*Ya.*' The voice was gruff, irritated.

'I've a message from Sari,' Mac said.

'You have wrong place.'

Mac held up his phone, its screen facing the man.

'I was sent this address.'

'Not here.'

'But there must—'

'*Tidak!*' The door slammed shut.

Mac stood in the dim half-light of the hallway, confused.

He heard footsteps approaching, and his name called.

'Captain McKenzie?'

Mac turned towards the voice. A short, squat, Indonesian man in a tired brown flannel suit. 'Yes?'

'It is Captain McKenzie?' the man asked.

'Yes.'

Mac barely registered the sudden bolt of pain as he was struck from behind. A glancing blow to the side of the head. He was briefly conscious of falling, of darkness closing in.

* * *

He woke to a blur of images. Particles of fractured light, intense and blinding.

Slowly, the light and the images fused, and he saw he was in a nondescript, sparsely furnished room. Plain grey walls. No pictures. No decoration of any kind.

He was lying awkwardly on a bed composed of a sunken mattress and a shaky, iron frame. There was a window covered by ordinary, faded venetian blinds. And bars. He sat upright and swung his legs over the side of the bed. There was a dull ache in the back of his skull and he was groggy, lethargic.

He stood, went to the door, and tried the handle. It wasn't locked. He opened it and stared straight into the eyes of an officer in a greyish-brown uniform.

'Please remain in room, Captain McKenzie.' The officer's English was awkward.

Mac did so without replying. He was both astonished and fearful. He certainly had no intention of grappling with an armed officer or soldier or whatever he was.

He sat back on the bed. Strength was returning to his limbs, but his head was getting worse. He became aware of voices further along the passageway and moments later, the guard stepped aside and a man of about forty in a dark suit and loosened tie walked in.

'You're awake, Captain. Stating the obvious, I suppose.' He smiled, pulling up a chair from the far side of the room, and running his left hand through his head of short, tight curls. 'How's the head?'

Mac made no attempt to mask his anger. 'Sore. Where am I? What's going on here?'

'Could we get some painkillers in here for the captain?' the man asked the guard.

'Yessir.'

'Why am I here?' Mac asked.

The man produced his wallet and flashed his ID. 'Robert Anders. I'm an attaché with the Australian embassy here. We are in a safe house with members of a special paramilitary branch of Indonesia's national police, POLRI. You're in no danger here, let me assure you. And my apologies for the bump on your head. Unnecessary, and rest assured that is being conveyed here to the powers that be.'

The paramilitary man returned with the painkillers and a cardboard cup of water.

Mac swallowed the tablets. 'You haven't told me what's going on.'

'And you have every right to know,' Anders said. He relaxed his wiry frame in the chair and loosened his tie a little further. 'I've never quite got the hang of the heat here.'

Mac simply glared at him.

'For the past few months, a special unit has been monitoring the movements of a young woman. She is a member of an underground network of political activists that can be traced to terrorist acts.' Anders took a swig from his glass of water and wiped his brow. 'She is suspected of relaying coded messages within the group and arranging contraband.'

'I'm an airline pilot, Anders. What the hell has any of that got to do with me?'

Anders briefly held up the palm of his hand. 'I'm getting to that.' He put the glass down on the table to his right. 'The woman goes by the name of Nancy Wu. She operates a fresh fruit stall at the city markets. Recently, our investigations have identified her real name as Sari Sanjaya, a young woman who went missing after her father was killed during a raid on a rebel group meeting. Our surveillance shows she was using an unlisted smartphone, which she recently dumped.'

Mac was beginning to see where this was headed. 'You retrieved the phone.'

'Yes. Sanjaya sent you a text message before discarding the phone. We haven't been able to locate her again since she sent that message, and she hasn't resumed any of her normal routines.'

'That was why you were waiting at that address.'

'Yes. Unfortunately, there was no sign of Ms Sanjaya.'

'You said I was in no danger here. Why would I be in danger?'

'First, let me tell you the authorities here have thoroughly checked your background and they suspect you of being involved in these activities–'

'That's ridiculous,' Mac said.

Anders cut back. 'They've established you were in Makassar on that evening three years ago and you'd been sighted staying with the Sanjayas.'

'Benny Sanjaya was a friend of a business colleague of mine. Martin de Courcey.'

'Nevertheless, it has raised suspicions with the Indonesians.'

'You can't be serious.'

'The authorities suspect the reason Sari Sanjaya sought your help was that she was planning to leave the country and betray the group. The fact she did not meet you at the address specified suggests she may be in danger from that group, and that you, by association, could also be under threat.'

Mac ran his hands through his hair and took a deep breath. 'So, am I under suspicion by the Indonesians or under threat from this… rebel group?'

'Both, it seems,' Anders said.

'So, I need a lawyer?'

'I'm organising legal representation for you. And I'm speaking on your behalf with the local law enforcement. Unfortunately, these things take time.'

'How long?'

'I'm pushing for a court hearing to take place within weeks rather than months. In the meantime, counsel for the Indonesian government is preparing a case against you.'

'Against me? On what grounds, Anders? I've got nothing to do with any—'

'I'm afraid the system here is a very different animal to the one we know back home,' Anders said. 'But please rest assured, I'm here to represent you, and we will get this cleared up, so you can return to Australia as soon as is possible.'

'I have a job...'

'I can communicate on your behalf with your employer and let them know the situation.'

'And what do *I* do?'

Anders spread his hands to show his empathy, and to take in the immediate surroundings. 'You shouldn't find it too unpleasant here, Mr McKenzie—'

'For God's sake, call me Mac.'

'This is a walled-in house on the outskirts of the city. It's used by POLRI units for purposes such as this. A safe house, and certainly a much better proposition to the local jails. You'll get used to the armed guards, and the bars on the window in this room, they're for your protection—'

'And to keep me prisoner.'

'For the time being but really, Mac, given the circumstances, and the seriousness with which the Indonesians consider these terrorist outfits, you're being given very special consideration.'

'Special... consideration.' Mac's tone didn't leave Robert Anders in any doubt of his client's anger and frustration.

FIFTEEN

The text message arrived the day Mac had been due back.

*Liz, I won't be back for a while. Complications. Sari
needs help right now.*

She sat on the couch in her apartment, her eyes transfixed on the message, reading it repeatedly. So few words. No actual explanation.

How could he leave her waiting anxiously while he stayed in Jakarta with the woman he'd loved years ago? What about his career? Friends? *Her?*

The tears came, and she was about to hurl her phone across the room when her rational voice urged her to stop, there was no point wrecking her phone.

Rational Liz.

I'm always Rational Liz.

There was an inner Liz, hidden deep inside, that wanted to break out occasionally and be irrational.

She brought Mac's number up and called.

No answer.

She tried again, and again.

Useless.

Why didn't he answer?

How the hell can you do this, Mac?

A large, gaping hole was opening up inside her.

My dad would never have done this to my mum.

Stupid! Why am I thinking like that?

She phoned Martin and blurted it all out.

'Doesn't make sense,' Martin said. 'Not like Mac…'

'No…'

'Let me see if I can track him down and find out what's happening,' Martin said. He rang off.

Liz paced the apartment. She was seen in the industry as one of the new queens of PR. Positive, passionate, quietly charismatic.

And yet right now she had never felt so overwhelmingly negative about anything.

An inner alarm was warning her Martin wouldn't be able to contact Mac.

Why?

Where was he?

SIXTEEN

During the week, Liz launched herself even harder than usual into her work. Driven, as she always had been.

Rational Liz.

Martin called her every day and dropped by her city office every few days. Supportive, understanding, always the calm, smooth reassuring presence. But Martin was also confounded, totally unable to understand the actions of his old friend.

'It's not the Mac I've known all these years,' he said.

At first, he thought something had happened to Mac, that he was in trouble, but the airline's HR had received a call from Mac asking for an extended leave of absence and a follow-up email from Mac's personal email address.

'I just can't understand why he won't pick up that damn phone and speak with us,' Martin had said to her.

It was a week and a half after Mac's expected return date; Liz had arranged a full weekend of social engagements to keep her distracted, but hadn't turned up to any of them. Instead, she'd sat on her balcony, staring into space, endless random thoughts swirling through her mind.

She missed Mac terribly.

On Sunday night her phone pinged. She grabbed it and brought up the text message screen.

> *Liz, forgive me for taking so long to write. It would take endless texts to explain what has been going on with Sari. She needs help. Being here with her has made me realise I still have feelings for her. I need to sort out how I really feel before returning, it wouldn't be fair to any of us otherwise. I hope you can give me some space. I will try to phone you soon.*

Liz put the phone aside. She didn't try to ring again. What was the point? A sense of acceptance came over her. She'd really believed during the six months they'd been together, she'd found "the one". If that was the case, then Mac shouldn't have been having any doubts. But his heart was elsewhere. She wasn't convinced Mac would call her, or even return, and if he did what was there to say now?

She wanted to scream but her throat felt choked, she had no voice.

Mac wasn't the man she thought he was, wasn't even the man she'd fallen in love with.

He was someone else.

SEVENTEEN

Robert Anders had visited Mac several times a week, keeping him informed on how his case was progressing. That was if you could call it progress.

Still no court date.

Still no details about the charges against him.

The interior of the house was basic and workmanlike, its rambling shape narrow in width and deep in length. A windowless hallway ran to the rear exit, the bedrooms, bathroom and laundry all off to one side.

Mac had noted that the asymmetrical living space at the front always had an officer stationed near the front door, with another man on the outside, watching the windows.

The rear exit led into a garden framed by steep brick walls, a covered corner courtyard section with a few pieces of gym equipment for Mac's use.

On the last visit, Anders brought along the Australian lawyer, resident in Jakarta, who worked closely with the Australian embassy, a man named Pryor. Mac found his legal representative to be both impressive and world-weary in the same instance. He hoped that was a good thing.

It was incredibly frustrating he was denied direct contact with Liz or Martin or anyone back home. Contact had to be via the embassy, and the answers given to Mac when he questioned that, had been vague. It had been two weeks since he'd written down a message for Anders to have emailed, via the embassy, to Liz. He'd urged her not to worry, and expressed his hope the embassy would have sorted out the misunderstanding as soon as possible.

No reply.

What was going on back home?

Today's visit from Anders was unexpected. He hadn't been due back for another two days. Mac hoped against hope there was some good news, or at the very least a response from Liz.

'There may be good news on the horizon,' Anders said as the door swung open and he entered the room as the guards stood to the side.

'A court date?'

'No, not yet anyway, but news about Ms Sanjaya.'

'*Sari*. What…?'

'The POLRI report a woman answering Sari Sanjaya's description has been sighted in Malay, staying at a country residence that's been under surveillance as a rebel relay point.'

Mac noticed his hands had started to shake. He still found it hard to come to terms with the world he'd been confronted by here, the other side of Indonesia, the side the tourists don't see. This was the hidden world of a dissident, underground network of rebellion that bridged Indonesia and East Timor, and of secret Indonesian anti-terrorist police units. A world Sari had once chosen instead of the life she could have had, back in Australia.

'Obviously I can't be too specific or reveal details,' Anders said, 'but a raid is currently being mounted on that house. Sari will be arrested and returned here for trial, and hopefully there should be no problem in having her testimony exonerate you completely.'

'What will happen to Sari?'

'That is for the Indonesian justice system, Mac. Not something we have any influence over. I'm sure you'd understand that.'

'But is she guilty of any actual crimes?'

Anders spread his hands in ignorance. 'We have no information on what the Indonesians have on her. As you're aware, she's not an Australian citizen. We simply have no jurisdiction and no knowledge of those proceedings. We're here to help *you*.'

After Anders had left, Mac asked the guards to escort him to the walled-in garden at the rear of the safe house. He sat for a while and watched the sun as it began its slow descent against a clear blue sky. It was all he could see from this outside area. But his mind wasn't focused on his own freedom, or on Sari, or the past here.

His thoughts were filled with Liz, memories of those intimate moments with her, strolling along the Circular Quay harbourside with the sails of the Sydney Opera House across the water. Precious moments.

He ached with the need to see her face, hold her close, touch her skin.

Why hadn't she sent a message back via the embassy? Liz, what's happening with you?

EIGHTEEN

It was 6.10 on Friday evening. Another long, hard week, Liz thought, but not because of the work. She believed she'd handled every aspect with more grit and determination than ever, feeding on the adrenaline, *no*, it was the emotional toll.

She was trying like hell to get Callan McKenzie out of her mind.

Not so easy when you were still up to your armpits in the TPA campaign, with those blasted images of the super-handsome, super-sexy Captain Mac staring, smiling, winking back from so many screens, pages, and posters.

Then again it wouldn't matter if I wasn't surrounded by all that. It would still be hell trying to forget him.

She heard the outer reception door opening.

Her assistant Sally had left for the day, *so who—?*

Liz had told Sally not to worry about locking up, she would do it, and she wasn't expecting anyone. And who would have been able to pass the security downstairs?

A voice on the other side of her office door. 'Hello?'

Should she be concerned? *No.* It's the cleaners, of course. She flung open the door to her office and Raf Vetrani stood there, a bunch of roses in hand, his rogue smile allaying any fears.

'I'm so sorry, Liz, I've scared you—'

'Not at all.'

'The security guy was still in the front lobby, he knows me of course, and let me in. I had no idea it was this late and Sally would be gone, time gets away—'

'Stop rambling.' She went forward and took the flowers. 'They're really quite stunning. Not necessary, of course, you'll still be billed the usual fees for–'

'Ha. I *know* that. Not at all what these roses are for. Just a little gesture really, from Bruno and I and everyone at Big Bear. Bruno and I have been a little worried. You haven't been yourself this past week–'

'My apologies,' she said, moving to a cabinet at the far end of the reception area where she organised a vase for the roses. 'Incredibly busy week, not that there's any excuse for–'

'*My* turn to jump in and stop you right there. No apologies necessary. The work has been brilliant, and the results… well, you've seen the same data I have, the campaign's going gangbusters.' He paused for a moment, took a breath, adopting a reflective tone she hadn't heard from him before. 'No, Bruno and I are just concerned for you, Liz. It's none of our business, and probably a little impertinent of me dropping by unexpectedly like this, not too unprofessional I hope…'

'Of course not.'

'It's just good old *Uncle* Martin, you know how he can run off at the mouth without realising it. He let slip you've been having a rough time personally. I gather there's a bit of a problem at TPA, and their star pilot's gone AWOL? Anyway, none of our business as I said, but we already think of you as family and we wanted to let you know… we're not just clients at Big Bear, Liz, we're your friends, and… I hope you're ours.'

'Oh… well, thank you…' Liz didn't expect the sudden surge of emotion that engulfed her, tears welled, and she fought to hold them back. 'Oh… sorry, *now* who's unprofessional–'

'You're probably the most professional person I've ever known,' Raf said, and he gently touched her shoulder. 'I should be the one apologising. I've turned up unannounced, caught you unawares, invaded your personal space, and spoken out of place. Mind you, no one's perfect…'

Liz felt an inner sense of calm at his words and the comforting smile that followed them.

'Actually, I really appreciate your words, and the flowers. Thank you, and please thank Bruno as well.'

'Why don't you thank him yourself? Have dinner with Bruno, his wife Caterina, and myself, tomorrow night, Bruno's place. Be a distraction for you, and we can all get to know each other a little better. That's if you'd like that. And you'll love Caterina, everyone does, she's the original and best earth mother.'

'You're really being too kind.'

'Is that a yes?'

She couldn't help but grin despite her watery eyes.

'Yes,' she said.

'Best word in the English language.' Raf gave her both a brief wave and the thumbs-up sign as he headed off.

Liz nodded and mouthed the words 'Thank you,' as he went.

The Vetranis were right, of course. She needed a distraction. She needed to socialize.

She was heading back to her office when she stopped, looked at the campaign posters on the walls of the reception area. Mac, devilish grin, captain's uniform.

Captain Mac.

TPA Air.

Let us fly you to your dreams.

We're always part of your journey.

Catchy lines.

Corny lines actually, thought Liz, but they'd worked. Big time.

Regardless, that was the Mac she knew, that was the Mac *everyone* knew.

Always part of your journey.

She felt a shiver and had an inkling something wasn't right. Something didn't gel. She'd felt that all along. Martin had felt the same. She gathered up her handbag and coat, locked up and left. Even if it was for one last time, for closure, for peace of mind, she needed to speak directly with Mac. She needed to find a way to contact him.

NINETEEN

The man who came through the door was an Australian in a tailored grey suit, but it wasn't Robert Anders.

It had been over eight weeks and Mac had barely contained his anger on the last couple of Anders' visits.

This time he was ready to explode.

The sight of a man other than Anders coming through the doorway didn't help.

'Where's Anders?'

The man offered his hand. 'Mark Adler, Australian embassy. I'm Robert's replacement.'

Mac didn't take the extended hand and after an awkward moment, Adler let it fall back into place.

'What do you mean replacement?'

'Robert's been reassigned and I'm the new attaché here. Please, can we sit?'

Mac remained standing. Glaring. 'I've been here over two months, no court date, no actual detail on the so-called charges against me, no contact with my family and friends and employer, and quite frankly I'm going troppo. I want to speak to Anders now. Forget that, I want to speak to the Australian Minister for Foreign Affairs.'

'Mac, please, let's sit and talk this through. Believe me, I understand your frustration—'

'I'm way beyond frustration, Adler.'

'It's Mark, please. Let's sit. This sudden new assignment is a surprise to me as well, and I want to represent you in the very best way possible. Let's talk.'

Reluctantly, Mac sat as Adler pulled up chairs to the small table in the room.

'As Anders made you aware, the raid some weeks ago on the rebel outpost failed to capture Sari Sanjaya, and whilst they felt they would close in on her quickly with the leads they had—'

'Didn't happen. I know all that.'

'It's put everything back to square one. So, what I am doing now, in unison with our legal team here, is pushing for a special hearing and to have any charges against you thrown out.'

'It's never been made clear what those charges are.'

'Suspicion of complicity with anti-government insurgents. Anders would have outlined all that.'

'Doesn't mean it made any sense to me. Why has Anders been reassigned on such short notice?'

'I'm sorry, I don't know the details.'

Mac slammed his fist down on the table. 'No one has any damn answers.' He stood, fists clenched. 'I need to get the hell out of here.'

The khaki-clad soldier by the door tensed and began to move forward. Adler motioned for the guard to stand back.

'Mac, please trust me, I'm on your side. I'm going to get these ridiculous charges quashed and get you back to Sydney.' He stood, and once again offered his hand.

Reluctantly, Mac took it. Whatever words he might have said in response, were stuck in his throat.

He didn't trust Adler any more than he now believed anything Robert Anders had said to him over the past... what was it? Eight weeks or more? He was losing track of time.

He was going mad traipsing from this bedsitter of a room to the walled-in garden, and back again. He'd been here far too long. At first, he'd been prepared to allow for the government's processes... hell, he'd had no choice anyway, had he? But any patience he'd had was at an end. Something wasn't right about this "safe house", these military-uniformed house guards, the visits from the Australian attachés, the wait for a court hearing, the charges of collusion with rebels.

He was tired of doing the right thing and waiting for due process to exonerate him.

I need to get out of here.

TWENTY

It had been six weeks since Liz had first taken Raf up on his invitation for dinner and since then it had become a welcome staple of the week, every Saturday evening at the home of Bruno and Caterina Vetrani. Raf was always there, of course, and occasionally another friend, business colleague, or family member of the Vetranis. Liz had come to enjoy these little social events. They helped to break up the weekend.

One week it might have been a traditional Aussie backyard barbie, another time pizza or Chinese takeaway, another time a sumptuous three-course Italian meal prepared and served by Caterina, a gracious, talkative young woman.

Each week, as Liz arrived, Bruno – gesturing towards Raf – would open with the same comment, 'Despite his ego and his swagger, some people actually *like* my brother. They're in the minority, but they *are* out there.'

Caterina, Bruno and Raf would always be teasing one another and the easy banter around the dining table became a regular backdrop to their evenings. Caterina would often talk to Liz about the possibility of her "fabulous PR skills" being used in another way: finding a wife for her "aging playboy brother-in-law". Tonight was no exception and as Caterina and Bruno teased him, Raf recoiled in mock outrage.

'You see what I have to put up with,' Raf said as an aside to Liz. He shrugged. 'Warped opinions. Lousy humour.'

Liz had been a little awkward the first time she'd come to the Saturday get-together, but she'd quickly been made to feel comfortable. They had made her feel like one of the family. Caterina was like the big sister she'd never had.

Tonight was a clear, balmy night. A little later, with Caterina clearing dishes and talking on the phone with her sister – she never did just one thing at a time, Liz observed – and with the brothers engaged in discussion, Liz took a moment to walk out into the courtyard at the rear with its surrounding gardens. Glass in hand, she looked to the night sky full of stars, and she started to count them.

There had been many nights like this, so long ago in Fisherman's Inlet. A sky full of stars was not uncommon out in the country, and she recalled quiet evenings, just her and her dad, in quiet discussion, and yes, sometimes she'd counted the stars.

After a while she was aware of a presence behind her.

'Beautiful evening.'

'Yes.'

'Not wanting to upset the equilibrium,' Raf said, 'but have you, or anyone, heard anything further from Captain McKenzie?'

'No.'

'I'm sorry to hear that. I understand you were close.'

'I really needed to speak with Mac. Clear the air.'

'Of course.'

'If he really felt he needed to stay in Jakarta, with this woman he knew from before, then I could understand...' She caught herself, surprised she was opening up like this, on *this* subject, to Raf. It hadn't been her intention. He was a client.

But he and Bruno had also become her good friends.

'Martin and I have been in touch with TPA's Jakarta office and with the Australian embassy, just trying to get another contact number or address for Mac or for Sari.'

'No luck?'

She took a moment to answer, tears welling up in her eyes again… damn! Her heartbeat accelerated. She took deep breaths, cleared her throat. 'No.'

Raf's hand touched her shoulder. 'Then you've done what you can,' he said.

Later, Raf walked her to her car out the front.

'You haven't had too much to drink?'

'No, I always keep my eye on that.' *Rational Liz*.

'Good. But always remember, if you ever think you're over the limit, Bruno and Caterina have a spare room, or I can always drive you.'

'Thanks. You're like a big brother, looking out for me.'

She was behind the wheel now. He leaned in, and gave her a goodbye peck on the cheek. 'Drive safe. I'll speak with you during the week.'

He waved, walking back inside as she pulled out from the curb.

As she drove, she looked in the rear-view mirror, caught a glimpse of him disappearing through the front door, but she also noticed a silver Toyota Corolla pull out from the curb and fall into place behind her.

She had a sense of déjà vu. A silver Corolla had pulled out directly behind her just last night, or was it one night this past week?

And… last week, as well?

She was aware the car remained behind her, turning when she turned.

And again.

Onto the Pacific Highway. Over the bridge.

When she came to the turnoff that led back to the eastern suburbs, the Corolla stayed on the main thoroughfare, heading south.

I'm being paranoid.

She laughed to herself. *Not so rational.*

And yet, although she hadn't been able to make out the person behind the wheel – because of the glare of the headlights – she had the peculiar sensation this same car had followed her on those previous occasions.

Now you're just being a crazy bitch.

She shrugged the thought away and turned into the driveway of her apartment block.

TWENTY-ONE

Mac was losing track of time. One day blurred into another.

Three months? Four?

The time between Mark Adler's visits seemed longer and longer. One week between visits? Two?

For a while, he'd had Mac convinced a trial date was imminent and he could expect the matter to be cleared up. Adler had brought along government representatives to confirm there was some progress.

Still nothing happened.

Despite his frustration and his anger, Mac found he was regularly becoming lethargic. Was that because of the long hours of boredom?

Every day Mac worked out for a while on the gym equipment in the courtyard, watched closely by guards, but despite that, he was aware of a growing inertia.

He no longer believed a word they told him.

There was one occasion weeks earlier when, no longer caring about their weapons or what waited on the outside, he'd tried to push past the guards. He'd been tackled to the ground and taken to his room, the door locked, and it wasn't until hours later that Adler arrived to console him. Then he'd been let out of the room.

At night, he found himself lying awake for longer, repeatedly reliving the events of that night at Paotere Harbour.

Three years ago. It seemed like another lifetime.

* * *

After hearing the gunfire during their stroll, it took all Mac's strength to drag a hysterical Sari to the side of the promenade. 'We have to stay back.'

Sari stopped resisting then broke down, the tears flowing freely, the sobs wracking her tiny frame. 'What if my father was hit? I was so afraid something like this would happen.'

Mac held her tightly.

The firing and the raised voices had ceased. The quiet that followed was unnatural.

'Listen to me,' Mac said, 'I'm going to go and find out what's happening. Promise me you won't move from here.'

'But, Mac—'

'If your father's in trouble, then quite possibly by association you are as well. So please just stay still and quiet. I'm a visitor here, with no known connection to your family. Do you understand?'

'*Ya.*'

Mac approached the area of activity. He recognised a mix of Indonesian National Police, the POLRI, and military personnel. Soldiers were posted in front of Benny Sanjaya's *pinisi* and they blocked the way past that.

'Halt,' one of the soldiers said.

'Can I pass?' Mac called out. 'I'm returning to my hotel on the other side of the promenade.'

'Identification.'

Mac inched forward and produced his passport.

'Go back and take the long way around,' the soldier said, returning his passport to him.

Mac didn't move. 'I'm not sure the streets are safe the other way,' he said.

'Wait here.'

Mac inched forward a little more, his eyes scanning the boat for some sign of what was happening, his ears primed and honing in on every sound and every scrap of conversation. He heard the muttered tones of the soldier asking his superior what to do with the Australian tourist who wanted to pass. From the direction of the boat, he heard a gruff voice declaring the other man had dived into the water and seemingly disappeared.

The other man?

Who were they referring to?

His silent question was answered sooner than he expected. Two soldiers emerged from the boat's cabin carrying a stretcher with a covered body. As they stepped down from the deck to the pier, the cover slipped from the head of the corpse, revealing the frozen-in-fear features of Benny Sanjaya.

Mac's heart sank.

The soldier guarding the scene returned to his post. 'You may pass. Quickly.'

'What happened here?' Mac asked as the soldier ushered him past.

'No questions, move quickly. *Cepat!*'

After a while, Mac noted the police had left the area and he doubled back.

The promenade was quiet. The serenity of the moonlit seaport betrayed no evidence of the tragedy that had played out here only a short while before. He reached the area where he had left Sari. She was gone. He kept moving, hoping she'd simply moved further back, retracing their steps from earlier in the evening. He hadn't been walking long when he heard her voice – a whisper calling out from the shadows in a narrow laneway opposite the promenade. He turned and moved cautiously towards the lane, his eyes and ears alert.

'Mac...' She appeared out of the darkness, her face warped by fear, her eyes already pools of grief.

She embraced him. 'Carl is with me.'

Vickerson stepped out of the shadows, water dripping from his hair and his clothes. 'They seemed to come out of nowhere, Mac,' he said, his voice a croak. 'Dozens of shooters, firing madly. Is Benny...?'

'He's gone,' Mac said. He felt Sari stiffen. 'I'm so sorry, darling.'

She stood frozen, a reaction against the waves of shock. Then she began to sob, the tears sliding down her cheeks.

'Were those men after you, Vickerson?' Mac didn't attempt to keep the edge out of his voice. He wanted to explode in anger, but he couldn't do that, not here, not now, not with Sari in his arms.

Vickerson seemed oblivious to Mac's accusation. 'Sari and I are going to need to get out of Indonesia,' he said to Mac. 'And I can arrange that. But can you help us tonight, can you book a hotel room we can sneak into?'

'Can you?' Sari said, pleading, blinking away the tears.

'The Hotel Borobudur isn't far from here,' Mac said matter-of-factly.

'Then let's go,' Vickerson said.

* * *

Later that night, Mac, Sari, and Vickerson had sat at a small table, drinking the hotel's coffee.

'I have the contacts to arrange a charter in the morning from a country airstrip,' Vickerson told them. 'I can take you with me, Sari, and land you safely in Malaysia. From there, you can board a commercial flight to Sydney. You won't be safe here, not if they suspect you, as they obviously did your father, of being involved with the insurgents.'

Sari remained silent, tightly gripping the coffee mug in her tiny hands.

'Just what are you really doing in Indonesia?' Mac directed this to Vickerson, more demand than question. 'The secret police here don't shoot to kill a journalist because he's writing about the rebels. And journalists don't have contacts who can spirit them away from the country under the noses of the military.'

Vickerson didn't respond.

'Sounds to me as though you're part of something else,' said Mac. 'Guns?'

'All you need to know is I can help Sari leave the country without incident. And as hard as it is to put this behind us – Benny was a great friend, it's a terrible loss – he'd want the three of us, and especially Sari, to be safe and to move on.' Vickerson leaned across and placed his hand over Sari's.

'My father was a part of… the rebel group as well, wasn't he?' Sari asked.

Once again Vickerson remained silent while Mac glared at him.

TWENTY-TWO

A thin stream of dawn light spread across the urban landscape of Jakarta. In an ordinary street on the outer rim of the city, the early morning quiet was briefly shattered by the sound of breaking glass. Mac sat bolt upright in bed to a scream and what sounded like muffled gunshots. Then a deathly silence that seemed even more unnatural than the noise that preceded it.

He expected the locked door to his room would burst open. With his heart racing he eased open the door to the wardrobe and squeezed in, pulling the door to, hoping whoever had raided the house wouldn't think to check a rickety, narrow cupboard. His muscles tensed as he heard whispers, rushed footsteps, and the doors of the other rooms being pushed open.

A key turned in the locked door to his room.

He held his breath.

There were hushed voices and then a flurry of retreating footfalls.

And then nothing.

No sound.

What had happened out there?

Where were the men who guarded his room?

After a few minutes he stepped from the cupboard and grabbed hold of an old stool by its legs, wielding it as a desperate weapon. He opened the door gingerly, inch by inch, and peered out. The guards were not there. Still no noise or movement. What caused the gunfire? A raid with silencers on the weapons of the raiders? If that was the case, where were the raiders? And where were the secret police stationed at this so-called safe house?

He ventured out into the hallway, his crude weapon held out in front of him, at the ready. He opened the door to the first of the rooms along the corridor, rooms he knew were quarters for the guards. He swung the stool to his side as he leaned in and surveyed the room. Two of the guards had been shot, their bodies strewn across the floor. Pools of blood spreading underneath them.

Mac stepped back, looked away, nausea swelling from the pit of his stomach. He sucked in a lungful of air and steadied himself.

Stay calm. Alert.

He gripped the old stool tighter and inched his way down the hall and into the main living room and the adjacent entry portal to the house. A third man – they would never tell him their names – the more talkative of the guards, the closest thing to a friend Mac had ever had in this place, was splayed on the floor, gun still in hand, pain frozen into his face, soaked in blood.

The assailants, whoever they were, had fled, leaving behind a twisted wreck of furniture and glass, riddled with bullet holes, and their handiwork; three murdered men and pools and smears of blood.

Why am I still alive?

Didn't they know I was in here?

Were they interrupted?

Thoughts tumbled frantically through his mind.

Should he get in touch with Adler at the embassy?

If the Indonesians suspected him of being part of the insurgency based on the contact from Sari, then what would they make of this? Three of their highly specialised secret police gunned down, and Mac still alive and unharmed?

Their suspicions would be worse, their case against him stronger.

He retraced his steps to his bedroom and dressed quickly, casual shirt, jeans, and sneakers. Just another tourist, except he was anything *but* a tourist.

I need to get out before the alarm is raised.

He wondered if any of the nearby residents had heard anything.

He knew there were stores and money in the house. He went to the guards' room first and searched through their valuables. Wallets with petty cash. He collected ninety rupiahs, but he needed more.

His eyes fell on a solitary key on a chain. It was placed at the front of a shelf in one of the wardrobes. He knew instinctively this would be the key to their "operations" room at the far end of the hallway.

The key worked, and he entered a space much larger than the other rooms, stacked with equipment and rows of compact metal storage units. He rummaged through the units, cutting his finger on the sharp edge of one of them. Despite the early hour, it was warm, and he felt the heat on his back and across his brow. He thought he heard the wail of a siren in the distance.

Shouldn't risk staying too long.

I have to go now.

He pulled open one last unit and luck was on his side. If you could call any of this luck. Money. He jammed plastic bags of the notes in his pockets and into his waistband. Four thousand rupiahs or thereabouts, he surmised.

He raced out the back entrance then crept around the side of the house, the shadows still long enough to provide some cover but with the morning light intensifying by the minute.

He walked the streets, keeping an eye out for POLRI vehicles. Before long he came to an old part of the waterfront. Men were already at work on their fishing boats and in the rundown buildings that must have stood by this stretch of shoreline for over seventy years.

He would look suspicious wandering around here.

There were undeveloped patches of ground dotted around the place, leading back up a hill towards a derelict-looking cluster of buildings. He found a spot under a large tree, away from any passers-by or prying eyes, at least he hoped it was, and he sat and forced himself to breathe calmly, and to think.

Where can I go? How the hell can I get out of this godforsaken country?

TWENTY-THREE

'Something different this weekend,' Raf said. He stepped up alongside Liz at the photo shoot for a new Big Bear in-store point of sale campaign. 'You, me, Bruno, Caterina, and we're inviting Martin, out on the Hawkesbury River, Saturday and Sunday.'

'You're hiring a boat?'

'We own a boat.'

'You haven't mentioned that before.'

'You don't get to hear about it until you get an invitation to join us.'

'I'm honoured.'

Raf laughed. '*We'd* be honoured to have you join *us*.'

'Then I can hardly refuse.'

Raf's eyes twinkled. 'Thirty-three-foot houseboat. We keep it moored at a marina out there.'

'Next you'll be telling me you have a plane, a helicopter, a satellite.'

'No satellite. Not yet, anyway.'

Liz wasn't sure if he was joking. You could never tell with Raf. Mischievous, exuberant, strategic, but what was pure fun and what was serious business, you had to get to know this guy a lot better, dig a lot deeper, to know any of that for certain.

Raf said goodbye – he'd just been checking in to see how everything was going at the North Sydney photographic studio – he had a meeting to go to.

The shoot dragged on for another two hours.

When Liz made her way through the parking station underneath the building she had that sudden, inexplicable sensation; a pricking of the hairs at the nape of her neck. She was being observed.

Really? This paranoia again?

Her eyes searched the parking area, but it was quiet, she was the only person there.

As she pulled out onto the street, scanning the road ahead and behind, she was sure she caught a glimpse of a silver Corolla parked a block further back beyond the photo studio.

Coincidence? she thought.

Must have been, as the Corolla didn't pull out and follow. It didn't move at all, and it was too far back for Liz to see if there was anyone inside.

Was this unease just a remnant of the despair she'd felt over Mac abandoning her? Manifesting as insecurity. Jumping at shadows.

She'd never been like that before.

That's not who I am, she decided.

She picked up her speed as she drove onto the interchange that led to the eastern suburbs. Occasionally, though, she couldn't help but glance in the rear-view, scanning the cars on the freeway behind her.

Watching, in particular, for one certain kind of car.

TWENTY-FOUR

Ringed by lush, forested slopes, the Hawkesbury River, which entered the ocean around fifty kilometres north of Sydney, was a wide, winding waterway, dotted with bays and inlets.

Liz was standing by the rail of the houseboat, head tilted back, enjoying the sensation of the breeze on her face. She'd let her blonde hair grow longer and it streamed out behind her.

Martin joined her.

'I read the Aboriginal name for the Hawkesbury is *Deerubbin*,' Martin said, 'which means deep water.'

'Plenty of that,' Liz said.

'These brothers know how to work *and* play,' he said.

Liz grinned. 'They certainly know how to live it up.' She angled her head toward the galley. 'And if I keep eating those sumptuous meals of Caterina's, I'm going to put on some serious weight.'

Martin placed his hands on his own belly. 'Tell me about it.'

They stood in silence for a few minutes, looking out over the waterway as it rolled past. The river was a glorious blue, reflecting the almost cloudless sky, the sun glittering across the river's surface like sparkling aqua fireworks.

'You'd almost think that Raf, the consummate dealmaker, had done a deal with Mother Nature for today,' Martin said.

Liz cocked her head towards Raf who was standing by the rail at the bow end. He was speaking animatedly on his phone. 'The deals are never far from these brothers' minds,' she said.

'And one brother,' Martin said, following Liz's line of sight to Raf, 'has, I think, a hot-blooded personal interest in his PR lady.'

Liz flashed him a bemused expression. 'I don't know about that.'

'*I* do,' said Martin. 'Big personality, loads of fun, but be careful. He has a reputation.'

'For the ladies?'

'For the ladies.'

'He's a client, and he's become a good friend, but that's all that's going on there. I haven't seen any sign of the so-called playboy, as Caterina likes to call him.'

'Maybe you won't, but I'd say he's sweet on you. Can't say I blame him.' He cast her a friendly wink. 'But if I may speak out of turn, and I usually do' – they both grinned at that – 'it's only been four months since… Mac left… you need some space, you certainly need some fun, but perhaps be wary of jumping into anything on the rebound.'

Liz dipped her head and smiled. 'There's a time limit for rebounds?'

'Oh yes.'

'Which is?'

'Twelve months… eighteen months… the jury's still deliberating on that.'

'Either way, it won't matter.'

'No?'

'I'm not interested in Raf in *that* way,' she said.

'I'm not sure if you've heard,' Martin said, 'but not having been able to contact Mac, the airline's had to stand him down.'

Liz didn't say anything. She kept her gaze firmly on the river.

They dropped anchor at midday and sat cross-legged on the deck. Caterina, who had, of course, spent much of the past two hours in the galley, served barbeque chicken with a fresh garden salad and herbs, topped with a tangy, tropical-style dressing that was her own creation.

'So, this is the *secret* weekend lifestyle of the Vetranis,' Liz said.

'You would think,' said Caterina, 'with the amount of time these two' – she gestured at Raf and Bruno – 'spend on the job, and with the success of the business, we'd be doing this every weekend.' She threw her hands in the air in her usual manner. 'Fact of the matter, this is *rare*. Very rare.'

'But when we do it, we do it in style, and in great company,' Bruno said.

Raf raised his glass of wine. 'I second that.'

They all raised their glasses.

A short while after, Raf pushed himself to his feet and peeled off his T-shirt. 'Great food, great wine, great people. And the best river in the world for taking a dip.'

Liz couldn't help but admire his lean, lightly muscled physique.

He went to the side of the boat, to the space between the railing, looked back, grinned, then jumped.

'Always the show-off,' Bruno said.

Moments later Raf clambered up the side ladder and back onto the deck. 'Fantastic,' he said. 'Liz, join me.'

'Perhaps not.'

'It's exhilarating, believe me. Come on, let your hair down. Martin, give her a nudge. You can't come all the way out here and not jump in those glorious waters at least once.'

'You can do it for both of us,' she called out to him.

'Come and jump, you won't regret it. You don't always have to be so… rational.'

Rational? What made him say that? Am I that transparent? Rational Liz.

'Pressure's on,' Martin said, joking.

'The hell with it,' Liz said. She stepped to the railing, casting her lightweight beach shawl aside. She felt Raf's eyes on her body, on her black bikini, then his eyes meeting hers.

He jumped, letting out a Tarzan cry as he did.

What a character.

Then Liz followed him over the side.

TWENTY-FIVE

Mac wandered the foreshore, from one ramshackle cluster of buildings to another; from one fisherman's wharf to the next. No sign of any police activity anywhere. No one paying him any attention. Shouldn't the POLRI be scouring the area, searching for him?

He was beginning to feel safe around these waterways.

Crazy.

Perhaps the search was concentrated on the city areas. Hell, he didn't know what they would be doing or thinking. None of this made any sense. It hadn't from the beginning. Maybe the raid on the safe house had signalled a bigger threat to the government agencies. Maybe he wasn't the priority.

Something else is going on.

After a while, he found another spot to sit and he watched the activity on the wharves. This was far from the major hub of the harbour, just small-time operators here, he surmised – fishermen, cargo runs, small boats, and some of the older-style *pinisi*.

A small plane flew overhead, and Mac looked up.

He was reminded of Benny Sanjaya's old cargo plane and the day of that flight to the Klaten district near Surakarta, with Martin. Sari had joined them, and she had taken him riding in the rainforest. He'd kissed her. It all seemed like a fantasy now.

Those Java ponies had belonged to breeders who had a stud farm there in the country region. Friends of the Sanjayas. Mac dredged his memory for their names.

Ahmad and Tika. An older couple. Mac had met them only briefly.

And now Mac wondered if there had been more to that stopover.

If Benny had been relaying messages to insurgent groups, had this been the method? Innocent stops along the way on their cargo trips. Delivering messages by direct contact, thereby avoiding phones, texts, emails. Nothing that could be traced.

Was the Java pony breeding couple a part of that network?

Mac needed help getting out of Indonesia. And he needed to find Sari.

Gut feeling told him Ahmad and Tika would know where to find her, especially if she was not part of that world herself.

He needed to find passage to Surakarta.

* * *

Mac's attention was drawn again to the activity on the wharves.

Would these people help him?

He wandered down to the shore. He knew he looked out of place here, but there wasn't anything he could do about that. He had the impression appearances didn't matter to these people. They were poor workers, toiling away in the furthest reaches of the industrial spots. He hoped they had no interest in the authorities, or in whether laws were being abided by, or not.

He approached a couple of labourers who were hauling barrels. They stopped what they were doing and regarded him with suspicion.

'Do you speak English?' Mac called out to them.

The taller, stringier of the two men said, '*Inggris?*'

'Yes.'

He looked at the other man and shrugged.

'Would you know if any of the boats here go near Surakarta?'

'Ah. Surakarta?'

'Yes.'

The stringy man looked to his right and bellowed. Then, his eyes meeting Mac's, he pointed to the group of men he'd shouted at. '*Berbicara Inggris,*' he said, '*Surakarta.*'

Mac headed towards the other group. They, too, were loading items onto a *pinisi* schooner.

One of the men was broad-featured, florid-faced. He reminded Mac of Benny Sanjaya. 'Englishman?' the man said.

'Australian. You speak English?'

'*Ya.* And you want to go to Surakarta?' the man said.

'Near there. Klaten District. Can you—'

'This is a fishing and cargo wharf. We don't ferry passengers.'

'I understand. Do you know—'

Florid cut him short again. 'You in trouble? POLRI?'

Mac stared back at the man and shrugged. How much should he reveal? He had no idea where he stood with these harbour workers.

Relief surged through Mac as the Indonesian offered his hand. 'They call me Corky. Help us load. We'll drop you near Semarang Port. I have a friend who can drive you to Klaten. Money?'

'Yes, I can pay him to drive me.'

Corky explained they made several stops along the coast, sometimes anchoring overnight, offloading in some places, loading in others. It generally took them two or three days before they passed Semarang Port in Java.

It occurred to Mac later, as the small, battered schooner pulled out from the rotting, wooden wharf, this crew were likely carrying illicit cargo. Whispered conversations and furtive glances out over the waters seemed to confirm it. The last thing these men wanted was anything to do with the National Police. These were not the kind of men, and this was not the kind of life, Mac could ever have imagined for himself. And yet, right now, he couldn't have been in better company.

He had come to Indonesia to see if he could be of help to Sari. Now it was clear he was the one desperately in need of help.

TWENTY-SIX

Corky and his crew did not want to enter Semarang Port, so they had one of the crew take Mac, in a small rowboat, from the *pinisi* to the shore. Here, the crewman took Mac to a workman's cottage where he introduced him to Corky's friend.

This man, with heavyset features and thick eyebrows, did not look at all happy as the crewman relayed a message from Corky.

'*Non*,' he said several times as the exchange between the two men became increasingly agitated.

Mac wasn't comfortable with any of this. He was about to say "forget it", when money was mentioned and the thick-eyebrowed man's mood lightened.

Now the crewman glanced back at Mac. 'He is good. Enough rupiahs make him happy to drive you.' The crewman flashed Mac a wide grin, then just as quickly waved, and left.

Mac's new friend introduced himself only as Rama. 'We leave the day after tomorrow,' he said, offering no other explanation. 'Pay first.' He held out his palm.

Mac placed the rupiahs in Rama's hand and attempted to make conversation. 'I appreciate the help from you and Corky.'

There was no response. Mac was given a bowl of rice and some tepid water, and then shown to a sparse room, where he slept on a torn mattress on the wooden floor.

Despite his exhaustion, it wasn't easy to sleep there. It was a long way from the comfort of the hotel room in Kuala Lumpur where he'd stayed over three years ago, the night before the reunion with Sari that had never happened.

Where had she gone?

He wondered, in her life as a fugitive from the Indonesian authorities, whether she'd had nights like this.

Why hadn't she stuck with Vickerson's plan?

Mac tried to resist, but once again his mind was whisked back through that vortex of memories.

* * *

The morning after Benny Sanjaya's murder at Paotere Harbour, Mac had hired a car and driven Sari and Vickerson into the countryside. He had stood on the edge of a clearing in the forest and watched the small private plane Vickerson had arranged take off and climb into the open blue.

The plan had been that Mac would take the next available commercial flight to Kuala Lumpur in West Malaysia and meet Sari in the coffee shop of the Raffles Hotel.

It had not been long after dawn when his flight touched down. He'd eaten breakfast in the airport cafe, then wandered the streets. The sight of another Eastern city coming to life paling into insignificance next to the urgency of his impending reunion with Sari.

Midday came and went and there was no sign of her. He'd waited in the hotel coffee shop until 3 p.m. then decided to check with the hotel registry to see if there was anyone of Sari's description staying on the premises. There wasn't.

He had walked out of the front lobby and stood in the street in desperation, looking about. Of course, there was always the possibility they hadn't reached Malaysia, that some calamity had overcome them. He didn't even want to consider that.

At the local Australian Press Syndicate office, Mac was told that Vickerson was at a courthouse on the other side of the city. The reporter was on assignment for a Malaysian newspaper.

Vickerson was on the front steps of the courthouse when he glimpsed Mac approaching.

'Mac! What the hell…' Lines of concern crossed his face.

'Vickerson. What happened to her?' He spat out the words and grabbed hold of the lapels of Vickerson's suit. 'Where's Sari?'

'She didn't meet you as planned?'

'No!' Perspiration gleamed from Mac's forehead, his eyes bloodshot from lack of sleep, his cheeks flushed red.

Vickerson pushed Mac's hands away. 'Get a hold of yourself. Sari and I arrived in Malaysia as scheduled. No problems. I hired a car and dropped her at the hotel the night before you were due to meet her. She had enough money to stay a few nights, and the necessary papers to travel on to Sydney.'

'Bullshit.'

'For Christ's sake, McKenzie, listen to me. Benny and his daughter were my friends too. I would never put Sari in danger, or abandon her if she was in trouble.'

'Then where is she?'

'I don't know. I wish I did.'

The two men glared at each other.

'Doesn't make sense,' said Mac.

'We have to face facts, Mac. Sari had money and an airline ticket, which she could have exchanged for another destination. She could be anywhere. Perhaps still in Indonesia or Malaysia.'

'She wouldn't have taken off without a reason.'

'Wouldn't she, Mac? How can you be sure what her state of mind was? Her father was murdered, and she had to be smuggled out of her own country.'

'We were headed to a new life.'

'Perhaps she was no longer sure what she really wanted,' Vickerson said.

Mac had wandered off, knowing he'd need help finding Sari.

In the days that followed, neither Kuala Lumpur's leading firm of private detectives nor the Australian embassies in Indonesia and Malaysia had been able to find any information on Sari's whereabouts.

The four weeks of Mac's annual leave were expended. He was running short on funds. He had returned heavy-hearted to Sydney and spent a couple of nights at Martin de Courcey's home, pouring his heart out to him.

The following day he was due back at Trans Pacific Air. Back to work. Back to the day-to-day reality of normal life.

In time, he came to accept Sari had chosen to go to a new life, just not the one they'd planned.

The death of her father had changed everything.

* * *

Eventually, Mac drifted to sleep, and the memories faded to black. If he dreamt that night, then he wasn't aware of it.

The following morning there was no sign of Rama. The cottage was otherwise empty, and quiet, and Mac spent the time wandering from the back veranda, with its view of surrounding countryside, and into the house and back again.

He began to worry the man called Rama had taken his money and left, and this rundown cottage in the middle of nowhere might not be as safe as he'd been led to believe.

TWENTY-SEVEN

It was a week and a half after the Hawkesbury cruise. Liz's birthday. The morning had seen a flurry of Happy Birthday emails and phone calls from friends and clients.

She didn't have any meetings scheduled for today – a quiet day in the office catching up on paperwork, there was plenty of that – and maybe a quiet dinner with her assistant. She wasn't expecting an impromptu visit from Raf, but then perhaps, she thought later, she should be expecting the unexpected at any time from him, it was clearly his forte.

No flowers this time, but he did have an envelope which he handed to her when she went out to the reception area to greet him.

'From Bruno, Caterina, and yours truly,' he said.

'Thanks.' She opened the envelope and pulled free a ticket.

'Happy birthday,' he said.

Liz glanced over the ticket.

'A tandem skydive?' Her eyes widened in surprise.

'I hope you're not scared of heights.'

'I wouldn't say I was particularly comfortable with them.'

'Perfect op, then, to face your fears.'

'I guess.'

'Ready?'

'For what?'

He held up another ticket. 'I have one as well.'

'Now?'

'Well, it *is* your birthday today. Right?'

He threaded his arm through hers. 'I say we get a move on. And if you chicken out once we're there, *no problemo*, you can stay on the ground with Bruno and Caterina and watch me.'

'Bruno and Caterina will be there?'

'They wouldn't miss your birthday skydive any more than I would.'

Liz flashed a look at Sally as she and Raf headed for the exit. 'You were in on this?'

The gleam in Sally's eye was a dead giveaway. 'Don't know what you're talking about,' she said.

It was an hour's drive to Wollongong, on the south-east coast. The tiny plane took off from an open field with the landing area on the wide expanse of North Wollongong parkland, near the beach.

Liz found herself going with the flow, caught up in the moment. A skydive was something on her to-do list, something she might very well never have gotten around to.

Adrenaline kicked in as the skydive team prepped them, and the banter swung back and forth between Liz and the Vetrani brothers. Bruno and Caterina watched eagerly from the sidelines, calling out their encouragement.

'Why isn't Bruno coming?' Liz called across to Raf as the two of them were fitted with the jump gear.

'Someone has to be the resident coward in the family,' Raf said.

'And someone in the family business has to keep their feet on the ground instead of their head in the clouds,' Bruno called back.

Brotherly banter. And yet, once again, Liz detected the undercurrent. Raf always goading his brother. And Bruno responding light-heartedly, though Liz could hear the edge in his responses.

There was another surprise in the plane's hold as the pilot began to taxi across the field. The instructor attached a wire to Liz with an accompanying earplug. Raf's instructor was doing the same to him.

'Your friend there will be able to talk to you, through this, during the jump,' the man said.

'Is that a normal feature on these dives?' Liz asked.

'Not at all. Something special Mr Vetrani arranged, just for this jump, just for the two of you.'

The plane lifted into the air.

Twenty minutes later they were cruising at the necessary altitude. There were four others also doing a tandem jump with an instructor.

'Okay, everybody,' the lead instructor shouted to the group as they huddled in the hold. 'Showtime.'

Liz, strapped to the front of her instructor, tensed.

This is it.

'You ready?' her instructor, a strong, lean man in his early forties, said.

'No,' said Liz.

'You'll be fine,' he said.

Raf and his instructor went out first, followed almost immediately by Liz and her co-jumper.

This was one of the most spectacular jump sites along the east coast. It afforded a breathtaking panorama of the mountains, the shoreline, and the ocean.

The powerful rush of fear gave way to sheer exhilaration as Liz and her instructor dropped, the world spinning around them.

Liz caught a glimpse of Raf in freefall just below her and a little to her right.

Then she heard Raf's voice crackle through the earpiece. 'Liz!'

'I hear you.'

'Quick question; will you have dinner with me tonight?'

'What?!'

'Dinner. Tonight.'

The earth was rushing up to meet her and this lunatic of a man was asking her out on a date. She could barely think. She gulped in air as the G-force strength of the wind pushed her face out of shape.

'Liz! We're running out of time!' Raf's voice was a shout, ringing in her ears.

'Okay, yes,' she shouted back. '*Yes.*'

She'd had no intention of dating Raf Vetrani, but up here in the open air, in freefall, with the sky, the sun, the earth, all whirling around her, nothing was the same, everything was different.

Just seconds later the ripcord was pulled, there was a sudden jerk upwards then she was floating, free as a bird, taking in the majesty and the calm of the heavens.

Then Raf's voice again. 'I took the liberty of booking a table for two for 7 p.m., fabulous seafood place overlooking Wollongong Harbour.'

'What do we do until then?'

'I don't know about you,' he said, 'but I think I'm going to need a stiff drink or two after this.'

She laughed. Giddy with the exhilaration.

'Is this how you always ask a girl on a first date?'

'Only PR queens,' he said. 'So much harder to get their attention.'

Then the soft landing, pulling her knees up and lifting her feet, gliding gently to a stop on her butt, the instructor also on his seat, his legs straddling hers. Untangling from the chute. Stepping free of the straps.

'Perfect,' said the instructor.

She looked across to Raf. He was rising to his feet, his eyes on her, his face beaming – young at heart, spirit of adventure – and she could not help the flutter of excitement in her breast or the warmth that flooded her heart.

The mic and the earpieces were still in place. She spoke into the mic. 'I don't normally date clients.'

'Normal? What's that?'

'Just one date,' she told him, smiling.

'God knows what I'm going to have to come up with,' he said, 'to get you on a second one.'

TWENTY-EIGHT

Liz wasn't sure if it was the perfectly easy charm Raf exhibited at dinner, or the mad spontaneity of the skydive, or the intoxicating kiss they shared as he dropped her back at her apartment at 2 a.m., but as she stood on her balcony, watching him drive away, she realised the effect he'd had. She was a different person. She felt new. Renewed.

She was still determined she wouldn't be entering a relationship with the man, but she did like the risk-taking adventurer in him, and the way it made her feel.

Different Liz.

She laughed to herself.

When she walked into the office six and a half hours later, she said to Sally, 'Do *not* get up to any more secret little projects like that with our clients.'

'How'd it go?' Sally asked.

'It was a good day.'

'If you're not interested in him, then I'm waiting in the wings.'

'You are far too young for him, and I repeat, no shenanigans with clients.'

'I'm twenty.' Sally's tone was cheeky, but Liz could tell she was half-serious. Raf Vetrani was, after all, a bit of a catch.

'You're a baby,' Liz said as she stepped through into her private office.

'When are you going out with him again?'

'I'm not.'

'Okay, just let me know if you need me to make any reservations.'

Liz glared back at her light-heartedly and Sally giggled to herself as she resumed typing.

It was later in the morning when the call came through. 'All the expert advice,' Raf said, 'states after a first date the man should wait a few days, which creates a bit of romantic tension, before following up with a phone call.'

'Sounds like good advice,' Liz said.

'Which I'm already breaking.'

'Raf, it was a great day, it really was, but there's no need–'

'We have our usual get-together, Bruno's place, Saturday night, but I thought it would be great for you and me to get together before that.'

'Perhaps if we leave it for now, Raf–'

'You don't date clients.'

'No.'

'Which is why I've spoken with Bruno at length this morning, and from here on in, he will handle all our communications with your agency, and me… well, I'll be way, way back in the background.'

'You're still a client.'

'What do I need to do? Resign from my own company?'

'Yes.'

'If I'm going to leave my own firm, then I'll at least need a night out with you to determine if it's worth it. Just one date.'

'We already had one date.'

'That doesn't count, it was your birthday.'

Liz relented, smiling to herself. 'Okay, a decider date.'

'Wednesday night sound good?'

'I've got a feeling I'm going to regret this.'

'Regret?' said Raf. 'There's no such word.'

'Oh yes there is.'

'I guarantee I will never let you regret anything, Miss Carter.'

They took in a show at the State Theatre in Market Street, followed it with a late supper at a nearby cafe, then Raf suggested a nightcap at his home in the northern suburbs.

'I've got a secret I've been waiting to share with you,' he said.

'Is that right?' said Liz, bemused.

'I've got some of the very latest coffee machines and I'm a bit of a closet barista.'

'Barista?' Liz said, laughing.

'My guilty pleasure.'

'I'm impressed.'

'You should be. I love coffee. Did a barista course a few years ago for my own amusement, and nothing relaxes me more than preparing a perfect cappuccino or latte or whatever I fancy at the time.'

'You've never revealed this hidden talent on Saturdays at Bruno's.'

'It's only for very special occasions, believe me.'

Liz was sure he was simply skylarking but once they entered his spacious, four-bedroom house in the leafy suburb of Chatswood, she saw his coffee machines in the kitchen and watched with a widening smile as he went into action, hamming it up as he went along.

It was a balmy night, so they sat in the garden courtyard adjacent to his back patio and he talked for a while about growing up with Bruno. He told her how they'd lost their father when they'd been very young. Ten years later a further great sorrow when, as young men, they lost the mother they adored. She'd worked tirelessly to raise them on her own and it was from her, Raf said, they'd learned their work ethic and, equally as importantly, their sense of humour.

'No doubt you got your infectious charm from her as well,' Liz said.

'Everything came from her,' Raf said, on a serious note. He glanced at his watch. 'One o'clock. Time to get you home.'

Liz didn't know what they talked about in his car as he drove her back to the eastern suburbs, but they talked non-stop the whole way.

'Looks like I'll be resigning in the morning,' Raf said at the door of her apartment.

'Does it?'

'Unless date three is definitely out of the question.'

'I thought this was our first date?' Liz said.

'Let me rephrase; unless date *two* is definitely out of the question.'

'I'll tell you what. You're such a good barista, it was such a nice surprise, I'll let you keep your job, and we can give that third date a try.'

'I knew that barista course would come in handy one of these days!' Raf raised his fist triumphantly, then, allowing a moment to pass, he gently leaned in and kissed her.

Liz returned the kiss and whenever she looked back in the days and months that followed, she saw it as the defining moment. Raf's heart and soul and energy, so much of all three revealed on that evening, made her feel alive. There was no good reason to be working so hard to resist him.

No good reason.

Something inside opened. They kissed for a while as though it really was their last chance to kiss, then Liz eased him through the front entrance, closing the door behind them. They kissed a while longer before they moved without any apparent effort to the door of her bedroom, and there, she cast any lingering doubts aside and removed, first, her blouse then her skirt as Raf peeled his shirt off, and then the rest of his clothing.

What am I doing?

The thought was a fleeting one, spirited away as Raf's strong hands touched her like waves of electrical current, smoothing their way over her hips and her thighs and the flatness of her belly.

She arched her back as his muscles pressed against her naked body. His fingertips lightly traced her spine, coming to rest at the small of her back.

Liz inhaled deeply. It was as though her body was remembering all over again how incredible this could feel. The right man. The right touch. The right moment.

She ran her own hands over his chest and the hardness of his biceps.

He was on top of her, across the bed now, his lips on her lips, his tongue seeking hers, pressing, exploring, his hands melting her skin. His touch was like a feather caressing her breasts and her nipples responded.

Somewhere in the jumble of her thoughts that night, as her body hummed, and her senses soared, Liz felt she had bypassed the present, stepping from her past and into her future.

TWENTY-NINE

Mac actually breathed a sigh of relief when he saw Rama approaching the cabin as twilight settled in.

The Indonesian didn't reveal where he'd been all day. He was his same gruff self, a man of few words, grunts really, and hard stares, but he did offer to share a meal of chicken and vegetables. It was about as far away from five-star cuisine as you could get but Mac was hungry and wasted no time consuming his share.

'So, we're heading to Klaten district in the morning?'

'*Ya,*' the man said.

'You're not much into conversation then,' Mac said.

The man simply glared back at him, as though he hadn't understood.

The previous night, Mac had slept badly and this night was no different. He tossed and turned, his body ached, and he couldn't switch off his thoughts.

Why did I ever think I should come here on some misplaced sense of duty for a woman who disappeared when it suited her?

And yet here he was, over four months incarcerated in a foreign country under the most unusual of circumstances. And now, a fugitive desperate for a way home.

They left early, 6 a.m., and as they drove, keeping mostly to back streets, Mac looked out on sprawling suburbs of old-style bungalows and buildings, followed by swathes of country with farms and croplands. Then, tracts of forest and the isolated stands of trees that were a feature of the Klaten area.

He began to recognise the landscape from the time he had visited here, with Sari. He could never have imagined back then, the circumstances in which he'd be returning now.

'I checked out breeders of Java ponies,' Rama said. 'There's only one farm of that type in Klaten. It's the people you spoke of.'

'You were able to get an address?'

'*Ya.*'

Mac had been wondering how he was going to find the horse farm, it had been a part of his anxiety all through the previous night.

'You could have filled me in on that last night,' Mac said, allowing his frustration to rear its head.

True to form, Rama ignored him.

Later in the day, Rama's utility van pulled up outside a farmhouse Mac recognised immediately.

'I shouldn't be long here,' Mac told Rama. 'I just need to find out from this couple, where to find–'

'Okay,' Rama said impatiently.

Mac walked up the rest of the driveway, across the wide expanse of frontage, to the front door of the large but rambling house. He rapped on the front door. There was no answer, but he heard voices from the rear of the property. He walked around the side of the house, remembering there were fenced-off areas and barns housing the horses further back. And as he rounded the edges of the house, he saw the older couple. Whatever chores they'd been attending to, they'd stopped and had turned towards the house at the sound of Mac's knock.

Mac called out as he approached. 'Ahmad! Tika! Sorry to intrude. You remember me? Mac. Benny and Sari's friend.'

The farming couple looked at him inquisitively.

Mac tried to remember how good their English had been.

'What is it?' Ahmad said.

Mac extended his hand. 'Mac. Sari's friend. It's been a long time, so I don't know if you remember me?'

Tika remained silent, watching him closely.

Ahmad shrugged. 'Sorry. Don't remember.'

'Oh.' Mac's shoulders sagged. He'd come so far, and he was so incredibly tired.

He couldn't lose his resolve now.

'I'm sorry to intrude like this. But can you help me? I'm a friend of Sari's. I was with her the night her father died. I need to find her.'

The older couple watched him, waiting.

'I'm in trouble and I need her help.'

Now Ahmad frowned and shrugged expressively. 'We don't know anyone named Sari.'

At least his English is good, Mac thought.

He realised the Indonesian couple were not going to say anything that linked them with rebel activists.

'I'm not working with any authorities,' Mac said. 'I'm an Australian pilot. I was detained by the government, who seem to think I'm involved with Sari's underground activities. I'm not. But I had a message from Sari and I really need help now getting out of Indonesia.'

'So sorry. Don't know a Sari. Can't help.' Ahmad motioned for Mac to go.

'Thanks anyway. And, again, I'm sorry to have disturbed you.' He turned to leave then paused, just for a moment, looking back at the couple. 'We rode your beautiful Java ponies into the woods there,' Mac said, sweeping his hand towards the nearby forest. 'About fifteen minutes' ride that way, there was a wide stream. We stopped and rested in the shade there. It was a beautiful day.'

He continued on his way.

Rounding the front of the property he saw the ute was no longer there. He ran forward across the long, wide driveway, scanning the road further along.

Rama had left him.

The arrangement had been that Rama would drive him out to this district then return him to the coast. But then had it been clear? He'd barely been able to communicate with the gruff, unresponsive local the *pinisi* crew had left him with.

He had no plan for what he'd do or where he'd go now. He'd been hoping against hope the horse-breeding couple would have remembered him and been prepared to put him in touch with Sari.

A desperate hope, perhaps, but he was in a desperate situation.

He wasn't sure how long it would be before it got dark, but it seemed he had no choice but to walk. And to keep walking.

Or running.

It worked for Forrest Gump.

With a wry flash of humour, he pictured himself running, mile after mile, sweat running rivers down his back.

Huh, he thought, walking will have to do.

It was a winding, dusty road. The sky was cloudy, there was a light breeze blowing which helped with the heat. He didn't recall how far it was likely to be to the nearest township. He'd been walking for ten minutes when he heard a motor behind him. He stood to the side of the road and turned to see a small old-style truck with an open tray at its rear. It pulled up alongside him and Tika peered out from the front cabin.

'My husband wasn't sure whether to trust you, but we remember you and I have a good feeling.'

'Thanks,' said Mac.

'We have to be very careful,' she said by way of further explanation.

'Of course you do.'

'Get in.'

She drove without another word for twenty minutes until they came to a village. The truck stopped in front of a dilapidated motel. 'The owner is a friend. I called ahead, and he can put you up for a couple of nights. He may be able help. Best we can do for you.'

'And Sari?'

'Go now,' Tika said.

He stepped out of the car and watched as Tika backed up, turned, and drove away. He didn't notice the two men seated in a car further along the street, one of them on a phone, the other taking covert shots of him with a compact camera.

THIRTY

A middle-aged woman with a long face, tired-looking eyes and thick black hair pulled tightly back from her forehead, showed Mac to a room. It wasn't the Ritz-Carlton, but it was a damn sight better than the beaten mattress on the floor he'd slept on the past two nights.

From a shop across the road, Mac bought an *ayam goreng* meal – fried chicken served with chili sauce and rice – and ate in his room, watching local news on the TV. He expected news about an Australian who was being sought by Jakarta's POLRI. He expected reports about an attack on a house on Jakarta's outskirts that had killed several men. He waited for any mention of the Australian consul, of Anders, or the man who'd replaced him.

There was nothing.

They're keeping it quiet.

He'd never felt so ragged, so lost. So alone.

He didn't have the energy to feel the anger he knew was seething just beneath his skin. Right now, he just wanted to get out the country.

It took him a long while to get to sleep, and only a couple of hours after, he woke to bright lights outside the window, raised voices, thumping on doors.

God no…

His door eased open and the woman with the tired eyes peeked in, speaking softly. 'I was told there'd be no trouble, now POLRI are everywhere, they know you're here.' She pointed to the rear door of the room. 'Go quickly. My brother will take you from here.'

Mac didn't dress, he simply grabbed his clothes and his shoes, held them against his chest and he raced out the back and into a small two-door sedan. The man at the wheel steered the sedan slowly, quietly, without lights, down the dark lane at the back of the motel and onto a dirt road that ran alongside the woods. He didn't speak, but he constantly jerked his neck and looked back to see if the POLRI had marched around the rear of the motel and spotted them.

'We might be okay,' he said after a few minutes, and he turned the car onto another road that took them further into the country. 'We were told there'd be no trouble when we agreed to help.'

Mac's throat was dry. He licked his lips and cleared his throat. 'Thanks for your help, anyway.'

'You're a friend of Sari's, they say.'

'Yes. Do you know where she is?'

The man didn't respond. Mac watched him as he drove, and he saw the man shared the long features and worn expression of his sister.

'I'll leave you at our uncle's farm,' the man said presently. 'You wait there.'

An hour later they pulled up at an old farmhouse. Mac heard an owl hooting as he stood beside the car, listening to the exchange between his driver and the farmer that was supposedly his uncle. Mac didn't know the names of any of these people. He didn't understand them when they spoke in the local *Bahasa Indonesia* language. He was no longer sure why they were even bothering to help him. It was clear, however, they didn't want the authorities associating any of them with any underground rebel activities. They didn't want to be found harbouring a fugitive.

The man who'd driven Mac, now got back in his car, and without a word, drove off. The farmer introduced himself as Dimas and he took Mac around to a cramped, sparse living quarters in a barn behind the farmhouse.

'Safe here,' he said. 'But do not stay long.'

'I don't know how police would have tracked me to that inn,' Mac said, bewildered.

'I don't think they did.'

'What do you mean?'

'POLRI have been watching my nephew's inn for some time. Suspicious of them. They would've seen you arrive, a white man, not a tourist, and suspected drug activities.'

'You think that's why they were knocking on the doors at dawn?' Mac asked.

'*Ya*,' said the farmer. 'I need to ask; where are you going?'

Mac tensed himself, breathing in sharply, stifling his frustration.

'Do you know anyone who can help me get out the country safely?' he asked.

The farmer pondered this. 'There is an Australian man – newsman – often in contact with our people. We'll get a message to him. He can help.'

'Newsman?'

'*Ya.*'

'What's his name?'

The farmer cocked his head and grinned. 'Ah. Best not to use names, *ya?*'

'Is it Carl Vickerson?'

Dimas showed his surprise, and he nodded.

'*Ya*, Vickerson,' he said. 'You know him?'

THIRTY-ONE

Sally's red curls appeared in the opening of Liz's office door. 'Your 10 a.m. appointment is here.'

'Yes,' said Liz. She glanced at the diary on her PC screen. 'This is the marketing lady from MakeHay. A fashion start-up.'

Sally mouthed the words, 'What did you find out about them?'

'Nothing,' Liz whispered back. 'Nothing comes up on Google, no website, no articles.'

'Sorry, my bad,' said Sally. 'Should've checked her out without blindly making the appointment.'

'She's here now,' Liz said. 'Let's hope she's actually got some money to spend.'

Sally ushered the young woman into the office, then closed the door on her way back out.

Liz offered her hand. 'Liz Carter.'

The other woman took it and responded with a firm shake, her steely grey eyes fixed on Liz. She was well-groomed, but considering she was in the fashion business, Liz noticed she wasn't wearing anything special. She had soft features, loose, auburn hair, yet Liz sensed an intensity about her.

The woman pulled up a chair but didn't reply by introducing herself. 'Thanks for seeing me at such short notice,' she said. 'Fabulous campaign you created for TPA.'

'Thank you. And I understand you're in the fashion business?'

'I'm going to kick right off with an apology, Liz. Okay if I call you Liz?'

'Of course. An apology?'

'Yes. I'm not in the fashion business. I'm not even here to speak about your publicity work. I felt I had an–' she took a moment, searching for the appropriate word '–obligation.'

Liz was hesitant. 'Okay…'

'My father was a good man. Built a great business. Grew it quickly. Nationwide, and very profitable. My ex-husband stole it.'

'Oh.' Liz wasn't sure what was going on, or even how best to handle this woman. If anything, she felt foolish she'd allowed a complete stranger to book an appointment without knowing anything of their business background. 'I'm sorry to hear that.'

'You seem like a nice person. You have a good business of your own. So, I'm here to warn you.'

Now Liz's interest was piqued. 'Warn me? Against what?'

'Against *whom*,' the woman said. 'My ex-husband.'

'I'm sorry, but this really isn't making any sense–'

'Raf Vetrani,' the woman said. Her grey eyes were piercing into Liz, the lines around her mouth set hard as though holding something back. Anger.

'Monica?' Liz said. Raf had told her about his short-lived first marriage. He'd been far too young, he'd said, but he'd never really elaborated beyond that.

'Yes.'

Liz began to rise from behind her desk. 'I can see you're upset, Monica, but I'm really going to have to ask you to leave.'

The woman didn't move. 'Please, *Miss* Carter, sit, hear me out. He will do the same to you.'

Liz remained standing. She was conflicted between fury and pity. 'This isn't any of your–'

'While I was grieving after my father's death, he divorced me and took over the company,' Monica said. 'All the time having one dirty little affair after another.' She pulled out her phone and tapped frantically on the keys. 'I've just sent your business email the names and numbers of seven of them, just the tip of the iceberg, but you can check them out for yourself.'

Liz picked up the landline phone on her desk. 'I'm calling security.'

Monica stood, a smirk spreading across her face. 'Don't bother, I'm leaving. I don't know why I wasted my time. Thought you needed to know but maybe you deserve him. Anyway, good luck, sister, you're going to need it.'

She stormed out, and seconds later Sally – having observed the furious woman marching out – rushed into her boss's office. 'Liz?' She saw Liz was shaking. 'What happened?'

'I wish I knew. That was… bizarre.'

'*Who* was she, exactly?'

'Never mind that. Maybe just… give me a few minutes to collect my thoughts. Hold any calls.'

'Sure. And can I get you something… water? Coffee?' She reconsidered. 'Scotch?'

Liz glanced at her watch. 'A little early for Scotch.'

'Fair enough. Anything then?'

Liz sat down, steadied her hands on the desk. 'Scotch,' she said.

Sally left, and Liz's phone pinged, the alert that she'd received a new email. She opened the email account on her PC and there was the message from Monica, with the seven names and phone numbers she'd promised.

Liz wasn't inclined to believe anything Monica had said to her. She certainly didn't intend to phone any of those numbers. The very thought of Monica's accusations made her feel sick to the stomach, and a dull ache had wormed its way into her head. She glanced over the names on the list. Six of the names meant nothing to her.

It was the seventh name that brought a catch to her throat.

THIRTY-TWO

Liz busied herself for the rest of the day, but as soon as she arrived home that evening she phoned Raf.

'I had a visit today,' she told him. 'From Monica.'

Raf was still in his office. 'I'm coming straight over,' he said.

'I'm sorry you had to deal with Monica and listen to any of her BS,' he said, as Liz opened the door and he stepped in.

Liz shrugged. 'None of my business. It's just that—'

'It gave you a hell of a shock.'

'Yeah.'

They sat on the sofa.

'We're together, Liz. So, of course it's your business.'

'Exes can be bitter. I get it.'

'None of what she's likely to have told you is true. At least, not the way she slants it.'

'Okay…'

'I think we could both use a drink,' he said.

'Agreed.'

Liz began to rise off the couch but Raf touched her on the knee. 'Let me,' he said.

A few minutes later he returned from the kitchen with two glasses of Scotch and dry. 'I didn't marry Monica to get my hands on her father's company, which is what she tells anyone who'll listen. I was just a kid. I was crazy in love. But I was too young, we both were.'

'You must have been what… twenty?'

'Nineteen when I met Monica. Her father took a shine to me, I joined the company and yeah, I was ambitious, and I was married to the boss's daughter, and I advanced very quickly. So, shoot me.'

'What happened?'

'When Monica's dad died, he left the controlling shares in his business to me and Monica.' He took a sip of his drink. 'Over the years Bruno and I bought small parcels of shares in the business for ourselves. Not a hell of a lot, we only had our salaries to draw on for small investments. Then, when Monica and I split, our controlling shares were split in half.'

'And together with yours and Bruno's personal shares, you ended up with a controlling interest?'

'Yeah. I took on the MD role with the board's support, and brought Bruno in, to work alongside me. We started to expand into other companies. Monica, as you may have gathered, had never shown much interest in the firm, she'd never even bothered to work there. She's become obsessed with the idea I only ever married her with this intent all along, to take control of the family fortune then divorce her.'

Raf paused. He took a breath. 'You might not have thought so, but if there's one person who can rattle me, then it's Monica. She became impossible to live with, always hitting the bottle, wanting me to spend more time away from the office, jealous of my relationship with her father, always out partying…'

Liz looked into his eyes. There was a vulnerability there she hadn't seen before. He wasn't a man who liked to reveal his innermost emotions.

'Affairs…?'

'She accuses me of that, but Monica was the one out running around with every Tom, Dick and Playboy. Like mother, like daughter.'

'Her mother?'

'I never met her. She took off overseas with some rich toy boy when Monica was quite young. Hasn't been seen or heard of very much since.'

'So, Monica's been through a lot.'

'Well, yeah.'

'You have to at least keep that in mind. Her mum taking off, and her dad gone now as well. How did he die?'

'Car accident. Tragic. He loved cars, had a fleet of 'em. He loved nothing more than taking them for a spin on country roads, told me his real passion was motor racing. He wished he'd been another Lauda or Brock.'

Liz reached out, took his hand, and held it reassuringly. 'You really liked him, didn't you?'

'Yeah. He did a lot for me.'

'Don't let Monica get you down like this. It's been tough for her, as well. Give it time. I've actually got a… *feeling*, she might have been following me and that's how she knows we're seeing each other.'

He stiffened, a sudden alarm in his eyes. 'What?'

'A few times recently I had a suspicion the same car was behind me–'

'What sort of car?'

'A Corolla.'

'She has a Corolla.' Raf jumped to his feet. 'Crazy bitch. I need to stop this–'

Liz pulled him back down. 'Let it go. Now she's been around here and said her piece to me, I'd say she's got it out of her system and that will be that.'

'Don't be so sure–'

'If I see that car again, and if I get the chance to say anything to her, I'll tell her what I just told you. Message received, now let it go. And eventually she *will* move on with her life. Like I have.'

Liz saw the tension release from his shoulders, and he relaxed.

'You're incredible and you're the complete opposite to her,' he said. 'Talk about going from one extreme to another.'

Liz kissed him. Seeing this vulnerable side to Raf Vetrani was most definitely a turn-on.

She didn't believe Monica was anything but a bitter woman with a story and a list created specifically to create chaos. If she'd felt a pang of doubt, then it was erased by those sensitive eyes of Raf's which revealed themselves at certain intimate moments. Like this one.

Raf returned her kiss with a deep-seated hunger, his hands moving to the small of her back. She sighed, shivering from his touch, and his fingers pushed up under her blouse to the straps of her bra.

'And speaking of getting extreme…' she whispered in his ear.

THIRTY-THREE

Liz was soaring. Her weekday evenings and weekends were spent entirely with Raf and the pace was never dull. They dined, took in movies, and plays, and spent long, leisurely hours on the boat. For the first time ever, she spent less time at work, promoting Sally to take on account management, and hiring a new office PA.

Raf was always full of ideas, and on one of their dine-outs in a North Sydney steakhouse, he suggested an impromptu holiday in Fiji.

'That would be incredible, but I can't up and leave work right now.'

'When did you last take a vacation?'

She turned the question over in her mind. 'It's been a while…'

'You have no idea, do you?'

She laughed. 'Actually, no.'

'Take it from a committed entrepreneur,' Raf said, 'getting the right balance between work and play is the key to success.'

'I know—'

'Prove it. A short break, just a week. The world won't end. And your protégée Sally Markham can look after the show while you're getting some much-deserved R and R.'

'It's tempting.'

'Two weeks in paradise. And I'm footing the bill.'

'In that case, why don't we make it three.'

Raf beamed. 'Done.'

* * *

They arrived at Nadi Airport and travelled by motor coach to a luxurious, sprawling resort called The Islander. It was a world unto itself, complete with tennis courts, a golf course, pebbled beach, and shallows for snorkelling. It had its own restaurants, cafes, and shops.

They stayed in a *bure* on the beach. Each day they woke early, took a swim in the pool, followed by a leisurely breakfast. They'd spend the rest of the day exploring some exotic section of their surroundings, dine in the restaurant in the evening, and dance to the resort's own band. They sat up until late sipping cocktails on the porch of their *bure*, listening to the sound of the surf and looking out on the silvery reflection of the stars on the dark ocean.

'I'm starting to think,' Raf said, on their third evening there, 'that this might be the first time in my life I've ever really, truly *relaxed*.'

'It can happen to anyone,' Liz said, 'even workaholic entrepreneurs.'

'Look who's talking, the woman who's never been on a vacation before.'

'I've been on a holiday before.'

'Name it.'

'Privileged information.'

'Ha. Non-existent information.'

'Tell me about your previous hols.'

'I went on a couple of trips with a crazy bitch, but they're best forgotten.'

'Cruel. She has a *name*; Monica.'

'I wouldn't even call this a holiday,' he said, changing the subject.

'What would you call it? Paradise?'

'Not even that.' He put his cocktail to one side, leaned towards her, his hand brushing hers, their lips almost touching. 'Heaven on earth,' he said.

It was the middle of the third week, three nights before they were due to return, and Liz no longer felt like the same person. She'd become a wild, free spirit of the islands, and Raf had transformed in front of her eyes into a laid-back, sun-worshipping beachcomber with an endless fascination for exploring what was beyond the next cove.

They were meandering along a vast stretch of sandy shoreline, Liz in black bikini and wide, floppy hat to shield her from the sun, Raf sporting several days' stubble, in T-shirt and board shorts, almost unrecognisable from the go-getting, business-obsessed Vetrani brother.

They stopped for a rest, sitting cross-legged on the beach, and Raf said, 'Let's stay here.'

'For how long?'

'For good.'

Liz threw her head back and laughed like a madwoman. 'Who are you?'

'I don't think I know anymore. Let's become blow-in locals and find out.'

'Once upon a time I would have thought that was a crazy idea. Now I'm not so sure.'

'So, you're in?'

Liz flicked her gaze over the incredibly handsome, rugged man beside her.

'I think we both know we have to go back,' she said eventually. 'But we still have three more days.'

Raf pulled out a small, neat box from his back pocket. 'We're not the same people,' he said, 'so let's not go back as the same people.'

Liz's eyes widened. It was a jewellery box.

'What are you talking about?'

'Let's go back,' he said, 'as a humble, lucky man and his incredibly beautiful wife.'

Liz's mouth opened but no words came. She was momentarily startled as Raf then slid the lid from the box to reveal both an engagement and a wedding ring. Her eyes locked with his, looking for signs of the joke, but she saw only an earnest expression and a longing.

'Liz, will you marry me?' he asked. 'Here in paradise?'

She held his gaze and it was as though she was out in the water, being pulled in by a powerful tide towards those eyes.

She had never imagined she might one day elope. She had come a long, long way away from Rational Liz.

She broke into a smile and she could feel the deep sense of belonging between them.

'Yes,' she said.

THIRTY-FOUR

She was in a daze for the rest of the day.

Raf went to the resort's front office to make arrangements for a local marriage celebrant, confident he would be able to pull something together at short notice for the following days. After all, they were on the spot and could have the ceremony at any time of the day or night that suited.

Later, he would tell Liz the resort staff loved the idea, and would all be on hand to witness and join in with an on-the-spot party.

Liz had returned to the *bure* to decide on what she would wear when she was overcome with a sudden bout of nausea. She raced into the bathroom and threw up.

Minutes later, as she sat quietly, her phone rang.

It was Sally. 'So how is the great, once-in-a-lifetime vacation?'

'It's... wonderful.'

'You okay, boss, you sound a little... off.'

'Queasy. I just threw up.'

'Everything all right?'

'Probably nerves. Raf and I...' Her voice trailed off. Should she reveal she was about to elope?

'Raf and you what?' Sally said.

Before Liz had decided how to respond, Sally said, 'Is it the first time you've felt nauseous this week?'

'Yes.'

'You had your period?'

'You really don't have a filter, do you?' Liz said with a laugh.

'So I've been told. Well, have you?' Sally said, pressing for an answer.

'Actually, I'm a little late.'

'Have the test, Liz.'

'I'm on the pill.'

'Always best to be sure.'

Now Sally had put the idea in her head, Liz felt it best to eliminate any suspicion she might be pregnant. Now. While Raf was out.

She purchased the kit from the resort's pharmacy. In the bathroom, she peed on the strip then waited. Her pulse quickened as the seconds ticked by. Her eyes never left the strip.

Then she gasped as she saw it turn to blue.

* * *

She was sitting, still as a rock, when Raf walked back in the front door.

I have to tell him.

'Raf–'

'There's good news and bad news,' he said anxiously.

'Okay?'

'The celebrant has one spot only when she's available to fit us in.'

'Is that the good or the bad?'

'The good.'

'And the bad is?'

'That time is now.'

'Now, as in *now*?'

'As in half an hour from now.'

'Raf, I can't–'

'You know that gorgeous white strapless dress you brought along for nights out?'

'Yes.'

'It will be perfect.'

'I have to tell you something.'

Even as she spoke the words, Raf was heading back out. 'Hold the thought,' he called back. 'I've got the urgent matter of a suit to sort out.'

'Raf!'

'Won't be long.' The door closed behind him.

An hour earlier, Liz had been certain about everything that was unfolding at whirlpool speed. Now she wasn't sure how Raf would respond to this shock news or that they'd be able to proceed with this… wedding? Elopement? Whatever it was.

Her heart was thumping.

There was a knock at the door. Liz opened it to one of the resort's *talai* butlers, a gracious young Fijian woman.

'I'm Alice,' she said, introducing herself. 'So happy for you, Ms Carter. I'm here to see if I can help you get ready. Can I assist, please?'

'Come in.' Liz stood aside.

'Your husband says you have a fine white dress, a lovely dress for the wedding?' She opened the bag she had with her. 'We have beautiful white flowers for your hair, to go with your dress.'

* * *

With Alice's assistance, Liz dressed and before she knew it, Raf had walked back in, with the celebrant, a big-bodied, dark-skinned, smiling woman with a striking headband and flowing garments.

'Now don't you worry about a thing,' the celebrant said, embracing Liz. 'It may be a little sudden, but we'll make sure this is an evening to remember, eh?'

'There's a small group assembling on the beach,' Raf said. He came forward and took Liz's hands in his. 'You okay? No… reservations? Cold feet?'

'There's been time for cold feet?' Liz sucked in a deep breath.

The celebrant gave a hearty laugh. 'Honey, you keep a sense of humour like that in your life, you're going to be absolutely fine.'

One of the young, male *talai* butlers poked his head in the door. 'Looks like a storm coming in soon,' he said.

'Then we'd best get this show on the road, eh?' said the celebrant.

A strong breeze was already brushing the shoreline as Raf, arm in arm with Liz, walked across the sand, flanked on either side by a small group of staff and guests. Liz's hair whipped about her face, as they approached the spot where the celebrant had set up. Liz's voice was a croak, her nerves on edge.

'Raf, something I've been trying to tell you.'

'Sorry.' He cleared his throat, his own nerves making a rare appearance. 'I've been running around like a headless chook. What is it?'

'We're going to have a baby,' she whispered.

THIRTY-FIVE

It was mid-morning and the humidity was rising. A warm breeze carried the smells of the croplands. Mac was seated on an old timber bench at the back of the barn, when Dimas came around the side. Mac had been there three weeks when the farmer told him his "friends" had finally made contact with Carl Vickerson. Dimas had explained the journalist had been surprised but had agreed to come out to the farm.

Now, a week after that, Dimas stood before Mac, a grin on his face. 'Your friend is here.'

'He's not my friend,' Mac said. He was drawn and hollow-cheeked, the exhaustion of his plight in this country etched into every line on his face.

He followed Dimas back to the farmhouse and into the large kitchen and dining space.

Vickerson rose from his chair at the table and extended his hand. 'Long time, Mac.'

Mac ignored the outstretched hand and simply glared at the reporter. 'You managed to have Sari spirited away all those years ago. Can you help me get out of this country?'

Vickerson lowered himself back into the chair. 'Mac, why don't you sit?'

'Yes, sit, sit,' said Dimas, 'I'll bring you water.'

Reluctantly, Mac pulled up another chair.

'I only arranged for Sari to get to Kuala Lumpur,' Vickerson said, 'with forged documents so she could carry on, with you, to Sydney. I don't know why she changed her mind and disappeared.'

'I tried to get in contact with you after you wrote that damned article about me,' Mac said through clenched teeth. 'Couldn't track you down.'

'I'm here now.'

'You get your kicks betraying people's privacy and spreading lies?'

'It was just an article drawn from someone in the news,' Vickerson said matter-of-factly. 'I file the stories, sometimes I lose friends because of it – goes with the territory.'

'We're not friends, Vickerson.'

'I'm told you're in trouble and need help getting back to Sydney?'

'Yes.'

'Then what's stopping you getting on a plane?'

Mac stared at him in exasperation. He motioned towards Dimas, who was loitering at the back door. 'It wasn't explained to you?'

'I got the main thrust of it. Something about being held by secret police, you escaped and are being hunted?'

'The authorities here have some cockeyed idea I'm involved with rebels.'

'Mac, I checked that story out on my way here.'

'And?'

'There is no special police unit operating out of a safe house in Jakarta. No records of you being detained and questioned or held.'

Mac stared at him, ashen-faced, and waited for him to continue.

'I've been to the Australian embassy,' Vickerson continued. 'There is no Robert Anders or Mark Adler. No information on a case by the Indonesian authorities against you. In fact, they've never even heard of you.'

Mac wanted to explode. He clenched his fist and held the anger in. 'They're covering it up.'

'Mac, I've got good contacts at different levels, both with the embassy and within the government. Trust me, you're not on any fugitive list. They don't even know who you are.'

'That's impossible. For God's sake, Vickerson, I was held in that house for over four months. At least two uniformed guards stationed there 24/7. Bars on my bedroom window.' Mac rose, too agitated to remain seated, waving his hands to make his points. 'The embassy officials visited every couple of weeks and showed me the documentation, discussed the legal process and the investigation they had underway into Sari and her so-called rebel associates.'

'Mac, let me assure you, there's nothing stopping you from going through the airports and flying home–'

'They took my passport, my ID.'

'Then we'll get that side of things sorted, and I'll arrange your ticket. But, Mac, when you're back home, you need to see someone about all this–'

'You don't believe me?'

'Mac–'

'You think I've lost my mind!'

'Mac, I have no idea what's going on with you. I've been in touch with your employer. No one's heard anything from you or from the Indonesians. TPA had to stand you down. I tried to phone Martin de Courcey but couldn't get through.'

'This can't be real,' Mac said through heavy bouts of breath. He looked down at his hands. They were shaking.

Dimas came forward and put his hands on Mac's shoulder. 'Sit, Mac. Drink.' He placed a glass of water on the table in front of Mac. '*Drink*.'

'Why did you come over here in the first place?' Vickerson asked.

'I had a text message from Sari,' Mac said.

'After all this time?'

'Yes. Said she was in trouble and could I help.'

'So white knight McKenzie came running.'

Mac shot him a look that was pure rage.

Vickerson shrugged, as if to say "Just saying".

'Have you still got the phone with the text?' Vickerson asked.

'No. Everything was confiscated. The safe house was raided, the guards were shot dead. I ran. Didn't have time to try to find any of that.'

Mac took a long swig from the glass of water. Then, wiping his mouth, he returned his gaze to Vickerson. 'The raid, the murders—'

'None of it happened.'

'I *saw* it.'

'Then it was staged,' said Vickerson.

'You're saying it was all… a hoax?'

'I'm not saying anything, Mac. Only that you were not detained by the Indonesian government and visited by the Australian embassy.' Vickerson stood. He stretched his long arms and legs, exchanged a glance with Dimas, then resumed his seat.

'You're talking about a hoax that went on for months,' Mac said, 'and involves a property and people posing as police and diplomats and enacting violence? That's… crazy.'

Vickerson sat and stared across at Mac, saying nothing. He took a swig from his own glass of water then said to the farmer, 'You got anything stronger?'

'I've got beer,' Dimas said.

'I'd appreciate it.'

Dimas brought the bottle to Vickerson, while glancing at Mac. 'For you?'

'No, thanks,' said Mac. The last thing he needed was to cloud his already tired mind.

Vickerson drank from the bottle. He continued to watch Mac closely.

Presently, he broke the silence. 'Mac?'

'What?'

'I believe you.'

'I should be so honoured.'

Vickerson ignored the sarcasm. 'I'll help you find out what's been going on.'

'How?'

'First things first. We get you to Jakarta and you report this to the police. The real police. After that, we get you on a flight back to Oz, get you settled. You need rest. Then we start investigating, for ourselves, every aspect of what you experienced, in conjunction with the police work. We find out how and why this happened.'

THIRTY-SIX

Martin de Courcey was at his desk. He looked up and broke into a wide grin when he saw his unexpected visitor. 'Liz. How was the holiday?'

She strode in. 'I wanted to be the first one to tell you. In person.'

'Tell me what?'

She held up her hand, fingers extended, revealing both the yellow gold engagement ring and the diamond-studded wedding ring, both sparkling. 'You're looking at a newlywed.'

Martin was up out of his chair and embracing her in an instant. 'You certainly know how to surprise a person. *You're married?*'

'Raf and I eloped. Last thing anyone expected, I know. *Last thing I expected.*'

Martin stood back, appraising her in a fatherly manner. 'You're beaming.'

'Haven't stopped,' she said. 'I don't think it's actually sunk in yet.'

'If you're happy then I'm happy.'

Liz noted the mild tone of apprehension in her old friend's voice. 'I know what you're thinking. Too soon, too fast.'

'It's been… what? Close to six months since Mac's been gone–'

'Yes,' Liz said. 'Believe me, I never thought I'd be that girl who gets caught up in a fast-track romance then elopes during an exotic holiday. But you know what? Everything just… *clicked* into place.'

'As long as it's not a rebound, eh?'

'No. Not a rebound. You know, when Raf and I first started seeing each other, I thought the same. It's too soon, and besides, he's not my type. And yes, he was persistent, and yes, he's a charmer. But right from the start, everything between us felt so… natural. I stopped resisting. Figured I'd have some fun and it would either run its course or… develop into something deeper.'

'You didn't think it would be the latter.'

'No. He's kept surprising me.'

Martin took her hands in his. 'And I think you surprised yourself?'

'I think I did.'

'You fell in love.'

'Yes.'

'Then that's what matters.'

Liz gave him a peck on the cheek. 'I've got to run. I just wanted to drop by, share the news.'

'I'm glad you did. Say hello to Raf.'

'We'll be getting together with everyone very soon.'

She left, still beaming, leaving Martin with a big wave. She wasn't planning on telling anyone about the baby for at least a few more weeks. One big announcement at a time.

It was important to have called in on Martin. She knew how close he was to Mac. He'd been the one closest to the two of them. And she knew how devastated he was, as she had been, about Mac's decision to break contact and stay in Indonesia. She'd always sensed, too, Martin was a little wary of Raf.

She hoped, in time, that would change.

* * *

After Liz had left, Martin picked up his phone and made a call, but it wasn't Raf's number he tapped in.

It was the other Vetrani brother.

Martin cut to the chase. 'Bruno, have you heard?'

'Just got off the phone from Raf, yeah, he told me. Wow!'

Martin had known the brothers for a number of years, but it had always been Bruno he'd found easier to talk to, the more realistic and down to earth of the brothers.

'I know Raf and Liz have been seeing each other for a while. But I never expected anything like this. I'm the one who introduced them, for God's sake.'

'And you don't think Raf is right for Liz?'

'She's barely had time to get over her break-up from Callan McKenzie. And your brother—'

'Has a reputation,' said Bruno, 'I know. Look, I'm as surprised as you. But, Martin, Raf has been a different man these past few months. I wouldn't have believed it, but it seems Liz has had a real effect on him. He's… a hell of a lot more settled. And I've never seen him so besotted with a lady as he is with Liz.'

'Who are you trying to convince, Bruno? Me? Or yourself?'

Bruno didn't hide his irritation. '*You.*'

'Do me a favour. Keep an eye on him, on the two of them, for me.'

'Martin, it's been over two years since that incident—'

'I know. But will you let me know if anything—'

Bruno cut across him again. 'Martin, I think the world of Liz too. Believe me, if my brother mistreats her in any way, as he did with Monica, he'll have me and Caterina in his face, and this time *he'll* be the one with the black eye.'

THIRTY-SEVEN

Raf's secretary looked up as Bruno swept by, throwing her a dismissive wave as he entered Raf's office. The secretary ignored the intrusion, she knew from past experience to stay out of it whenever the brothers were on the offensive with one another. And she knew that expression on Bruno's face. He was on the warpath.

'What the hell do you think you're doing?' he said to his brother.

Raf turned from his PC screen. 'Funny way to congratulate your brother on his wedding.'

'Wedding? Is that what you call it?'

Raf's tone was flippant. 'Elopement. Betrothal. Whatever.'

Bruno spoke through clenched teeth. 'Congratulations.'

'Thank you.'

'Liz isn't just our ad contractor,' Bruno said, 'she's got a profile in the PR community and she's become a family friend–'

'And now she's my wife.'

'Do you know what you're–'

Raf cut him short. 'This is different, Bruno.' This time his tone was one of annoyance.

'Different? It's *always* going to be different.'

'This isn't like Monica or any of the others. Liz is something incredibly special.'

'I know that.'

'I'm in love with her, Bruno. I've been a different man since she's been around, even you commented…'

'And I've been telling everyone that. But we both know it's bullshit.'

'Not this time, Bruno.'

'You really expect me to believe you're a changed man? Now? After all this time, after all these years?'

'This time, yes.'

Bruno sat, briefly holding his head in his hands. 'Raf, I'm serious. Neither Caterina nor I want to see Liz hurt in any way.'

'Neither do I, bro.'

'Don't *bro* me. I've had enough of cleaning up your messes.' Bruno stabbed his finger in the air. 'We've built up a reputation in the business community. None of us need any trouble. The business doesn't need it. This time, I'm holding you to account.'

'I'm going to pretend I didn't hear that,' Raf said with steel in his eyes. 'No one holds me to account, little brother.' He leaned towards Bruno. 'All you need do is show a little faith. Liz has made me a better man. No more bad boy. This is for real. *This*' – he brought his hand to his chest and tapped it – 'is the new, improved Raf Vetrani.'

THIRTY-EIGHT

Liz woke early and glanced at the clock on the bedside table. 5.45 a.m.

It was still dark, the edges of the room touched by the first soft traces of dawn light. She slipped quietly from bed. Raf was still asleep. She pulled on a pair of blue jeans and a blue-striped blouse and went along the hall and down the stairs.

It surprised her now to realise she'd only ever been to Raf's Chatswood home once before, the night he'd revealed his hidden barista side – she was always amused when she thought of that cute, quirky moment – and on that occasion, she had seen very little of the double-storey home.

Yesterday, when they'd arrived home as man and wife, Raf had briefly taken her on a walk-through. It had been late afternoon, they were both exhausted after the flight back from Fiji and the quick trips they'd each made, individually; Liz to see Sally at the PR office, and Martin over at TPA; Raf to his own office, where he called Bruno.

She hadn't felt like lying in this morning and she wanted to explore. She was spellbound by the magnificence of the colonial-style interior with its spacious rooms, high-vaulted ceilings, and the exquisite furnishings of rosewood and carved teakwood. She went out the double sliding doors to the back veranda. She felt a rush of exhilaration, followed by an overwhelming sense of calm, as she watched the strengthening rays of sun rising and filtering over the leafy suburban landscape.

Bruno and Caterina had a beautiful home, just a few suburbs away, but it was modest compared to this large, almost-stately house which Raf had, up until now, had all to himself.

She'd understood it was a big house but there was more to it than she'd imagined. Raf and Bruno were wealthy and successful young businessmen, but this place must have been worth more than a few million.

I've barely begun getting to know this man who is my husband.

'Good morning!'

She turned to see Raf, in his satiny white robe, coming through the double doors.

'I'm glad to see you're up bright and early,' he said. 'I've got a trip to the Hawkesbury planned.'

'You want to go out on the boat?'

'No. There's a spot in the country nearby.'

'We're going for a country drive?'

'Not just a drive. There's something I want to show you.'

'What?'

'You'll have to wait and see.'

'How many more surprises have you got up that sleeve of yours?' she said, tugging his robe at the wrist, flashing a cheeky grin.

He took her face in his hands and kissed her deeply.

'I'm just getting started,' he said.

THIRTY-NINE

The drive north to the Hawkesbury area took a little over an hour. Raf took one of the turnoffs from the freeway and pulled over to the side of the road. He reached into the back seat and grabbed hold of a scarf.

'Now this may seem odd,' he said to Liz, 'but play along with me, okay?'

'What are you talking about?'

He placed the scarf around her neck then lifted it up past her chin, saying, as he did, 'I want to cover your eyes, just until we turn into the next street.'

'What?'

'Those surprises you say I've got up my sleeve; got one coming up.'

'And you don't want me to see it?'

'All will be revealed,' he said, and she allowed him to place the scarf over her eyes then tie its ends behind her head. 'Okay. Ready?'

'As I'll ever be,' she said, grinning. 'I feel like I'm eight years old, playing hide and seek.'

Raf drove along to the next turnoff, made a left turn and a few minutes later he pulled over to the side of the road and switched off the ignition.

'Hold tight,' he said.

He stepped from the car, came around to the passenger side and, taking Liz by the hand, guided her out then led her several steps onto the grass that ran alongside the road. He reached behind her again, untied the scarf and removed it.

'Voila!'

Liz gazed out over a two-acre block, a field of long grasses with blades of emerald green, a tuft of trees off towards the western aspect. The property afforded a view across the valley and down on the great, vast expanse of rolling river that was the Hawkesbury, magnificent under the mid-morning sun.

'Beautiful,' she said. 'But what are we doing here?'

'It's ours,' he said.

'Ours? You... *bought* it?'

'Long-time dream of mine,' Raf said, 'to have a piece of land overlooking the river and to build my dream home on it. Except, now, it will be *our* dream home.'

'I know Big Bear is going great guns, but… on top of the home you already have, you can afford this?'

Raf placed his arms around Liz's shoulders and began leading her forward across the land.

'We're doing very well all right but, Liz, it isn't just Big Bear that's doing great. When Bruno and I took over my father-in-law's company – Leeman Enterprises – it consisted of the rent-a-car firm he'd started, VIP, and a few smaller businesses, including the Big Bear stores. We expanded Big Bear, as you know, but we also purchased several other companies you wouldn't yet be aware of, including a couple of real estate development firms. And we've had an incredible year.'

'Feels like these surprises are going to go on forever.'

Raf laughed. 'I'll see what I can do.'

They reached the far end of the property, where a sharp incline dropped away to the wilderness reserve that bordered this side of the river.

'Bruno and I appointed a CEO to the real estate side of the business. He runs the projects, and with the ongoing real estate boom…'

'Where are the developments?'

'One is an apartment complex in Sydney's south, right near the coast, at Cronulla. There's another on the Central Coast. And a third one in Queensland, just south of Brisbane.'

'I'm starting to feel like I've married into the Murdoch family.'

He pulled her closer, kissed her on the cheek. 'Not quite, ha!' He grinned. 'I'd say the media's too volatile for the Vetrani clan. But advertising and PR, now they are fun and there are profits to be had.'

She elbowed him in the side. 'Hey, that's my turf.'

'You're a Vetrani now, so we'd be crazy not to invest in your business. How do you feel about a national network? A Liz Carter Advertising & PR office in every Australian capital city?'

'You're kidding.'

'I've already floated the idea to Bruno. We're both keen if you are.'

'In case you've forgotten, I'm pregnant. With our child.'

'We employ the crème de la crème to run the local offices. You've already had your PA, Sally – clever girl – looking after Sydney while we were away. You'd oversee it, the national face of the business, the quietly vivacious publicity queen who created the super-successful TPA and Big Bear campaigns.'

She playfully brushed her nose against his. 'I could get used to being treated this way. Love it. But you're kind of overstating my achievements.'

'If anything, I'm *under*stating them. World's your oyster now, Liz. No reason it can't be not just TPA's, but *your* window – *our* window, on the world.'

She sucked in a deep breath. 'Wow. Lots to think about. One thing at a time, maybe?'

'Of course.'

'Anyway, what's all this about your dream home?'

'Bruno and I have been coming to the Hawkesbury since we were kids. It's why we bought the boat and why we moor it out here. So, to have a big house on the hill, looking out over all this, is something of a boyhood fantasy. I put a deposit on this block a few years ago and have been paying it off in big chunks. Waiting for the right time to build.'

'And that's now?'

He squeezed her hand. 'With you. Yes.' He sat down on the spot where it began to slope, drawing her down to sit alongside him. 'The architect we used on the developments has also designed houses for wealthy clients. Great guy, just the right kind of mind to custom-design something based on our own ideas. We'll go and introduce you. He's got an office at Circular Quay, overlooking the harbour. Good for inspiration, he says.' Raf laughed.

'So, he doesn't do things by halves?' Liz said.

'Oh no, not our Richard Santini.' Raf snapped his fingers for effect. 'He approaches everything like it's his own personal Hollywood blockbuster.'

Liz's eyes connected with Raf's. 'Sounds like someone else I know,' she said.

They sat silently for a while, watching the boats on the river below, when Liz thought she heard a car and turned, looking back across the field to the road. There was a car, fading into the distance, rounding the bend in the road. *A silver Corolla?* From this distance, she couldn't be certain.

Monica Leeman? Still loitering, stalking? Surely not.

She was going to comment to Raf, but she checked herself. No point in spoiling the moment, based on something she might or might not have seen correctly.

'Let's go and meet this Spielberg of a house-builder of yours,' she said.

FORTY

Liz glanced about at the spacious suite of offices, the wall-length windows affording a glorious view of the harbour, of the Opera House with its famous sail-like structures, the Sydney Harbour Bridge, the bustle of people around the foreshores and the ferry terminals.

Richard Santini's receptionist could have stepped out of a glamour magazine, with her perfectly styled hair, high cheekbones, and Armani outfit. She beamed at them and took them through to the architect's office, complete with its couches, spectacular view, and an area that displayed model designs and floor plans.

Raf and Santini clasped hands and embraced and there was some easy banter about the last time they'd met – but

Liz was only half-listening. The opulence of the decor here, the Paris fashion-type attire, none of it put Liz at ease. Quite the opposite.

This wasn't a world she'd initially felt was the Vetrani style. It certainly wasn't the impression from the Saturday barbeques at Bruno's home. Raf's North Shore home, his Hawkesbury property, his gravitation to this higher end of town, wasn't what she'd anticipated.

Her reverie was interrupted. 'Liz?' said Raf.

They'd motioned her over to a table where a floor plan was spread.

'This is the design Richard has created, based on some of my ideas,' Raf told Liz.

She cast her gaze over the plan.

'What I want to do now, Liz,' Santini said, 'is to start incorporating some of your ideas.'

'Ideas? Okay…' She'd been caught up by Raf's enthusiasm but now she realised she wasn't really ready for this.

For a moment Liz's mind was blank.

Then, she thought of the familiar old Fisherman's Inlet home where her father had raised her. She felt the breeze on her face, felt the heat of the tropical sun at her grandparents' Cairns property, and heard the chirp of the birds.

Her finger touched the sheet where the back patio, overlooking the river, was depicted. 'This is great,' she said, 'but I'd like to see this extended all the way, a wrap-around veranda with colonial-style wooden posts and a fibreglass covering, garden beds incorporated into the design' – her finger traced the paper – 'and here, on the western side, a breezeway that leads to a walk-through aviary.'

'Young lady,' Santini said, 'you missed your calling. You would have made a brilliant architect.'

Outside the building, as they headed for the car, Liz said, 'What a day. I'm whacked.'

'Let's get home and crash,' Raf said.

'I need coffee. You can do your barista thing while I log on remotely. I want to check on a couple of things at the office.'

'Workaholic.'

'Look who's talking.'

Half an hour later, Liz kicked off her shoes, changed into T-shirt and sweatpants, and phoned Sally, who brought her up to speed on the creative ideas their team was developing for one of their newest clients. Ending the call, Liz logged on to check her emails. She scrolled through the usual emails and questions from Sally and the freelance creative team they'd been using.

Then she saw the email from Monica Leeman.

You should have listened to me. You should have called the women on that list. You've made a big mistake, but there's still time to walk away.

Her thoughts flashed on Monica's mention of the list and she recalled the names Monica had attached to the previous email, weeks before. One name had stood out to Liz, but she'd dismissed the whole thing as Monica trying to create suspicion and chaos. Liz had put it out of her mind.

She was about to delete the email when she reconsidered. She should keep the email as evidence she was being harassed by her husband's ex. She didn't want to alert Raf. Not yet. And she didn't want to have to call in the police. Not if she could avoid it. Not if she could convince Monica to leave her alone, to forget about Raf, to let it go. She created a folder and saved the email to it.

She was racing through the remaining emails when her smartphone buzzed. A text message. She checked the screen and saw it was from Monica.

It wasn't hard to get hold of Liz's number. Her agency's website had the office address along with both the office landline and her smartphone so clients could always get in touch. Good for business. Not so good when you have an unwelcome nuisance like this.

Her pulse quickened as she opened the message.

Has he promised to build your dream home yet?

FORTY-ONE

The Indonesian detective was a small, lean man with intense eyes and a manner so dry it gave Mac the impression of disinterest.

'Can you describe the men who detained and guarded you?' the detective asked.

'Yes.'

'Then we will have you sit with our identikit man. What about the house in which you were imprisoned? Could you locate it?'

'Not sure,' said Mac. 'I never actually saw it from the outside. When I fled from there it was dark, I didn't look back. I went out the front but slipped almost immediately into a side street.'

'You say you were not far from an area of docklands. Could you identify the spot?'

'I think so.'

'Then we will drive you around the harbour, looking for signs you recognise. But first, the identikit. Let's get started.'

Vickerson was with them when the police drove Mac along the streets that ringed the harbour. Mac's description led the officers to a stretch outside the main commercial zone, where smaller fishing trawlers and cargo boats operated. The rundown boathouses and wharves along there were difficult to distinguish from one another. Mac couldn't be sure of the exact location where he'd first reached the shoreline, but the general area seemed right.

They drove the streets that were set further back from the docks. Once again, these streets had a similar appearance; rows of small, dilapidated warehouses, factories interspersed with low-level residential houses and apartment blocks.

'Anything familiar?' asked the detective.

'Nothing specific. No.'

'Perhaps if we get out and walk some of these streets.'

They walked up and down several roads; there was an incline there, and Mac remembered he had run down a hilly road in the half-light of the dawn. There were dozens and dozens of houses that were pale imitations of one another.

'We need to knock on every door and look inside,' Mac said.

'That would take weeks and a great deal of manpower,' the detective said. 'And permission.'

'I don't have any other way of finding the right house.'

'Can you launch a comprehensive search?' Vickerson asked the Indonesian.

'That remains to be seen,' replied the detective. 'However, we will, of course, make enquiries of known identities in this general area.'

Mac was frustrated. He wished he could be of greater help, but apart from the identikit pics, which were fairly accurate, he'd been of no real assistance.

Back in the motel room Vickerson had rented, Mac asked, 'What did you make of the detective? He seemed… distracted.'

'These guys are inundated with cases.'

'We spent half a day with him and I didn't get a read on him at all.'

'He's not as excitable as some.'

Mac ran his hand through his hair. It had grown much longer than usual. 'What was your take?'

'I don't think he believed you,' Vickerson said.

'What? Why?'

'Look at it from a harried, overworked detective's viewpoint. You say you were arrested by POLRI, and it wasn't them. That means a group impersonating both local authorities and embassy diplomats. There's no evidence. There's certainly no apparent motive. You can't locate the place you were held. There's nothing to suggest to them a crime has actually taken place.'

'Other than my word?'

'Other than the word of an Australian, who came here because he received a text from a former lover, who also happens to be a suspected rebel.'

'So, what do they think? That I'm delusional?'

'Who knows what they think? Maybe.'

'Then how do we convince the cops this is for real?'

'We keep working at it,' Vickerson said. 'But I suspect if you want answers, you and I are going to be the ones doing the heavy lifting.'

'I'll knock on every door myself and ask the occupants if I can look inside.'

'Waste of time, Mac.' Vickerson fixed a couple of Scotches and gave one to Mac. 'For the nerves. Try to relax a little, okay?'

Mac took the glass. 'Why is it a waste of time?' He took a sip and the cold spirit tasted good.

'Most of the doors would be slammed in your face. Suspicion of a foreigner at the door. Some of those homeowners will have secrets of their own. And besides, whoever did this went to a lot of trouble and expense. They won't have left the interior of the house looking the same.'

'They'll have renovated?'

Vickerson pulled up a seat, took a mouthful of the amber liquid and savoured it. 'Exactly.'

'Is there anything we *can* do?'

'I'm going to reach out to some of my contacts here, in real estate and local government,' Vickerson said. 'We're looking for any properties in this district that were purchased or rented out in the past twelve months. Someone has planned this in advance, and one of the resources they needed was a suitable house.'

'Okay.' Mac wrung his hands and looked closely at Vickerson. 'Why are you helping me like this?' he said.

'Like I said, I believe you. Something very screwy is going on. What's more, this is one hell of a news story, and just so we're clear, I intend to report it. So, if you want me out of the picture, Mac, just say so. Your call.'

Mac didn't respond straight away. He drank the Scotch. Conflicting thoughts ricocheted through his mind. He didn't like Vickerson. Didn't trust him. At the same time, Vickerson had extensive Indonesian contacts.

He put the glass down on the adjacent coffee table. He wiped the sweat from his eyes. 'Seems I'm going to need all the help I can get,' he said.

FORTY-TWO

Mac woke and glanced at the bedside clock. 4 p.m.

Vickerson had rented a two-bedroom hotel room for a couple of days. He'd pointed out that, in addition to communicating with police, Mac needed plenty of rest. Mac had initially wanted to jump on the phone to Liz, Martin, and TPA but Vickerson had cautioned against that.

'You need to have a clear head,' Vickerson had said. 'At the moment you're exhausted, you're rambling, you're all over the place. And we don't know what's happening back home where you're concerned. It will be a shock to everyone to hear from you suddenly, so let me ease the way, let me make the first calls.'

Mac hadn't agreed. He wanted to make the calls. Sure, he needed some rest first, but hadn't expected being dead to the world the rest of that evening, the whole night and most of the next day. He padded out into the living area, groggy and lethargic.

Vickerson had set himself up at the dining table. He was on his phone, talking, facing his laptop, surrounded by notepads and papers. Mac went through to the kitchen, made a coffee and once he joined Vickerson at the table the reporter was off the phone.

'You described the place you were held,' Vickerson said, 'as having a large, paved walled-in garden at the back. Bars on your bedroom window facing onto that garden…'

'Yes.'

'A large house with a modern kitchen and tiled floor in the dining area, freshly painted walls, otherwise older-style but most of the rooms closed off to you.'

'And with a couple of guards at all times,' Mac said, 'one of them always positioned at or near the front entrance.'

'Your interior and garden descriptions don't fit with the rundown conditions in that part of the town.' Vickerson was tapping away at the keyboard as he spoke. 'I was making contact all morning with local builders, landscapers, and renovators. One of those landscapers has a record of paving a courtyard and building a stone wall at a house near the docks there, just over six months ago—'

Mac felt a sudden surge of adrenaline, sweeping away his lethargy. 'That has to be it.'

'I was able to get an address from the landscaper,' Vickerson said, 'and it was a simple search with local government to identify the sales history of the house.' He drew away from the laptop screen, his attention now on Mac. 'It was purchased three years ago by a company called C-Max Imports, and was sold just a few weeks ago to a local investor who plans to lease the property.'

Mac leaned forward. 'We need to get over there.'

'And as soon as I've been able to contact the investor, I'll arrange for us to go to the house posing as potential clients.'

'In the meantime–'

Vickerson cut across him. 'In the meantime, you need food.'

Mac didn't think he would settle that night but once again he fell into a deep sleep, this time being woken by Vickerson at 9 a.m.

'We've got an appointment this morning to look at that house.'

On the taxi ride down to the old docks area, Vickerson turned to Mac. 'When we get back to the hotel, once the time zone for Sydney is right, I'll make those advance calls so friends and TPA know you're coming.'

Mac shrugged. 'Did you find out anything about C-Max Imports?' he asked Vickerson.

'Shell company, no records of any actual business being conducted, set up by an Indonesian named Johnny Makawi who has his finger in a few pies.'

'What else have you discovered about this Makawi?'

'Nothing.'

'Why's that?'

'He doesn't actually exist,' Vickerson said.

FORTY-THREE

'Thank you for coming in,' the psychologist said to Mac as she ushered him into a room at the police station. 'The detective inspector is concerned about the psychological impact of your ordeal. I think it is a good idea for the two of us to have a chat. I hope you're okay with that.'

'Sure.'

The detective had contacted Mac while he and Vickerson were on their way back from the house Vickerson had located. The house didn't look the same as when Mac had been there, it had been completely renovated. The detective had asked them to drop by the station and it was there he'd asked Mac to have the counselling session.

'I don't need counselling,' Mac had said in protest.

'We always advise at least one session when someone has been the victim of a crime like this,' the detective inspector said.

'Can't hurt, Mac,' Vickerson had said, 'and while you're doing that, I'll bring the inspector up to speed on what we've learned about the house.'

The psychologist was a calming personality, as Mac would've expected, and she spoke with both compassion and authority.

'Let me start by asking you if there are any periods of time over the past several months for which you can't account; for which you have no memory?'

'No.'

'No missing days or even just hours, for example?'

'None. Why would you think that?'

'We simply want to eliminate any possibility the trauma has affected your memory or your perception of what's been happening. Memory loss is not uncommon in situations like this.'

'I didn't imagine being locked up for over four months. And the reporter, Carl Vickerson, has tracked down the house where I was held.'

The woman smiled encouragingly. 'That is good. The team will follow through on that. Now, having been held for such a long period of time, the mind can play tricks, particularly if you were unknowingly fed drugs.'

'I was tested for traces of that when I came in before.'

'And the inspector will have those results in hand very soon, however, casting your mind back, do you recall any instances where you could have had your perceptions distorted by–'

Mac leaned forward, his voice raised, his eyes burning with frustration. 'What are you implying here? That I imagined all this?'

'Nothing,' the psychologist assured him. 'Please, Mac, just relax, take a moment. I'm here to help you, and to make certain the inspector and his team can investigate this to the best of everyone's ability. Part of that is ensuring, after this traumatic ordeal, you're in the best mental state to assist.'

'And I am,' Mac said. 'Apart from the fact my abductors misled me into believing they were both Indonesian and Australian officials, my memory and my perceptions are one hundred percent crystal clear on everything. I understand there's no motive for any of this, and I have no hard evidence at this point to back any of it up, but it's real, and I need to be taken seriously.'

'You can be assured, Mac,' the psychologist said, 'it's being taken very seriously.'

The psychologist went on to speak to Mac about the need to accept that he'd been emotionally affected by his kidnap. Indeed, he wouldn't be human if he hadn't been. She encouraged him that in the short term he should talk this through, if not with her, then with another counsellor back in Sydney.

Mac agreed.

She cocked her head towards the glass-panel office wall. 'Ah, the inspector. I know that look, I think perhaps he has some news for you.'

The inspector was waiting to talk to Mac after the session, taking him through to another office. 'We have the results of our test,' he said, motioning for Mac to take a seat. 'Just to reconfirm, Mac, you haven't been a recreational drug user in the past?'

'No.'

'During your time in the house, were you unusually tired? Unmotivated?'

'I did push-ups and ran on the spot in the garden but apart from that, I obviously couldn't have the same level of activity I'm used to. So yeah, I started getting lethargic, I was restless and got tired, bored easily. Why?'

'We found traces of various substances in your system, Mac. One of them was a mild sedative that would have made you tired, even a little disinterested, without you probably being aware of it. And it would have worked in conjunction with very small doses of another drug to keep you from boiling over, becoming violent due to anger, perhaps creating an unrealistic feeling of comfort or relaxation at times.'

'What other drug?' Mac asked.

'Ketamine,' said the inspector.

FORTY-FOUR

Two months prior, TPA had advised staff and media that Captain Callan McKenzie was on extended leave, holidaying overseas. In his capacity as marketing manager, Martin thought it best to hold back on revealing the facts, including the news the airline had stood Mac down from his position. As their PR consultant, Liz agreed. They could fine-tune their strategy on this once Mac had been in contact and future arrangements had been negotiated.

With Sally Markham by her side as co-presenter, Liz was wrapping up a presentation to Martin and the TPA board. Since announcing her pregnancy, Liz had been training Sally to take over more and more of the daily management. This presentation was for the next phase of the *Window On The World* campaign.

For this cycle, the creative focus was on three new staff members – a pilot, an engineer, and a hostess – featuring each of them individually, and as an ensemble across print, digital and broadcast media spots. For this stage of the campaign, there was more emphasis on the quality of service and the diversity of flight destinations.

Afterwards, Liz and Sally made their way to Martin's office. He joined them there a few minutes later.

'It's been well received,' he told them as he strode in and eased himself into the chair at his desk.

'I'm relieved,' Liz said.

'Actually, they're happy the advertising focus this time around is less reliant on one individual. As we all know, no one expected the sudden media attention that fell on Mac.'

Sally playfully punched Liz on the shoulder. 'Told you they'd love it, worrywart. Although I'm not certain the media might not find another bandwagon to jump on.'

Liz and Martin shot her a look.

'What do you mean?' Liz said.

'The engineer guy is kind of hunky in a tradie sort of way.'

'Down, girl.'

'I could do that,' Sally said with a mischievous squint.

Martin grinned, wagging his finger at Sally. 'Keep it clean, ladies.'

The landline on Martin's desk rang. 'Give me a minute, girls,' he said as he picked it up.

'Martin,' his secretary said, 'I have a call from overseas. It's a reporter but he says this is an urgent, personal matter.'

'What's his name?'

'He wouldn't say. Do you want me to get rid of him?'

Martin's instincts were telling him otherwise. 'Put him through. I'll handle it.'

A moment later a voice he didn't immediately recognize came on the line. 'Mr de Courcey?'

'Speaking.'

'I'm calling from Jakarta. It's Carl Vickerson—'

'Vickerson?' Martin saw Liz's shoulders stiffen and she sat up straighter in her chair at the mention of Vickerson's name.

'I've got Callan McKenzie with me,' Vickerson said. 'He's been the victim of a crime here in Indonesia. He's coming home soon, and wants to speak with yourself and his girlfriend, Liz Carter, but given the length of time he's been gone, rather than just make a call himself out of the blue, we thought it best if I gave you some pre-warning. I've been trying to phone Miss Carter—'

'You're the one who wrote that ridiculous so-called exposé on Mac,' Martin said, barely containing his disgust. 'So, what the hell are you up to this time?'

'Mac was held against his will, cut off from all contact. It's a long story, Mr de Courcey, but he reached out to me for help. The point is, I simply wanted to let you know he is okay, he is free, and he will be on his way home and getting in touch.'

'Martin, what's happening…?' Liz said.

Beside her, Sally also sat rigidly, eyes on Martin.

'Put Mac on the phone,' Martin said.

There was some discussion at the other end, Martin could just make out the muted voices, then for the first time in almost six months he heard the voice of his old friend.

'Martin?'

'Mac, thank God, I've been trying to get in touch with you. We all have. What's going on? What are you doing there with Vickerson?'

Martin listened as Mac gave him a brief, bare-bones rundown on how he'd been held captive then escaped.

At first, Martin didn't respond. None of this sounded real.

'Martin?' Mac said.

'Mac, the HR people here received an email from you stating you were taking extended leave. Liz received a text saying–' he paused, searching for the right words but wasn't sure there were any '–you weren't coming home, you were staying with Sari.'

'What?' Mac said. 'Christ…'

Liz was motioning to Martin to hand the phone to her, but he instinctively felt it was best to hold back. At this point anyway. He could see Liz was on edge and he knew how much she'd been hurt. And now she was a married woman. Mac was sounding desperate, not like himself at all; the story he told made little sense, and Martin didn't like the simple fact that Carl Vickerson was involved.

'Mac, I'll pass all this on to Liz. Get in touch when you're back, we need to talk, a lot has changed here, okay?'

'What's changed?'

Martin saw Liz mouthing the words "Tell him".

He took a deep breath. 'Mac…'

'Yes?'

'I'm sorry to have to break it like this…'

'Break what?'

'Liz is married.' Martin wondered whether to add that Liz was pregnant but stopped short. One thing at a time…

'Married?'

'Yes.'

There was a long silence.

'Mac, just call me as soon as you're back in Sydney. Okay?'

Still no response

'Mac…'

His voice was a croak. 'Yeah.'

'Call me the moment you're at the airport. I'll pick you up. Okay?'

'Okay…'

Martin ended the call. He felt Liz and Sally's eyes boring into him.

'Liz,' he said, 'something's not right...'

FORTY-FIVE

Martin was at the gate when the passengers off Flight 416 from Jakarta came through. His first shock was Mac's appearance, his gaunt cheeks and hollow expression, although Mac's eyes lit up when he saw his old friend and mentor.

They shook hands then embraced. 'So damn good to see you,' Martin said.

'You bet.'

'I've kept the rent up on your apartment,' Martin told him as they made their way across the concourse towards the parking station. 'But you're staying with me the first few nights at least. You're going to need plenty of relaxation by the look of it.'

'No need, Martin, the last thing I want is to be any further burden.'

Martin flashed him a warm grin. 'You couldn't be a burden on me if you put your heart and soul into it. You're staying with me, no argument. Now, what about your luggage?'

Mac spread his arms. 'What you see is what you get.'

'At least you were able to get a passport arranged,' Martin said.

They reached the car. 'I've discussed your situation with the TPA brass,' Martin said, as they got in and adjusted their seat belts. 'I've arranged for the Indonesian police to send some correspondence, verifying the report of your abduction, and we'll set up a meeting with the chief. There'll be no problem reinstating you.'

They exited the parking station, Mac looking out on the familiar airport roads and freeway exits that surrounded Kingsford Smith International.

'I'm not sure what my immediate plans are,' Mac said.

'I understand, there'll be plenty of time to–'

'You said Liz was married,' Mac said.

'Yes.'

'Who did she marry?'

'One of her clients. Raf Vetrani.'

'The Big Bear convenience stores guy?'

'Yes.'

'She thought he was charming but arrogant. Full of it.'

'I'm sorry, Mac… I know it must all come as a hell of a shock. She received that text, supposedly from you.'

'It broke her heart.'

'It rocked her, Mac, and it took her a while to bounce back but you know Liz–'

'It didn't seem to take her very long at all. Just a few months.'

'It's not for me to say.' Martin adopted a diplomatic tone. 'I thought maybe it was a rebound thing, you know, but I guess they clicked and–'

'I need to find out who sent that text.'

'The Indonesians are investigating?' Martin asked.

'They're not making much progress. Vickerson doesn't think they believe me. They think I'm a bit of a nutcase.'

'How did Vickerson get involved?' Martin pulled into the driveway of his Bondi Beach home.

'After I escaped the house where I was being held, I sought out people who might have known Sari.'

'An underground network?'

'Yes. And they'd had dealings with Vickerson. They contacted him.'

'Mac, can you trust him?'

'No one can trust Vickerson,' Mac said, 'but his contacts, journalistic and otherwise, have been a lot more help than the police or our embassy.'

They had arrived at Martin's. They walked up the drive and through the front door.

'Has he had much success?' Martin asked.

'We found the house I was kept in. It's been resold and renovated, no evidence left behind of any kind. But Vickerson has traced the name of the company that owned and has now sold it.'

'And?'

'Just a shell company. No traces of any actual business taking place. And the director, Johnny Makawi, is a man that doesn't appear to exist. There are no other records on him and his contact details are fake.'

'I'm… stunned,' Martin said. He flopped down on the living room couch. 'And I'm bushed, and you must be jetlagged. I'll arrange some food in a moment. First, sit. Catch your breath.'

Mac remained standing. 'When was the wedding?'

'They eloped. Just a few weeks ago. And, Mac, there's something else–'

'I need to see her,' Mac said.

FORTY-SIX

Mac had longed for this moment for over six months. Now it was finally here, he was dreading it.

It was not the reunion he could ever have possibly imagined.

Martin had spoken with Liz and she'd agreed to meet with Mac, suggesting he come to her new home, in Chatswood, at 11 a.m. She would be there alone in the morning for their meeting, and would head off to work later.

It was one of those days made dull by heavy, dark clouds. The door opened and there she was, achingly beautiful, more so than he remembered. He sensed the awkwardness between them, something that had never been there before. It was to be expected, and was just one of a multitude of regrets that consumed Mac.

'Hello, Mac.'

'Hi.'

'Come on in.' Her eyes were wide with curiosity, he noted, while her face was a cast of disappointment. An unusual blend, but then of course nothing was remotely normal about this situation.

Mac followed her through the front alcove and into the main living area. He glanced about. 'Quite the place.'

'Yes.'

An awkward pause. Mac had rehearsed many times what he was going to say but now he found himself speechless, trying to recall just *one* of the words he'd planned. He hated this. He realised, in that moment, he wasn't the same person. And neither was Liz.

'Let me show you the house,' Liz said.

They walked through the kitchen and out onto the covered rear patio. They were silent, at first. A light rain had begun to fall.

Presently, as they looked out on the garden, Liz said, 'After I received the text saying you weren't coming back, I expected to take it easy for a while. But then, suddenly, things began to escalate at the speed of light with Raf. Sometimes I think that man is going through life like a whirlwind. He does everything at warp speed.'

'You know I didn't send that text?'

'Martin told me.'

'I'm so sorry this happened, Liz,' Mac said, 'but at the same time I'm genuinely pleased you've found happiness. You deserve it. And Martin spilled your big news. You're pregnant.'

'Yes.'

'Then congratulations are in order.'

He wanted to shout out, "I love you, I don't want to lose you, this should never have happened." But how could he? Everything had changed so quickly. Liz had believed he'd left her. She fell in love and married another man. She was pregnant with another man's baby. She'd moved on, swept up – in her own words – by the whirlwind that was Raf Vetrani.

'Do you have any idea who locked you up like that?' Liz asked.

'Vickerson suspects it was either rebel activity, opposed to Sari's group, or unsanctioned police action, with the intent of drawing out Sari and her network.'

'Is there any evidence of that?'

'No.'

'And there was no contact between your abductors with Sari or her people, no ransom demands, no traps laid to catch her?'

'If there was, I wouldn't know about it. And it seems I was being drugged, apparently to keep me docile and easy to handle.'

'My God. And you believed you were being held the whole time by Indonesian authorities?'

'Yes.'

Liz motioned to the outdoor seating. 'Let's sit.'

They pulled up the wicker chairs and Mac hoped the awkwardness between them would ease. It didn't. There was a distance.

His heart ached for this woman.

'So, what do the Indonesian police have to say about all this?'

'They're vague. Their investigations have gone round in circles. Truth is, they don't seem to believe me.'

The comment took Liz by surprise and Mac saw her body straighten. 'What? Why would you lie?'

'They had their psychologist talk to me before I left for Sydney. She raised the possibility I'd been suffering from a traumatic event. I could have been fantasizing as well as suffering severe memory loss.'

'What about the drugs? Surely they don't think–?'

'That I took them? That I'm an addict? They haven't said that, but I'm certain they consider it a possibility.'

'But you have proof of what happened to you.'

He spread his hands helplessly. 'Actually, I don't have anything.'

'But I have your text messages.'

'They don't prove anything one way or another. As far as the police are concerned, I could have sent those texts myself while in a state of acute stress.'

'What about the text you originally received from Sari?'

'I don't have the phone.'

'But I saw it,' Liz said, reminding him.

'Still doesn't prove a damn thing. Even if I did receive a message from her, doesn't discount me having this so-called potential psychotic breakdown when I arrived over there.'

'But you don't believe that's what happened to you?'

'No. I know it didn't.'

Liz reached out, took his hand in hers. 'I'm so sorry you've been put through all this, Mac.'

'I know.'

'I wish there was something, anything, Raf and I could do to help.'

'Thanks. But this is something I have to deal with myself, and I've got support. Martin, and–'

'Vickerson?'

'Yeah.'

'I thought he was the enemy, after *that* article…'

'I don't know what he is,' Mac said truthfully, 'but right now he seems as mystified and as determined to find answers as I am.'

'I guess, to him, it's another news story.'

Mac shrugged. 'I think that's what everything is to Vickerson,' he said. 'Anyway, I've taken up enough of your time. I just wanted to see you. Set the record straight.'

'It's straightened,' she said with a gentle smile.

Liz walked with Mac to the front door.

'So much has happened. For both of us,' she said. 'But, Mac, if things had been… different…'

'They weren't.' He gave her a departing peck on the cheek, lingering close to her a moment more than perhaps he should have.

'I wish you all the best, Liz,' he said, then he turned and walked quickly through the rain to his car.

'Stay in touch, Mac,' she called after him.

Joining the Pacific Highway traffic, his hands gripping the steering wheel tightly, Mac felt the anguish rise inside. The windscreen wipers swished back and forth. He wanted to smash his fist into the windscreen, he wanted to choke up and cry. He hadn't cried tears since he'd been a young boy.

He did neither. Instead, he just drove. And drove.

And drove.

* * *

Liz watched him drive away. She went back into the house and up to the main bedroom on the upper level.

Wide glass doors opened onto a balcony. She stood, hands on the railing, looking out over the garden and the rooftops and the trees of the surrounding neighbourhood. A wind had sprung up and the rainfall was heavier now.

She was in love with Raf, so what was this she was feeling for Mac? Sympathy? Regret? It had, after all, been only six months. But after that text she'd shut down her emotions, and after a few months her friendship and professional relationship with Raf had morphed into something else entirely.

She heard far-off thunder.

She couldn't stop herself from remembering the past and imagining what might have been in a different universe.

It's not what I feel now. It's not who I am now.

And yet, those locked-away emotions had come to the fore and she needed to let them loose. She wanted to scream them out.

Inside she was wailing like the bird that had given her nightmares in her childhood.

FORTY-SEVEN

It was the annual TPA address to shareholders, a gala business event at the InterContinental on Macquarie Street, just an easy walk from the harbour foreshore. Liz was seated at the directors' table to the front of the convention room, taking her cue with the others to applaud as Martin de Courcey was called to the podium.

'One thing I don't have to stand here and sound convincing about,' the CEO said to a smattering of laughs, 'is the positive impact our marketing and PR has had over the past year. You're all well aware of that, and we've all seen the uplift in our share price. So, I'm now handing over to our marketing manager, Martin de Courcey, who will highlight just how the campaign has expanded our national sales and profits.'

Martin took his place, raising the mic to his lips. 'Thank you…'

The months had flashed by quickly for Liz. She made every effort to push Mac and his dilemma to the back of her mind. She was caught up in the exhilaration of being with Raf, the excitement of the house they were building by the Hawkesbury, and the challenge of expanding her agency.

She'd texted Mac a few times but had no response.

'With both our profile and our national bookings in overdrive,' Martin said, 'TPA is now formulating plans to expand our market share further in key locations...'

Listening to Martin, Liz was reminded that her own business seemed to be in tandem with TPA when it came to this new wave of growth. With her agency rebranded as Liz Vetrani Communications, Liz had interviewed and employed bright account managers to run her offices in Brisbane and Melbourne. She'd expanded her suite of offices in the Australia Square Tower in George Street. Raf had said that later they would look at furthering the expansion into Adelaide and Perth. He was always thinking big, always enthused with new ideas.

When she said that to Raf, he patted her swelling belly. 'We've got an heir on the way,' he'd said, beaming. 'When we're finished, and he's grown, he'll be inheriting quite the empire.'

Raf had opened doors, and Liz and her team were adding a couple of major new accounts each month.

One of the directors at the table leaned towards Liz, interrupting her thoughts as he whispered in her ear, 'Good speech. Martin knows how to deliver...'

'Gift of the gab,' Liz whispered back, smiling.

'He's got good words to work with. Your words?'

'A collaboration,' Liz said, her smile broadening cheekily, 'but mostly mine.'

Martin was winding up his speech. '...and a special round of applause, if you will, to the young lady seated here, Ms Liz Vetrani, our PR and advertising consultant – give us a wave, Liz – whose exceptional contribution has certainly made my job a whole lot easier.'

After the speeches, a duo played soft jazz as the guests mingled. Liz's and Martin's glasses were refilled by a waiter. Neither of them could have been unaware that of the many promotional posters on the walls, several were of Captain Mac.

'How is he, Martin?' Liz asked, cocking her head in the direction of one of the posters.

'He's taking an extended break. He hasn't been in any rush to resume duties.'

'Is he okay?'

'He tells me he is, but to be honest I haven't spoken much with him lately. He hasn't been easy to contact.'

'I know.'

'I'm hoping he'll be back in town, and back in the cockpit, sooner rather than later.'

Martin was being drawn away by one of the directors when Liz caught sight of Monica Leeman in the crowd, approaching. Her hair was styled differently, her backless evening gown attracting stares.

Monica stepped in her path as Liz turned to move away.

'I see you fell pregnant even though you were on birth control,' Monica said.

'What are you doing here, Monica?'

'I'm a guest. You haven't forgotten I still hold my parcel of shares in Vetrani Investments, even though I have no control and hold no positions there?'

'No, of course I haven't forgotten—'

'I have a few TPA shares of my own as well, and this, after all, is a shareholders' event.'

'What do you want, Monica?'

Monica motioned towards Liz's belly. 'What happened?'

'Not that it's any of your business,' said Liz, 'but what makes you think I was on birth control?'

'You and Raf were only dating for just a few months. You eloped suddenly and clearly you were already pregnant at that time.'

'That doesn't mean I was still taking the pill.'

'Of course you were.'

'It's none of your business, Monica. You need to stop this. You need to let this obsession of yours go.'

'Have you looked into why the pills didn't work?'

'The doctors—'

'Said there's a small percentage of situations where this happens,' Monica said, completing the response for Liz. 'That may be so, but why you, why now?'

'Monica—'

'Were the pills checked?'

Liz simply glared back, her patience at an end. 'That's enough.'

'And where is the great man tonight? Is he still using that line about flying all over the country, building his beloved little empire?' Monica's eyes locked with Liz's, and she saw the hesitation there. 'Oh, of course he is.'

'I said that's enough.'

'I'm going,' said Monica. 'Really don't know why I keep worrying about you. You're just not getting it, are you?' She began walking away. 'I'm betting those pills have disappeared. But if you can find them, Mrs Vetrani, *get them checked.*'

Martin moved back alongside Liz. 'That's a mighty big frown on your night of nights,' he said. 'Everything okay?'

'Fine thanks, Martin.'

'Who was that?' He gestured to the exit as Monica walked out.

'Raf's ex.'

'That's Monica? She's still turning up uninvited, creating tension. I thought—'

'She'd given up? So did I. Apparently not.'

'What did she want this time?'

'Nothing worth talking about.'

'Liz—'

'Don't worry. I'm through giving that woman the chance to move on. If she makes one more approach, even though she hasn't done anything threatening, I'll be having a discussion with the cops.'

'You'd take an injunction against her?'

'Not sure there are grounds for that, but I'll at least discuss what the options are.'

The rest of the evening was like a flash. Liz had brief conversations with many of the directors and guests, but later couldn't recall anything that had been said.

Her nerves were on edge. She found herself battling to keep her hands from shaking. What was it about that woman that played on her mind? She couldn't seem to get Monica's words about her birth control pills out of her thoughts.

If you can find them, get them checked.

FORTY-EIGHT

Liz opened the front door and embraced Sally as she led her inside. 'Thanks for coming.'

'No probs,' said Sally, glancing about the Chatswood home. 'Nice digs. What's this about?'

'I need some help from someone level-headed and impartial. I don't know anyone who fits the bill the way you do, Sal.'

'Me? In that department, I'm just a rank amateur next to you.'

'Maybe once,' Liz said. 'Now I'm not so sure.'

'What makes you say that?'

'I eloped with a man I'd been dating only a few months.'

'Yeah… well… ain't love grand?' said Sally with a wink. 'So how can I help?'

'I want someone clear-headed to tell me if I'm being paranoid or not.'

'Okay.'

'I found out I was pregnant while we were in Fiji,' Liz said. 'So I had no need to keep taking the pill.'

'Of course not.'

'When I returned to Sydney, I threw the pack into the bathroom cabinet and forgot about it.'

'Has this got something to do with Raf's ex at the function last night? What did she say?'

'It's more what she implied.'

'Which was?'

'That I get the pills checked, *if* I could find them.'

'Right,' said Sally, 'we're now officially on the paranoia border.'

'The pills are gone.'

'And we're crossing over.' Sally took a moment to examine Liz's face. She'd never seen her boss frazzled like this. 'Seriously, Liz, you probably threw them out.'

'I didn't.'

'Liz, you've got to stop letting this strange woman get into your head.'

'I know. It's just...'

'What? You really think the pills could've been... what? Tampered with? Or switched?'

'I don't know what to think. That's where your level-headedness comes in.'

'You were on holiday, Liz, all out of routine. You probably just forgot to take the pill one or two nights. Not so unusual. And when you got home, the pills could easily have been misplaced. Happens all the time.'

'Thanks. I needed someone down to earth to speak some sense to me.'

'Anytime,' said Sally. 'So, is everything with you and Raf okay?'

'Great.'

'Where is he?'

'Out of town. Actually, he's been spending two or three nights away, each week, for the past month or so. Looking for companies to buy.'

'That's Raf.'

'Yes. And he's been spending more and more time with his buddies on a yacht they've recently purchased.'

'Training for the Sydney to Hobart?'

'Yeah. That race is a long-time dream of his. And now we're spending more time apart than I'd hoped.'

'You married Mr Busy-Taking-Over-The-World, so I guess it's to be expected.'

Liz patted her swollen belly. 'It's just the hormones talking.'

'And that's to be expected, too.' Sally bent down and placed her ear against Liz's stomach. 'No more stressing about missing pills. You're having a baby, which is absolutely fantastic – I can hear its little heart beating – and you're going to be the best mother in the world. Got it?'

'Got it.'

* * *

Later, after Sally had left, Liz was in the bedroom slipping into her negligee, when she was struck by a sudden thought.

I just can't switch off from this damn thing.

She went down to the study-office Raf used when he was at home. It adjoined the double garage at the side of the house. Liz remembered there was a storage area with shelving in an alcove between the two areas. Raf tended to stash all sorts of odds and ends in there. She'd never had any reason to go into that alcove herself, but she'd seen it from the study.

If Raf had removed the pills, then he would most likely have thrown them out with the rubbish. So, there was no reason to go looking in his storage spot.

And yet here I am.

She rummaged through the shelves. There was no sign of her birth control pills. She was about to retreat when her eye caught a medium-sized dark blue pouch she hadn't seen before. She recognised it as one of those handy travel packs she'd seen in department stores. She slid back the outer catch and opened it. The interior was a transparent Ziploc bag with multiple pill-holding compartments.

She took out one of the pills and held it between her thumb and forefinger. The edges were rounded slightly differently to her birth control pills, and the surface wasn't as smooth. However, those slight differences weren't noticeable, unless you were examining it closely and *looking* for differences.

What are these pills?

She kept the pill and replaced the travel pouch on the shelf. One of her recently acquired clients was a small pharmaceutical firm and she hoped her contacts there would do her a favour and have the pill analysed.

Back in the bedroom, she placed the pill in her handbag then lay down. The softness of the pillow against her head was pure heaven. She was tired, and she had an early start the next day. But the more she tried to push Monica Leeman and the pills from her mind, the more awake she became.

It's going to be one of those nights.

Damn.

The minutes ticked by. Just as drowsiness was finally overtaking her, she was startled by the shrill ring of her alarm.

6.30 a.m.

New day.

Yeah, right.

She dragged herself from her bed. Usually, she faced the mornings with a sense of exhilaration and excitement, but today she found herself filled with dread.

FORTY-NINE

Liz picked up the phone late that afternoon. She was instantly more alert when she heard the voice on the other end of the line. It was her contact at the pharmaceutical company, Dr Michael Su, a calm, genial, middle-aged man with whom it had been easy to establish a rapport.

'Hi, Liz. I've got the results you asked for.'

'I really appreciate your help, Michael,' Liz said. 'What did you find?'

'Absolutely nothing. I don't know where you obtained this tablet, it's nothing but a harmless powder. No medical properties whatsoever.'

'Like a placebo?' Liz asked.

'That's exactly what it is.'

* * *

'A placebo.' Sally had seated herself in front of her boss's desk. She'd been called in and told what had happened, after Liz had finished the call. 'And Raf has a whole heap of these stashed away?'

'Yes.'

'And you think he switched these out with your birth control pills?'

'It's too much of a coincidence.' Liz shifted her weight to ease the tension in her shoulders and her back.

'Why on earth would he think he needed to do that?' asked Sally. 'After all, you were getting married. And married couples *do* have babies.'

'Yes, but although he planned to propose to me in Fiji he didn't know I'd say yes and agree to elope then and there.'

'Even so…'

'Don't get me wrong, I'm thrilled about the baby,' Liz said, 'but it's not something I would've intended at this point in time, not with the marriage so new and the busyness of both Raf and myself expanding our businesses.'

'Too much happening all at once,' said Sally.

'Exactly.'

'Liz, if you think Raf did this, then you have to confront him and talk it through.'

'He'll come up with a perfectly reasonable explanation – that the pills I found were samples of some proposed business venture, something like that… he's always got an answer.'

'You can't let something like this just sit there in your mind, hanging between the two of you. You have to talk to him.'

'I know.'

'Before you do… maybe there's something else you should do.'

'Such as?'

'I can't believe I'm saying this,' Sally said, 'but perhaps… first… you should be the one to go and confront Monica Leeman, instead of it always being the other way around. She's been feeding you these suspicions… sending texts… dropping hints… instead of just coming out and saying what she means. Maybe you need to establish once and for all just what she knows, and how much of it is real and how much of it isn't.'

'I'm not sure I could trust anything that comes from her mouth,' Liz said.

She was silent for a moment, pondering this as Sally looked on.

'Before I talk to Monica, there is someone else I could talk to first.'

'Who?' Sally asked.

'Raf's sister-in-law.'

'Bruno's wife?'

'Yes,' said Liz. 'I've always got on well with Caterina. Happy, bubbly, but she's also the grounded, earth mother type. And there's something else...'

Sally waited expectantly while Liz considered her next words carefully.

'Something Monica sent me... I ignored it at the time... something that, I think I always knew, sooner or later, I was going to have to show to Caterina.'

FIFTY

Despite everything, Liz had always found something particularly comforting in the weekly Saturday evening barbeque at Bruno's home. As usual she was met with hugs by Caterina as she was led through to the dining room.

'So unusual to have Raf miss two of these in a row,' Caterina said, 'but I'm so glad you've come anyway.'

'He's been spending more and more time in Melbourne this past fortnight,' Liz said. 'Big deal on the verge of being signed off.'

'He's pushing everything too hard at the moment,' said Bruno, entering the room and embracing Liz. 'At a time like this, he should be here by your side.' He playfully pretended to kiss her baby bump. 'Getting close. How have you been?'

'Fine. A few niggling pains this morning, then just before I headed over here...'

Bruno's tone revealed his concern. 'Contractions?'

'I don't think so.'

'Raf *really* should be here,' Bruno said, 'instead of running around, sweating over this deal.'

'This is the Weatherup Financial Services deal?' asked Caterina.

'That's the one,' Bruno said. 'It's going well, and we want to keep the expansion happening, but why we need to relentlessly pursue a buyout of Weatherup right now, with the baby almost here, well… I've tried to get Raf to back off a little, just for a while…'

'But you know Raf…' Caterina said with an exasperated sigh.

After the dinner, and while Bruno was distractedly playing with their three-year-old daughter, Liz took Caterina by the hand and they walked to the far end of the rear courtyard.

'There's something I'd like to talk to you about, confidentially,' Liz said. 'But it's… a very sensitive matter…'

'Of course you can, Liz. And it doesn't go any further… strictly between us. Sisters doing it for themselves and all that.'

'It's… a family matter…'

'Meaning it's a Raf matter,' said Caterina. 'Don't worry about that, neither Bruno nor I have ever had any illusions about Raf. Wild boy, playboy, Mr Big Ego… you're the one who actually tamed him. But you know Bruno and I think the world of you, Liz, we don't ever want to see you suffering in any way. Has something… happened?'

'Monica Leeman turned up at a business function during the week.'

'Not *her* again.'

'She implied something about the pregnancy.'

'She's a jealous, bitter woman.'

'Before I get to that,' Liz said, 'there was something else… something she emailed me a while before. A list. I didn't take it seriously, of course…' Her voice trailed off.

'What list?'

'Monica claimed Raf had a string of affairs while she was married to him.'

'Let me guess. She gave you a list of women she claims he slept with?'

'Yes.'

'I'm not going to pretend Raf wasn't a bad boy. But Monica is behaving like a sick woman.'

Liz drew a folded slip of paper from her skirt pocket. 'This is a printout of the list Monica sent me.'

Caterina glanced over the names on the paper. Her eyes widened when she saw her own name.

'I know your name being on there is bullshit,' Liz said.

'The thought sickens me.' Caterina mimicked sticking her fingers down her throat.

'I know Monica is capable of lying and manipulating,' Liz said, 'but she also implied Raf switched my birth control, and I found fake pills hidden away that could have been used for that. I need to know what you think, Caterina… just between us… what do you think I am dealing with here?'

Suddenly, before Caterina could respond, Liz doubled over, groaning.

Caterina reached out, steadying her. 'Liz, what is it?'

'Pain…'

'Contractions?'

Liz nodded feebly, gripping Caterina's arm.

'We need to get you to the hospital.' Caterina's head whipped about, looking back across the courtyard. 'Bruno!'

FIFTY-ONE

The pain of childbirth, the sheer intensity of it, was not something Liz was ever going to forget. Despite that, she could hardly believe the euphoric wave of joy that swept through her drained body, just minutes after delivery, when her newborn child was placed in her arms.

This little miracle was worth it, every minute of it.

'A healthy, bouncing, baby boy,' the doctor said.

Bruno and Caterina, all wide smiles, had been there for the birth.

'You're one of the incredibly lucky ones,' Caterina said.

'How do you mean?' said Liz without taking her eyes off her baby.

'Short labour. Just three hours. Some people, me included, took three times that.' Caterina edged closer to the bed, arms reaching out. 'Now stop hogging your new son and let me give him a cuddle.'

Liz passed the baby to her. 'Say hello, Luke.'

'Luke?' said Caterina. 'You've named him already?'

'As you know Raf and I decided to wait for the birth to learn the baby's sex, although Raf was certain it was a boy. And we'd decided on Luke if it was the son Raf was hoping for.'

'I was on the phone to Raf just after we brought you in,' Bruno said. 'He's on his way, flying in from Melbourne.'

'Thanks, Bruno.'

He took her hand in his and gave it a gentle squeeze. 'I'm sorry he wasn't here with you for the birth. I could tell, from his voice on the phone, he was regretting it.'

'You and Caterina were here,' Liz said, 'so it's all good.'

Caterina handed the baby back to Liz.

The doctor paid a brief visit, nurses came and went, Bruno and Caterina hovered, and there was a congratulatory phone call from Martin. Liz engaged with everyone, but her mind kept flashing back to Raf, to her concern over those placebo pills, to his desire for a son, an heir, and to her disappointment he hadn't been here for the birth. Luke was premature, but they'd known the birth was imminent, and still Raf hadn't been prepared to roll back on his new business drive, or to hand this particular series of meetings to Bruno or one of the other executives.

She pushed those thoughts to the back of her mind.

Don't think about any of that now.

And she gazed down lovingly into the eyes of her little boy.

* * *

Liz opened her eyes.

Caterina was sitting in the chair beside the hospital bed. 'Poor tired girl,' Caterina said. She stroked Liz's arm. 'You probably didn't realise this, but you went to sleep while you were talking to me, mid-sentence.'

'That's not like me,' Liz said sleepily.

'Welcome to motherhood. You're now officially a different version of yourself.'

'Is that a good or a bad thing?'

'Both of those and a whole lot more,' Caterina said jokingly. Her demeanour shifted to serious, earth mother mode. 'We kind of got interrupted last night.'

'We kind of did,' Liz said.

'Raf ran around having lots of affairs when he was married to Monica, and she became convinced he was sleeping with absolutely everyone. He had plenty of flings, didn't particularly seem to even bother hiding it, but he didn't sleep with everyone. Certainly not with me, though he did make the odd brazen pass.'

'What? After you and Bruno were married?'

'Yeah.'

'Why on earth would he do *that*?'

'He was a lot wilder back then, Liz. He liked to push the boundaries, and see what he could get away with. He wanted to have everything that anyone else had, including his own brother. He liked to play with fire.'

'Did Bruno know?'

'That's one of the few things I've kept to myself. Better that way. And it was years ago. I made it quite clear I thought he was being an asshole. He's been the model brother-in-law ever since, and that's why I'm telling you all this now. He's a changed man and something tells me he'll be a great father.'

'You were about to tell me, last night, what you thought about those fake pills.'

'I really don't know about that one,' Caterina said. 'But, honey, I do think you need to be certain you're right about that before you talk to him. It's a nasty accusation if by any chance it's all a mistake and there's a rational explanation.'

As if on cue, Bruno popped his head in the door and said, 'Look who I found wandering around out here.'

Raf stepped in from behind him. He moved to the bed, taking Liz in his arms, kissing her, holding her tight. 'I got here as soon as I could.'

'We have a son.'

'Just saw him in the nursery,' said Raf. 'He's fantastic.'

'He's like a bundle of magic.'

Liz's tensions faded. It felt good to have Raf there, to be in his arms, to feel his lips on hers. But she was aware she didn't feel the level of joy she would have expected at this moment, with her husband at her side, and their newborn baby nearby.

Somewhere, deep inside her, something had changed.

FIFTY-TWO

Liz and the baby came home from the hospital three days later. She had appointed Sally Markham to take over as managing director and to run the agency while she took some maternity leave.

For the next three months, Raf was in and out. When he was there, he doted on both Liz and their new son. She liked this loving, caring side to him, but at the same time sensed an emotional distance growing between them, something that hadn't been there before. Something she hadn't been able to stop.

Each week, he'd been spending more and more nights away, interstate.

That was playing heavily on her mind again this morning. It was a Saturday and she'd spent the morning feeding and cuddling Luke. She couldn't help but notice Raf was on edge.

Again.

She watched as he wandered in and out of his study, tapping away on his laptop keyboard one minute, then in the next moment striding across to the large windows at the back of the living room to stare outside.

Back and forth.

'Raf, what is it?' she asked presently.

'What do you mean?'

'Ever since you came back from Melbourne, after Luke was born… it hasn't felt totally like we've been on the same page.'

'Just distracted. You know the Weatherup deal fell through, after all the effort that went into it?'

'Of course I know. We spent hours and hours talking about it.'

'I took my eye off the prize. Let it slip through my fingers.'

Luke began crying and Liz rocked him gently in her arms. 'Raf, it's not important–'

He cut across her. 'I'm building this empire as some people laughingly call it, for you and for our son.' His voice was like ice. 'So, don't tell me it's not important. It's *everything*.'

'It's not everything,' Liz said.

'*Christ*. I don't have time for this shit right now.' He grabbed the jacket that was draped over one of the lounge chairs and he strode out the front door.

Luke began wailing louder. Liz hugged him closer, tears welling in her eyes. It was the first time Raf had raised his voice like that. The first time he'd stormed off like that. The first time he'd sworn at her. She hated this gulf between them, hated that it seemed to grow a little more each day. She listened to the sound of Raf's car as it sped out of the driveway.

FIFTY-THREE

Less than half an hour later there was the sound of another engine in the driveway. Liz opened the door to see a smiling Bruno.

'Hi, Bruno, come on in.'

Bruno entered and took Luke in his arms. 'Just a brief visit to see this little fellow and to see how you guys are doing.'

'We're great,' said Liz.

Bruno shot her a knowing stare. 'Your eyes aren't saying you're doing great. Where's Raf?'

'He's… out.'

'Liz, what's up?'

Liz looked Bruno in the eye and instinctively felt she could open up to him. And it was a relief. After all, Bruno knew his own brother better than anyone.

'Raf stormed out a while ago,' she said. 'He just hasn't been himself since the baby was born. I thought at first it was the pressures of this new business drive, and being away a few nights a week, but now…'

'You think there's more to it than that?'

'I really don't know what to think.'

Bruno placed the baby gently in his bassinet. 'He's sleepy.'

'Yes. Nap time.'

'This is a very special time for you guys. I told Raf he needed to back off on the expansions, just for a short time, but he practically snapped my head off.'

'Exactly what just happened here,' Liz said.

'Just give it some time, Liz,' Bruno said. 'Raf's under a lot of stress at the moment. New marriage, new father. And this whole mania of his about making Vetrani Investments one of the country's biggest corporate success stories. He's spreading himself too thin, pushing himself too hard, but I believe it will all settle down soon.'

'You do?'

'Yes. And I'm doing my bit, believe me, to make Raf see that for himself.'

Liz gave him a hug. 'I don't know what I'd do without you and Caterina.'

'We're here for you,' Bruno said. 'Now, are the three of you coming over for the usual Saturday night tonight?'

'I'm not sure…'

'Come, Liz, even if it's just you and Luke.'

'Okay.'

Bruno, like Caterina, was so easy to talk to. Liz almost wanted to confide in him about the suspicions she'd had about the birth control, and the various accusations Monica had made. At the same time, she had to be careful. She didn't want to drive a wedge between the two brothers, so she held her tongue.

She'd intended following up with Monica, making it clear she wouldn't stand for any more harassment, regardless of how subtle. But with a newborn in the house, sleepless nights, and the fact Monica hadn't been in touch again, she'd pushed it to the back of her mind and the months had passed. Maybe this time Monica was gone for good.

Being a mother was such a glorious experience, and little Luke made her so happy, she'd decided to let go of her suspicions about the pills, and accept there *was* a rational explanation. And leave it at that.

And give Raf some space.

Now she was beginning to wonder if that had been a mistake.

FIFTY-FOUR

Liz and Luke were welcomed heartily when they arrived at Bruno's home. Caterina had a friend joining them and together they served up a sumptuous meal. Raf didn't arrive and no one was certain where he'd gone. After the meal, Caterina and her friend focused all their attention on the giggly, three-month-old baby. Bruno excused himself.

'Back shortly, ladies,' he said, 'just got a couple of quick business matters to address.'

Shortly after, Liz headed upstairs to the bathroom. At the top of the stairs, she heard Bruno's voice in his home office at the end of the hallway. Curious, she moved in that direction, stopping just short of the door, which was ajar.

She listened.

Bruno spoke urgently into the phone. 'Where the hell are you, Raf? What's going on?'

Bruno was silent for a moment, listening to the response, then he resumed. 'You were smitten by Liz from the moment you met her. Went out of your way to win her over. You insisted this was different, this was *it*, the real deal, she'd changed you, made you a better man and all that Robbie Williams bullshit. Got married, for Chrissakes, had Luke. I believed you this time, Raf. And now what? Less than a year later you're neglecting her, neglecting your son, rarely at home, casting her aside like some plaything. Same old, same old.'

There was another silence, longer this time, as Bruno listened. In the shadows, outside the room, Liz waited.

Bruno spoke again. 'I don't care what the other problems are. You should never have overextended. Always big-noting yourself. Always. If you won't look after Liz, then Caterina and I will.' He ended the call. Liz heard the sound of something heavy being thrown against the wall.

Liz backtracked stealthily down the hall, and made her way to the bathroom at the far end. She'd never heard Bruno speaking or acting so firmly. She was glad he was being protective of her, and critical of his brother, but what had Raf been saying?

She was standing motionless outside the bathroom door, lost in thought, when Caterina approached. 'You okay?'

'Fine,' said Liz.

'You look like you've seen a ghost.'

Liz decided to come clean. 'Don't say anything to Bruno, but I overheard him on the phone to Raf.'

'Heated exchange?'

Liz nodded. 'I've never heard Bruno angry like that.'

'Mostly he keeps calm when he's dealing with business or family dramas. Occasionally, he doesn't.'

'He's under a lot of pressure, then?'

'He's always running around behind the scenes putting out the fires and he can get anxious. But he bottles it up. Puts on a brave face.'

'It seems you're really the secret calming influence in the family.'

Caterina grinned. 'Oh, you better believe it.' She took Liz by the hand. 'Now, let's get back to taking it easy, eh?'

They headed back to the dining room but Liz couldn't switch off from what she'd overheard.

What were the other problems Bruno was referring to? The overextending?

And the "same old, same old" comment, was that about casting off romantic partners? Monica Leeman's warnings came bubbling back to the surface of Liz's mind.

I've let all this drift for too long, Liz thought.

She felt instinctively she needed to confront the issues once and for all.

FIFTY-FIVE

Mac stood on the edge of the dusty field, his head tilted upwards. Two small planes rose and fell in formation, like baby hawks playing on the air currents. He walked past the rickety gate and onto the grounds of the aerodrome at Schofields in the New South Wales countryside. He breathed in the fresh country air, with its scent of eucalyptus from the swaying gum trees beyond the fence.

'Restricted property,' called a gruff voice from behind him.

Mac turned to see a tall, lanky, middle-aged man in overalls ambling towards him.

'Sorry. Just admiring those flyboys.'

'They're showing potential.'

Mac held out his hand. 'Callan McKenzie,' he said. 'I'm a pilot with TPA.'

The other man shook his hand. 'Jack Reynolds.' He looked Mac up and down, sizing him up. 'You're that Captain Mac fellow.'

'I got talked into that gig by a very pretty lady.'

'They're hard to say no to,' Reynolds said. 'So, what can we do for you?'

'Nothing,' Mac said. But then he reconsidered. 'A job, maybe.'

'What about your great big jet airliner job?'

'TPA was good enough to give me some extended leave to do other things.'

'This isn't one of those hippie-era things like trying to find yourself, is it?'

'I'm looking for the real Australia.'

'You're a hundred years too late,' Reynolds said with a grin.

'What are those guys up there doing?' Mac asked, sticking his thumb skyward in the direction of the planes. 'Looks like they're practising precision stuff.'

'I run a flying school here,' Reynolds told him. 'Train quite a few blokes for the various air shows. Some of 'em have even been winners.'

'Sounds like fun.'

'But most of my customers are regular dudes looking to get a commercial licence. You reckon you could teach them?'

Mac was enjoying this man's rustic charm. He adopted a slight twang in his reply. 'Reckon I could.'

'Tell you what,' Reynolds said. 'Take me up for a spin so I know you're the real deal, and I can hire you to give a few lessons. Look good on my resume to have a *TPA man*' – he exaggerated that part – 'on my books, now won't it?'

Half an hour later Mac was in the cockpit of a twin-engine Cessna, flying Jack Reynolds over lush, green paddocks, and gently sloping hills.

'And what's your background, Jack?' Mac asked.

'Air force. Twenty years. Retired. Saw action in Afghanistan, amongst other places. This is a lot more peaceful, Captain Mac.' His permanent grin widened.

'Then you could do with a little excitement,' Mac said. 'How about you teach me some of that precision flying stuff?'

* * *

Mac found a room at a local boarding house. He spent the next two months in Schofields, flying, teaching, and learning. It was the first place and the first thing he had found that helped distract him from his ordeal in Jakarta, and from the loss of Liz. It was on a Tuesday night in his ninth week there he received a call from Carl Vickerson.

'Mac, I have some news. Nothing much, but–'

'What is it, Vickerson?'

'In my talks with the Indonesians and the embassy there, I've sussed out Johnny Makawi's name is on dozens of under-the-radar shell companies masquerading as importers-exporters. Those companies have dealings with various transport and shipping firms. The *news* is that, from one of my sources here, I've learned those shell companies are being investigated by the Australian Federal Police for links with organized crime.'

'What kind of organized crime?'

'Drugs. Cocaine, heroin, weed.'

'I thought all that stuff came mainly from South America and Europe.'

'It does,' said Vickerson. 'But Indonesia has a large heroin problem, and with its fishing trawlers and its ports it's being used increasingly as a distribution point for heroin, and now for all kinds of substances, into Australia and New Zealand.'

'It doesn't explain what they wanted with me.'

'Not yet,' said Vickerson. 'But, Mac, we've uncovered a trail and now we need to stay the course.'

FIFTY-SIX

The admin for all the Vetrani businesses was handled out of their North Sydney head office. Liz tapped on the door to the chief accountant's office as she stepped in. 'Hi, Arthur.'

Liz had always thought Arthur Sykes had the look of a man who suspected everyone of everything. She always expected his hand to urgently cover the papers he was looking over. He had a cop's face, but he was, in fact, an easy-going, polite, meticulous, finance man, married for over twenty-five years, and with three grown children.

He looked up from his desk. 'Liz.'

She pulled over a visitor's chair and sat facing him. 'How are those boys of yours?'

'Lazy,' he said.

'Typical teenage lads, then?'

'Two of them are over twenty now.'

'So, they're still works in progress, eh?'

'Epic works in progress.'

'And Mellie?'

Sykes cast an exasperated expression. 'She thinks the answer to all the world's ills is to go shopping for new outfits.'

'Now *that* I can relate to,' Liz said.

'To what do I owe the unexpected pleasure?' Sykes asked.

'A favour,' said Liz. 'I'm planning a totally over-the-top birthday prezzie for Raf–'

'It's his birthday?'

'Not for a while yet. But this will take some pre-planning, and… well, it won't be cheap.'

'Nothing about the Vetranis comes cheap,' he said with a wan smile.

Liz acknowledged the comment with a grin and a spread of her arms. She was inwardly pleased she'd managed to put Sykes at ease, no mean feat as both his quip and his weak smile were out of character.

'I know the companies are going well,' Liz said, 'but as this surprise present will carry a hefty price tag, I want to make certain, for my own peace of mind, it isn't going to cause any angst, income-wise, for me and Raf. So, I'd like to take a look over the accounts. I want this to be a really pleasant surprise, not an "oh my God no we can't afford it" kind of shock, if you get my drift?'

Sykes had lapsed back to his usual uncomfortable self. 'Shouldn't you discuss this with Raf?'

'Then it wouldn't be a surprise. And besides, he's out of town at the moment.'

Sykes shrugged. 'I see.' He considered this for a moment. 'Perhaps it's worth running by Bruno?'

'A two-year-old can keep a secret better than Bruno. The moment Raf looks at him he can tell if his brother is hiding something.'

Sykes nodded. 'Yes, I know what you mean.'

'So, if you could set up access for me.'

'I can run you through the accounts myself,' Sykes said.

'No, you've got enough on your plate with everything that's going on around here.'

Sykes pursed his lips. 'Well…'

Liz grasped the moment. 'Thanks, Arthur. I really appreciate it.' She leaned forward expectantly.

Liz had begun to worry that Raf was spending too much by purchasing the land by the Hawkesbury, hiring architects and builders to construct his dream home, not to mention buying and crewing the yacht which he was now sponsoring in the Sydney to Hobart race. Then there were the finances being invested in the agency. She'd questioned Raf on all this. He'd assured her it was just a drop in the ocean to the income he had flooding in.

She'd believed him, swept up as she had been in the early days by his confidence and his charisma.

Sykes scribbled on a notepad, tore off the leaf and handed it to her. 'This password will access the accounts for the various companies.'

Liz pocketed the note. 'That's great.' She stood to leave. 'And not a word to Raf, okay?' She placed her right forefinger to her lips.

The accountant nodded reluctantly. 'Just what is this super-duper surprise, anyway?'

She flashed a mysterious grin. 'Need-to-know basis, Arthur. But all will be revealed.'

* * *

Liz drove across the Sydney Harbour Bridge, back to her office in the Australia Square Tower. She told Sally she wasn't taking any calls. Closing the door to her office, Liz flexed her hands and sat behind her desk. She accessed the Vetrani Investments intranet, tapped the "Finance" icon and entered the password. What was she looking for? Anything, she supposed, that raised a suspicion with her.

She did know what she *wanted* to find; nothing.

Nothing at all out of the ordinary.

She spent an hour poring over one spreadsheet after another. All appeared to be in order. The businesses all showed healthy profits, although the amount of profit and income didn't seem to cover the level of spending Raf had undertaken with the house, and with the funds he'd poured into the expanding of her advertising business. Was she missing something?

The real estate developments were harder to understand. There was a lot of money being moved from one area to another. Liz had to admit she didn't have the financial head to follow every nuance of these spreadsheets.

When Liz's own business had become part of the Vetrani Investments group, she had stopped using her own personal accountant. Raf had insisted it should all now be under the one umbrella, and be administered out of their HQ. On an impulse, Liz picked up the phone and called the woman who had previously handled her accounts. Rosa Skamos was someone Liz knew she could rely on to be discreet.

'Hi, Rosa. I wonder if I could ask a big favour? I've got some spreadsheets I'd like you to look at.'

* * *

Everything about Rosa Skamos was larger than life. Big hair, big eyes, big personality. She favoured long, flowing garments, and she bustled in, with a wide smile, and spoke briefly with Sally before Liz ushered her through to her office.

She hadn't been available to help her old friend the previous day, when she'd received the call, but Rosa had made time this morning.

'I just want to get someone who knows figures the way you do to look at some accounts,' Liz said.

'You've got some concerns, honey?'

'Not really. Long story, let's just say someone with an agenda is trying to spook me.'

'And you want to put it to rest in your own mind?'

'Yep.'

'Then let's do this.'

Liz's fingers flew across the keyboard. She entered the password and froze when a dialog box appeared on the screen.

Password Incorrect.

She re-entered the password and got the same result. Rosa waited patiently, her eyes showing her concern. Liz tried a third time. Same result.

'They've changed the password,' she said.

'Sorry to state the obvious,' Rosa said, 'but someone didn't want you spending too much time with those spreadsheets.'

FIFTY-SEVEN

Liz had checked with Raf's secretary. There was nothing secret about his itinerary. Another series of meetings and dinners with the CEOs of several Victoria-based companies. These were the latest round of acquisitions Raf was pursuing. For each of his trips to Melbourne he stayed at the Mercury International Hotel.

While Bruno had always been tight with both the company's and his own personal finances, Raf had been the opposite. Money was no object. So, if that was the case, why was she being kept at arm's length from knowing anything about their finances? Was he keeping secrets? Had he tampered with those birth control pills? Why had there been such a rapid change in him since their elopement? Was he still the wild boy and womanizer both Monica and Caterina said he'd been in his early days? Was that the real reason for his distance and for these endless nights away? Even Bruno had advised him to cut back on these trips.

I'm being paranoid.

She came through the customs bay at Melbourne Airport at 9.45 p.m. and hailed a taxi.

What am I doing? This isn't me.

'No luggage?' asked the cabbie.

'Just me,' she said, sliding into the back seat. On an impulse she'd asked Caterina to look after Luke, and she'd gone to the airport in Sydney, managing to secure a seat on the next flight.

'Where to, Miss?'

'The Mercury International,' she said.

Now I'm the stalker.

She'd kept telling herself she was simply taking charge, that this out-of-character impulse would prove once and for all her suspicions, and Monica's warnings, were all unfounded. Then she'd know this surprise trip would have been in all their best interests. But as she stepped from the taxi and walked into the lobby of the hotel, she felt the panic rising in her.

Have I become the new Monica?

'Can I help you?' asked the receptionist.

Liz produced her ID. 'My husband is staying at the hotel,' she said. 'He's expecting me but he's out at a dinner at the moment. If I could just get a spare key...?'

Minutes later she swiped the key card and pushed open the door to Raf's room on the seventh floor. All that time on the flight and in the taxi, her mind had been in turmoil, her emotions not like her emotions at all. She hadn't been certain what to expect when she arrived and surprised Raf, but it was nothing like the sight that greeted her when she walked into the room.

FIFTY-EIGHT

Raf and two buxom girls – naked; their entwined bodies stretched across the plush lounge suite and onto the richly textured carpet floor.

One of the girls glanced lazily in Liz's direction. 'Who's this?'

Raf's head whipped round. He reached for his trousers and quickly pulled them on, his eyes locking with his wife's. 'Liz...?'

For several seconds Liz stood frozen, absorbing the scene before her. Her husband's eyes were glazed, as though he'd been on a bender.

'Go to hell, Raf,' she said. She turned and walked out, slamming the door behind her as she went.

FIFTY-NINE

Despite the hour, Liz caught a taxi back to the airport. She wasn't thinking straight, didn't know where she was going or what she was doing. Suddenly it seemed she was a different person, leading someone else's life.

The images were stuck in her head.

How can that be the man I love, the father of my child?

She held her smartphone in her hand. She thought about phoning Martin or Caterina or Bruno or Sally. She wanted to blurt it all out to someone who cared.

Instead, she found herself wanting to call Mac. Cry on his shoulder, share her grief, admit to the terrible mistake she'd made. But Mac had been off the radar for months. He'd suffered a traumatic injustice and who had truly been there for him? He'd gone off alone. Was he wandering aimlessly? Or had he started rebuilding a new life?

Her phone buzzed. She looked at the screen and saw it was Raf. She was about to press "Ignore" but then on an impulse, she answered. What could this manic stranger possibly have to say to her after what had just happened?

'Liz, I'm so sorry. I've been a fool. Come back. Let's talk.'

'Are you kidding me?'

'I know I've been spinning out of control, Liz. I need help and I'm going to get it. I don't want to lose you—'

'We're finished, Raf.'

'There's a devil inside me. I thought I'd left that part of me in the past, but I've slipped... the pressures...'

'What pressures?'

'Chasing the acquisitions, I've overreached, taken on too much debt, profits are down this quarter… panic started setting in. And I've been acting out, like a stupid kid, I know…'

'Does Bruno know what's going on with the finances?'

'Not the full story. He's always trying to hold back on any borrowing or takeovers.'

'You need to come clean with Bruno and try to do the right thing, but I doubt you're even capable–'

He cut across her, pleading. 'Don't shut me out, Liz. I need you–'

'You don't need me. What am I? One of your acquisitions?'

'Liz–'

'Were you on drugs in that room?'

'This is a wake-up call, I can change all this.'

Despite the fury she felt inside, Liz was surprised by how calmly she responded. Perhaps she should have remained Rational Liz all along.

'It's a wake-up call all right,' she said. 'I hope for Bruno's sake you get the help you need. But I'm divorcing you, Raf.'

He shouted down the line at her. 'I'm your husband. We need to talk about this.'

'Don't call this number again,' she said, and ended the call.

* * *

There was a 6 a.m. Qantas flight the following morning. Liz booked the one remaining business class seat from her phone and sat waiting in the airport lobby all night, wide awake, going over the rollercoaster ride of events from the past year. The memories flashed repeatedly in her mind until she thought she was going mad.

She dozed off and on in the last hour before boarding began.

176

I have to get my life back.

She'd phoned ahead to ask Bruno and Caterina if they could look after Luke for another day while she got her head together. She told Caterina what had happened, and Bruno had come on the line.

'So sorry, Liz,' he'd said.

'Yeah.' It was all she could manage to say. She was exhausted.

'I'll pick you up at the airport and drive you home,' Bruno said.

'No need, Bruno.'

'I'll be there,' he said.

* * *

Bruno pulled up outside the Chatswood house and walked Liz to the door. A soft breeze scattered leaves at their feet, across the doorstep, and through the garden at the front of the property.

'Will you be alright?' Bruno asked as Liz put her key in the door.

'I'll be fine, Bruno. I can't thank you enough for...' Her voice trailed, tears welling in her eyes.

'I'd stay, Liz, it's just—'

'You've done more than enough, Bruno, far more than I would've expected. You need to be with your own family... and you've got your hands full in the office. You're the one who's actually running Vetrani Investments day-to-day while Raf's off playing emperor. And you need to look at the accounting. I don't know how he's done it, but Raf's been hiding stuff from you. And what's more, I'm putting paperwork in motion to take back full ownership of my agency.'

'Understood. And I'll look into those finances. But Arthur Sykes has his finger on the pulse.'

'Sykes means well but I went to see him, and I think Raf's been manipulating him as well.'

'Okay. I'll get to the bottom of it.' He placed his hand gently on her shoulder. 'But you're still family, and I'm worried about you.'

'I'm okay. Really.'

'If you're certain.'

'Certain.' She gave him a tender push, a soft smile. 'Now go. And… thank you for the ride.'

'You can leave Luke with us as long as you need. You call me if you need anything. Anything at all.'

'I will.'

'Promise.'

'Promise. *Now go.*'

He waved as he went, and she watched him drive off.

How can two brothers be so different?

She closed the door behind her, all the emotion bursting out. She staggered to the sofa and burst into tears.

SIXTY

Two hours later Liz pulled up outside a commercial building in Milsons Point. The northern end of the Sydney Harbour Bridge dominated the skyline. She walked into Rosa Skamos's office.

'I need you back on board, looking after the accounts,' Liz said. 'Short notice, I know. Are you able to do that?'

'Of course,' Rosa said. She gestured for Liz to sit. 'You look stressed to the max, hon. What's happened?'

'I'm divorcing Raf,' Liz said, without any hint of emotion. 'There are only two things I'm demanding in the settlement. Full custody of my son. And full ownership of my company and its separation from the Vetrani group.'

'I'm sorry to hear you're going through that.'

Liz had cried for an hour after Bruno had dropped her home. It was as though she'd shed every last drop of anguish and self-pity. In its place was a steely resolve.

I need to take my life back.

'Bruno Vetrani will ensure you have full access to the accounts,' she said, 'and you can start dismantling the connections straight away. I need you to dig deep, and identify anything that's being hidden, anything that isn't strictly legal. I don't want any more funds from the parent company being used. And yes, that will mean pulling out of some of the new business pitches Raf set up, and possibly closing the interstate offices for now. We need to make sure the agency is in a strong financial position.'

'I'm on it,' said Rosa.

From there Liz drove across the bridge to the agency's offices in George Street. The next step was to rally the team at the agency and to take up the reins again. A classic soul song about love gone wrong was playing on the car radio. Liz marvelled at the irony of it. She drove into the underground parking station and as she stepped from the car, she saw Monica Leeman waiting by one of the pillars.

'I phoned your office and they said you were on your way in,' Monica said.

'And here I was thinking you must spend all your spare time lurking down here.'

Monica thrust a swathe of papers towards her. 'You might find these of interest.'

Liz swatted them away. 'I'm divorcing Raf, Monica. So, no need to keep up this bizarre surveillance of yours. It's over. Mission accomplished.'

Monica took hold of Liz's hand and forced the papers into her palm. 'I had a visit from some intimidating men this morning,' Monica said. 'I think you'll find they'll be paying you a visit at some point. So, you might think divorcing that scumbag is the end but it's just the beginning. Too bad you didn't listen to me in the first place.'

Monica walked away, slid behind the wheel of her Corolla, and pulled out of the parking space. Liz stood and watched, puzzled, as the car passed through the exit gate. She went back inside, pulled out her phone and called her brother-in-law.

'Bruno? Raf once told me Monica had a Corolla.'

'That's right. You suspected she was following you. Is she—?'

'Would she have replaced it recently with another model Corolla?'

'Not that I'm aware of but I wouldn't know what Monica is up to these days. Why would I? She may still be a large shareholder, but we don't have any info on her private business.'

'What colour was her Corolla?'

She listened to his answer, then said, 'Okay.'

'What's this about?' Bruno asked.

'Nothing,' said Liz.

She placed the phone back in her handbag and walked across to the elevators. The car she'd seen following her on those previous occasions had been a silver Corolla. Monica's Corolla was gold. If it wasn't Monica Leeman stalking her, then who was it?

* * *

After she'd addressed Sally and the team, Liz sank into the large leather chair in her old office. She fanned the papers Monica had given her across the desk and ran her eyes over them.

The first sheet was a photocopy of a purchase order, made out several years earlier to a Sydney food, events, and props specialist that serviced the entertainment and advertising industries. The order was for the creation of fake pills in a range of shapes and sizes that imitated specific products, and which the purchaser planned to use in an upcoming TV commercial. Liz read through the specifications. One set of the pills was to replicate the standard birth control tablet. Another set were to be shaped like a pill prescribed for patients with a heart condition. The purchase order was from one of the Vetrani companies. The signature was that of Raf Vetrani.

Liz leafed through the other papers. There was a copy of the death certificate of Warren Leeman. Liz recalled Monica telling her that her father died of a heart attack while driving. Picking up her phone, Liz tapped in the number she thought she would never call.

Monica came on the line. 'That was quick.'

Liz ignored the smug tone. 'What's this all about?'

'You can read and put two and two together.'

'You think Raf replaced your father's heart tablets with placebos?'

'He ordered fake pills for a non-existent marketing plan. Pills that were lookalikes for my father's tablets. Not long after, Dad has a heart attack. And the pills that look like birth control? I think he switched out my pills back then, except I didn't get pregnant. Years later he plays the same trick on you with the difference being that you fell pregnant straight away.'

'What on earth made you think of something like this?' Liz asked her.

'When you fell pregnant while eloping,' Monica said, 'I thought this plays perfectly into Raf's hands. He *has* to have planned this, but how? I thought maybe he switched your pills. It's not hard to create a placebo. You get hold of empty gelatin capsules, fill them with sugar or harmless powders, and have them shaped to whatever design you want.'

'And this purchase form? How did you find that?'

'The public can't just order up something like that from a pharmaceutical firm, but I did some research,' Monica said. 'I discovered prop specialists that custom-make anything for films, ads, events, you name it. I spent months phoning firms that do that kind of work, then I hit the jackpot. A firm that could trace just such an order. I was searching for evidence he'd tampered with your pills, Liz. You say it's none of my business, but I've got a score to settle with that bastard. What I wasn't expecting to find was he'd also had those fake heart pills manufactured.'

Liz swallowed hard. She was lost for words, barely able to believe she was having this conversation.

'I've given the cops those papers.' Monica's voice had a note of triumph. 'They questioned me this morning and they'll be coming to see you. They've told me they can't open an investigation on what I've given them. Too flimsy. But if they had physical proof of fake pills, that would change things. So, Liz, did you ever go looking and find those pills?'

'You really think Raf interfered with your father's tablets to inherit the firm?'

'I know what he's capable of.'

'Why should I believe anything you say? You gave me a list of women Raf supposedly slept with. Caterina Vetrani was on that list. She didn't sleep with him.'

'Who told you that?'

'She did.'

'She's lying. She doesn't want that weak, lily-livered husband of hers to find out. And she certainly wouldn't want Raf to learn she'd told anyone. She's scared of him, probably senses what I already know about him.'

'That's a hell of an accusation.'

Liz was chilled to the bone by Monica's response.

'That psychopath murdered my dad and stole the family business and I intend to prove it.'

SIXTY-ONE

Liz ended the call and sat staring into space. If she contacted the police and revealed the existence of those placebos, and if it proved Raf had interfered with Monica's father's heart tablets, resulting in his death, then her son's father would be on a murder charge. That was something that would hang over little Luke's head for the rest of his life.

But if there was any truth in Monica's words and if she kept her knowledge of the pills secret, then she was perverting the course of justice. Could she live with that?

Was her husband a murderer? He may be many things, he may have contrived to make her pregnant, but she didn't believe he would conspire to kill.

She decided to head for the Chatswood home. It was time to move out before Raf returned from interstate. She didn't want to confront him again.

Sally walked into the office. 'So good to have you back. You're not staying longer today?'

'I need to arrange a place to stay and move my things out of the Chatswood house,' Liz said.

'What?'

'I'm leaving Raf.'

'I'm so sorry, Liz.'

Liz was speaking as though on autopilot. 'Luke is being looked after by Bruno and Caterina. Once I've arranged a place, I'll pick him up—'

'Liz,' Sally said, 'I've got a spare room at my house. You can camp there until you've got a place sorted.'

'I couldn't—'

'Yes, you could. And you will. Deal?'

Liz felt a small sense of relief. 'Deal.'

* * *

Back at home, Liz threw several outfits for both herself and Luke into a suitcase and her family photo albums and personal belongings into a carry box. She'd sold off her own furniture when she'd moved in with Raf. There really wasn't very much she needed to take. She could send for anything else, but for the most part she'd simply start from scratch.

There was a loud knocking on the front door.

Raf?

But he wouldn't be knocking.

She opened the door to a man in a suit and a woman in a pantsuit. They introduced themselves as detectives.

'We'd like to ask you a few questions, Ms Vetrani,' the male detective said.

'What's this about?' Liz asked.

'It's in relation to accusations made against your husband by his ex-wife.'

'Come in.'

Liz stood aside as they entered. They stood awkwardly at the entrance to the living room. Liz didn't offer a seat.

'Monica Leeman, the former Mrs Vetrani, has made a claim her husband replaced her father's heart pills with specially manufactured placebo tablets, and she believes he did the same with birth control pills, used on both herself and recently on you.'

'I'm aware of her accusations,' Liz said.

'Were you on the pill at the time you discovered you were pregnant?' the female detective asked.

'Yes.'

'Do you have reason to believe your pills were tampered with?'

'No. Like you, I have only Monica Leeman's far-fetched suspicions to go on.'

'Is your husband at home, or due home soon?'

'He's been away on business. I don't know when he's getting back.'

'Would you object to us making a search of the house and removing any pills for testing?' the man asked.

They haven't asked me if I'm aware of any such tablets. So I don't have to be the one to reveal the pills. They can find the pills for themselves.

'I've no reason to object,' Liz said.

She stood back and watched quietly as the detectives removed pills from the bathroom cabinet, and wasn't surprised when the male detective emerged from the study with the travel carry case. When he opened it, the zip bag of fake pills was visible.

'Have you seen this case before, Mrs Vetrani?'

'I would have noticed it at some stage or other,' she said.

Keep it enigmatic.

Despite everything, she hoped the tests would show there were no placebo pills that imitated the heart pills. She prayed the police would establish Raf wasn't responsible for Warren Leeman's heart attack. The detective then held up another item he'd retrieved from Raf's storage area.

'Are you familiar with this, Mrs Vetrani?' the detective asked.

SIXTY-TWO

It had been a few years since Vickerson had been in touch with this particular Indonesian contact, a fast-talking man with sandy straw-like hair. He had a tattoo of a snake on his neck and everyone, including Vickerson, had told him it was crazy to attract such attention given his line of work.

His response was that he was hiding in plain sight, and it had worked just fine.

Vickerson asked him about the dodgy export company and the name Johnny Makawi.

'Whoever Makawi really is, he or she sends "assistants" to do their dirty work,' the straw-haired man said.

'What dirty work?'

'Transporting the merchandise to the ports and loading it onto boats, for shipment to Australia, New Zealand, New Guinea.'

'Drugs.'

'Your words, not mine.'

'Can you pull together a list of the owners and operators of those boats?'

'What's this about?'

'Makawi's a director of a shell company that previously owned a house I'm interested in.'

'Aha.' This was not a surprise to the tattooed man. 'That house was a clearing point for the shipments when they reached the port area. Grapevine says it was used a year or so ago for some secret bullshit, then sold off.'

'Why is your underground network involved with drug dealers?' Vickerson asked.

'Occasionally we lend them a hand in return for some much-needed financing.'

'You're political activists, not drug gangsters.'

'Like everyone else, we need money. Sometimes the funding gets low.' He cleared his throat. 'You want to know who's masquerading as this Makawi?'

'Yes.'

'Why?'

'A friend of mine was imprisoned in that house.'

'You're looking for a ghost,' said the Indonesian. 'I'll send you that list and good luck. You'll need it.'

Vickerson felt a tingle at the back of his neck; something else was going on here. When he received the list of companies, he initiated an online search for the listed directors.

He waded through bits and pieces of data well into the night. There weren't any names that meant anything to him. However, he did see, unexpectedly, a document that listed a boat that had been used to consign shipments locally. He accessed public records that showed the owner of that boat. He ran a search with the name of the boat and the name of the owner. Half a dozen articles were listed on the search page which he read through laboriously. It was in the fourth article a name leapt out at him.

He phoned Mac. 'You need to come to Sydney,' he said. 'You and I need to sit down with the Federal Police.'

SIXTY-THREE

Liz sat at her desk, staring at the computer screen, but she was really staring into space. She was finding it hard to concentrate. Raf had been texting her, asking her forgiveness, requesting they meet to talk things through. He was insisting she give him another chance for the sake of their son.

He was back in the house at Chatswood and he'd also texted, asking, "Why did you allow the police to enter and search the property? What was that about?"

She'd had voicemail messages from Bruno and Caterina. They wanted to know how she was doing. They were worried about her. It was a week since she'd picked Luke up from their care and settled herself and Luke into the spare room at Sally's Bondi Beach home in the eastern suburbs.

Liz had hated heading off to the office that morning, leaving her baby in the care of the nanny she'd hired. Little Luke had been wailing, and seemed to have a slight temperature.

'Don't worry,' the nanny, a conscientious young brunette named Connie had said. 'If there's even a slight rise in that temp then I'll take him to the doctor, and I'll call you. Now go.'

What had been the point? She wasn't achieving anything here, and Sally had everything in hand running the business. *Thank God for Sally.*

She heard voices out in the reception area then her door opened, and Sally stuck her head in. 'Liz, I've got the Federal Police out here.'

'Federal Police?' Liz headed straight out to where Sally was conversing with four men in suits.

One of the men turned to her as she approached. 'Mrs Vetrani?'

'Yes?'

'I'm Senior Detective Inspector Craig Ryan, with the Federal Police,' he said. He then introduced his colleagues, and handed her a printed document. 'We have a warrant to seize all work product.'

Liz swallowed hard. Her throat was dry. She managed to find her voice. 'What is this about, Inspector?'

'Part of an investigation into all businesses associated with Vetrani Investments.'

Liz's eyes looked over the warrant she'd been handed. 'You're confiscating *all* our computers and files?'

'That's correct.'

'But we're in the middle of several national campaigns for major clients.'

'I'm sorry, Mrs Vetrani, but this is a police matter now and we need to start removing the items in question, then we need to conduct interviews with yourself and your staff.'

The other four staff members had come from their offices and were standing at the inner passageway, watching. Liz stood aside, alongside Sally, as the agents began to move through the offices, collecting, labelling, and removing the PCs.

Sally, always a strong and calming presence, gripped Liz's hand. 'Just breathe,' she said.

* * *

When the detective inspector sat down with her, in her office, Liz found him to be considerate and he came straight to the point.

'I'm sorry for the inconvenience,' Ryan said. 'I can't put a time frame on it, but your equipment will be returned as soon as we've done our checks.'

'Checks for what?' Liz asked.

She shouldn't have been surprised the policeman ignored her question. After all, he was the investigator here to interview *her*.

'Can you tell me about shipments from overseas that have been directed to your offices in Victoria and Queensland?'

'We don't have any such shipments,' Liz said.

'Shipments have been seized that were consigned by your firm, Mrs Vetrani.'

'We're an advertising and PR consultancy. We don't have any requirements for shipments, large or small.'

'That's what I would have thought. So, can you shed any light on the nature of these deliveries?'

'Inspector, I've already said we don't have any such shipments.'

'I'm afraid there are boxes delivered with the name of your firm as the principal.'

'What do they contain?'

'Cocaine.'

Liz's breath caught in her throat. 'Then someone is falsely using our company's name.'

'The deliveries were made to your interstate office, Mrs Vetrani.'

Liz sighed in frustration. 'That can't be.'

'And the signature on the consignment documents,' he said, handing her a copy of the paper, 'is yours.'

SIXTY-FOUR

Liz sat frozen, shaken to the core.

She'd asked Ryan if she was under arrest. He'd told her she wasn't being arrested at that time, they would be searching the computer files and checking her signature against other documents, before considering formal charges. He told her to remain in the city until further notice.

Her father would have been so ashamed of her, she thought. Then she reprimanded herself. *Why am I thinking that? I haven't done anything wrong.*

Sally came in. 'The staff want to know what to do.'

'Tell them to take the rest of the day off.'

'Then what?'

'We'll have to come up with a plan,' Liz said, surprising herself with her own resilience. 'Can you look at getting some replacement PCs in urgently?'

'Of course.'

'We don't have any off-site backup networking, do we?'

'No.'

'Then I guess we just start from scratch, remembering as much as we can.'

'You don't think the PCs will be back before we do all that?'

'Doesn't sound like it to me.'

'Liz, you got any idea what's going on?'

'Raf. God knows what he's been up to.'

'The cops were questioning me about some shipments,' Sally said. 'We don't have any records of–'

'I know. They asked me the same. Someone's been using the firm as a cover, Sal.'

'Cover for what? That police dude give you any clue what's in these shipments?'

Liz held her tongue. Should she reveal anything? Then she thought, what the hell.

'Drugs,' she said.

There was a buzz at the front reception.

'Now what?' Sally headed back out the front.

She reappeared a moment later, accompanied by Martin de Courcey.

'A friendly face,' said Sally.

'Sorry to intrude,' said Martin.

'Don't be ridiculous,' Liz said, 'you're never intruding.'

'Let me get you guys some coffee,' Sally offered, disappearing out the door.

'What's going on?' Martin said, motioning at the desk. 'Place is looking bare.'

'Never thought I'd be saying these words,' Liz said, 'but we've been raided by the Feds. There, I've said it. They've confiscated all our PCs and filing cabinets.' Liz raised her hands in frustration. 'Somehow we're expected to run a business with all our damn work removed.'

'I wasn't expecting anything like that,' Martin said. 'I came rushing over the moment I saw the news break.'

'What news break?'

'Switch on the news channel,' Martin said.

She flicked the remote and the LCD screen in the corner of the office came to life. Images washed across the screen: footage shot outside the North Sydney office block that housed the Vetrani Investments HQ; aerial shots of the Hawkesbury River Liz had come to know so well, of her and Raf's multi-level home under construction on the hill; interspersed with grainy shots of Raf and Bruno and several other men.

'In breaking news,' the off-screen newsreader reported, 'a cocaine ring worth hundreds of millions of dollars has been smashed by police. Twelve men have been arrested – including Sydney entrepreneur and real-estate developer Raf Vetrani, an award-winning architect and several other well-known Sydney business identities.

'The arrests come after an exhaustive three-year top-secret investigation by Federal Police in conjunction with the NSW Drug Squad and the Marine Area Tactical Operations Unit. Police targeted fishing trawlers and leisure boats allegedly using the Hawkesbury River and NSW Central Coast waterways to traffic cocaine imported from Chile via distribution points in Indonesia.

'Late last night police pounced on a number of the men and seized 1000kg of the drug from boats as they pulled up to private ramps along the Hawkesbury River...'

'Good Lord.' Liz's voice was a whisper.

Martin stood behind her chair and placed his hands gently on her shoulders. 'I'm so sorry, Liz.'

'I've been such a fool.'

'Nonsense.'

'Everything about Raf... it's all been a façade.'

'You couldn't have known.'

'It's all been for nothing. A waste...'

'Liz, whatever Raf may or may not have been, there's no question he loved you deeply and you produced a beautiful baby son.'

Sally appeared with mugs of coffee. She placed them on the desk and turned to leave.

'Sally,' Liz said, 'stay with us.'

Sally pulled one of the visitor chairs over. 'I was listening to this out the back,' she said. 'The guys have got the radio news on.'

'I've been so damn blind,' Liz said.

'*Enough* of that,' Martin said firmly.

'...police will allege that one of the companies purchased by Vetrani Investments,' the newsreader was saying, 'a fresh seafood supplier called Seafish Pacific, operated a super trawler that brought the white powder in to local shores. The drugs were then shipped nationally under the guise of several of the Vetranis' local firms. One of those firms is the successful advertising and PR agency owned by Raf Vetrani's wife...'

Liz couldn't believe what she was hearing. 'Everything I worked to build...'

Sally reached out and hugged her friend. 'You'll bounce back, Liz.'

Liz wiped the tears from her eyes. 'They think I'm part of it,' she said.

Martin pulled up a chair of his own. 'The Feds know what they're doing. They'll soon establish that's not the case.'

'Perhaps, but the business I'm in is all about image. And mud sticks,' said Liz.

The news report was wrapping up. '...the charges will include conspiracy to import a border-controlled drug and importing the drug... and in a surprise development involving news services, police have revealed the investigation received a major boost just a week ago, based on information supplied by the well-known freelance journalist and former foreign correspondent, Carl Vickerson...'

SIXTY-FIVE

Liz had agreed to meet with the detective inspector at the Australian Federal Police's Sydney offices. She was seated in one of the interview rooms when Craig Ryan, dressed in a plain blue-grey suit, entered with a colleague – a serious, bespectacled young woman with a short blonde bob.

'Thanks for coming in, Mrs Vetrani,' he said, pulling up a chair at the long table.

'It's Liz,' she said.

'Liz, this is Detective Andrea Clifton.' He gestured to the young woman beside him.

He shifted in his chair, rearranging the papers he'd placed on the table. 'Liz, our handwriting analysts have confirmed your signature on the shipping documents was a forgery. Your computers will be returned to your office in the next forty-eight hours. I'm pleased to say our investigations have cleared you and your business of any complicity in the drug trafficking.'

'Detective, I'm separated from my husband' – Liz didn't elaborate on the reason – 'and my PR and ad agency is being removed from the Vetrani group. But Raf is still my husband and the father of my son and I've learned via the media he's been arrested on drug importation charges. And my signature's been forged on consignments related to those drugs. Could you please tell me what exactly has been going on?'

'I'm not at liberty to reveal specific details pertaining to the case,' Ryan said, 'but I can tell you the charges against your husband are serious and far-reaching.'

'What does that mean?'

'All I can tell you is that we've been tracking this drug ring for the past three years. The gang has been loading their contraband onto fishing trawlers in Jakarta and transferring them to a private super freighter that's been sailing into Australian waters. From there, the goods are loaded onto a series of local boats and yachts moored at marinas around the Hawkesbury and the Central Coast. An architect, Richard Santini, owns one of those boats and is a director of an export company registered in Jakarta. On the basis of that link we've been watching Santini, and have been able to establish their routine and the other contacts that are involved.'

Liz frowned. 'Santini?'

'Yes. The same man designing the house you're building on the Hawkesbury,' Ryan said. 'He and your husband are old friends, both members of the Calabrian Club in Sydney, the same club to which both of their fathers belonged.'

'Raf and Bruno came from Calabria when they were very young, when their parents settled here.'

'Calabria has an underground drug network, a Mafia-run operation. The Calabrian Club here has no involvement with that or with anything illegal, but we believe Raf and Santini contacted Mafia members through other Calabrians they met at the club. They used those contacts to set up their own operation importing from Calabria, via Chile and Indonesia, under the guise of fake exporting companies.'

'Have you been watching Raf all this time as well, due to his connection with Santini?'

'Yes. Raf and Bruno and family members.'

'Including me?'

'There has been some surveillance, yes, since you became personally involved with the Vetranis.'

'And one of the vehicles used to keep tabs on me was a silver Corolla?' Liz asked.

Ryan looked surprised. 'One of them, yes.'

The young female detective spoke up. 'A week ago, we were approached by a journalist, Carl Vickerson, whom I believe you know.'

'I know *of* him,' Liz said. 'He wrote a revealing article about my former boyfriend, Callan McKenzie.'

'Your former boyfriend claimed to have been imprisoned in a house in Jakarta. Vickerson's been looking into that for some time. He came to us with a paper trail that linked one of the directors of Santini's shell company, J Makawi, with a company that previously owned that house. We've now established through our Indonesian counterparts the house was used to store drug shipments and as occasional lodgings for the sailors who helped move the drugs.'

Liz's throat was impossibly dry, and she reached for the glass of water on the table. She drank.

'The same house?' she asked.

'Yes,' said Detective Clifton.

'How do you know it's the same house?'

'Captain McKenzie had already located that house and identified it, while in Jakarta with Vickerson. That was what led to Vickerson's search for its owners and any connections to those owners.'

'Which led to Santini?'

Ryan responded to that. 'Yes. And when Vickerson came to see us last week, he brought Captain McKenzie with him. We were able to show McKenzie photos of various Australian businessmen who are in Jakarta and who are connected with both Raf and Santini's companies.'

'Captain McKenzie identified a man in one of those photos,' Clifton said, 'as having masqueraded as Robert Anders, a diplomat who visited him while he was being detained.'

'An elaborate and lengthy ruse,' Ryan said, 'but child's play to someone with the drug ring's resources and finances at their disposal. They would have had men posing as police and government officials, using stolen uniforms and forged documents.'

Ryan shifted in his seat, once again briefly scratching his head. 'When our colleagues removed those pills, suspected of being fakes, from the Chatswood home,' he said, 'they also found a phone, which they asked you about on their way out.'

Liz recalled being questioned about the item. 'Yes. I hadn't seen Raf with that phone before.'

'The phone used a highly sophisticated encryption app for texting,' Ryan said. 'We broke the encryption and found Raf used the phone for regular contact with Santini and various freighter staff and men in that Jakarta house. Johnny Makawi was a pseudonym used in those calls and texts. It was enough for us to move our sting to its next phase: a raid not just of Santini's boat, but of several others, including the Vetrani yacht being used to train and crew sailors for the Sydney to Hobart race.'

Liz breathed deeply. 'My God...'

'Within the previous twelve hours,' Ryan said, 'all those boats had taken possession of cocaine and heroin from the super freighter just off the coast.'

'At the same time,' Clifton said, 'we established Raf had manufactured those pills. They are replicas of both birth control and the particular heart tablets used by Warren Leeman. Monica Leeman has given us a statement that Raf would have had easy access to her father's medicine, at the time of her marriage to him, to make that swap. We believe he swapped those pills, leading ultimately to Mr Leeman's death.'

Liz barely registered any of that.

'But that house–' She coughed, the words catching in her throat as though they were choking her. 'You're saying Raf was involved in Mac's abduction?'

'Yes, Liz, he appears to have arranged it.'

SIXTY-SIX

Liz left the police office and drove straight to the one place she thought she would never visit, the maximum security prison where Raf was on remand. Given all she'd now learned, she could not just walk away, not without confronting him one last time, not without saying what she had to say.

They brought him out to the visitor area where he sat behind a glass wall opposite her. Liz stared at him for a long time before she spoke.

'You're the father of my son,' she said. 'I let you into my life, I let you change my life, but I don't know who, or what you are.'

He looked at her with doe-like eyes, and spoke calmly, rationally. 'I loved you with all my heart and soul, Liz. I still do.'

Visibly shaking, Liz took a long, deep, calming breath. This was important. What she had to say was important. 'You never loved me. You don't know the meaning of the word. You loved the idea of me. What was I, Raf? A trophy? A showpiece? Another woman you could conquer, a woman with a business you could add to your empire. Like you did with Monica? Like you did with the others?'

'No.'

'And to win me, to make sure I was available, you *kidnapped* Mac and had him imprisoned. What kind of monster does that?'

'Don't believe any of that, Liz.'

'Don't believe it?' She stared deeply into his eyes, and looked closely at every contour of his face. She no longer recognised him as the same person. 'Why me, Raf? Did you *select* me as the best female to give you a son... like selecting a thoroughbred mare for a stable?'

'I fell in love with you, Liz. Do not listen to any of these accusations. I will prove them wrong.'

'Are you delusional?'

They sat silently for a moment, watching one another.

'You need to stand by me, Liz.'

'I cannot believe I'm hearing this. You're a drug dealer, a kidnapper, a murderer.' She rose from the table. 'The divorce is underway, and I'll make sure it's as speedy as possible. And I don't think it's a good idea for you to *ever* have anything to do with your son. Luke doesn't deserve you for a father.'

She wasn't sure what she'd been expecting from Raf at this meeting. Anger, threats, turning the blame on her. Not this calm, reasonable, total denial. She was unnerved by the passive exterior he was projecting.

'Don't do this, Liz,' he said with a penetrating gaze.

'Goodbye, Raf.' She walked out without a backward glance.

SIXTY-SEVEN

Carl Vickerson strode into the office of a man he'd known for many years and who was now the editor of the highest circulating Sydney daily newspaper.

'How's my favourite Aussie Irishman?' Vickerson said.

'I've never been your favourite, but I am an Aussie Irishman, true blue.' The newsman shook Vickerson's hand vigorously. Paddy O'Brien was big-boned with piercing brown eyes, well-known for his dynamic handshake. He and Vickerson had always had a healthy rapport. 'Only time I ever see or hear from you freelancers is when you want to sell me a story.'

'And I've got the best one I've ever had.'

'Full o' crap.' O'Brien's laugh always sounded like it was coming through a bullhorn. 'You say the same thing every time you grace me with your oh-so-precious presence. I should reject your pitch based on that alone.'

'Don't reject this one,' Vickerson said, sliding into one of the visitor chairs as casually as if this was his own personal living space. 'It's linked to the major drug bust that's going down right now.'

'Already got my best people all over it,' said O'Brien. 'Why do I need a lowlife like you getting in on the act?'

'Same reason as always. I've got the best angle.'

'Which is?'

'One of the men arrested, Raf Vetrani, a millionaire businessman, is also linked to another case I'm about to break. And I'm the one breaking that story because I've got a personal link to it.'

'I'm listening,' the editor said.

'I've been investigating Vetrani ever since I found out he was involved in a major fraud and conspiracy. He had a fellow Australian imprisoned in Indonesia using forged documents and men posing as government officials. The man he had abducted is an airline pilot and will be known to most Australians because he was the star of an ad campaign that went viral eighteen months or so ago.'

'Who are we talking about?'

'Captain Mac.' Vetrani handed O'Brien a printout. 'Read this. First in a series of articles.'

O'Brien adjusted his reading glasses and looked over the copy.

> *The arrest this week of Sydney business identity Raf Vetrani, as part of a multi-million-dollar drug ring, is just the tip of the iceberg. Vetrani is also implicated in a wider series of crimes that may well be the most scandalous the harbour city has seen in over a decade.*
>
> *It involves the false imprisonment in Jakarta of media personality and pilot Callan McKenzie, better known as Captain Mac.*
>
> *The pilot was lured overseas by a phony text message supposedly from a former lover. He was allegedly detained there by Vetrani's henchmen, complete with stolen police uniforms.*
>
> *The reason for this remarkable plot? A beautiful and successful advertising and PR entrepreneur named Liz Carter, loved by both men and now the mother of Vetrani's son and heir.*

For Liz Carter it is a nightmare that's just beginning. For each of these three, and the others drawn in by Vetrani's web, it is an emotional tourniquet of deceit, heartache, and treachery.

I became a small part of this extraordinary series of events well over a year ago, when newspapers carried my story about how Captain Mac had fallen in love with an Indonesian girl. That romance happened long before the ad campaign, and was with a girl who subsequently vanished after the death of her father who was a suspected rebel sympathizer.

Perhaps Vetrani read that article. Perhaps he didn't. Either way, armed with the knowledge of Captain McKenzie's misfortune, he began to formulate his cruel plan...

O'Brien looked up from the printout, his gaze settling on Vickerson. 'And you've got more on this?'

'Loads. The very stuff your dreams are made of, Paddy.'

'We'll start running the series from the next edition,' the editor said.

SIXTY-EIGHT

Vickerson's articles were simply the beginnings of a mass media storm centred on the case against Raf Vetrani. Once again, Captain Mac was in the news. This time, Raf and Liz Vetrani were household names as well. To the media, Vetrani's drug ring arrest was of secondary interest, behind the more sensational story of his obsession for Liz, and his Byzantine plot to win her heart while she was led to believe her boyfriend had left her.

Liz had remained behind the doors of the Markham family's Bondi Beach home. She still had the babysitter, Connie, come by for a while each day, allowing her to spend some time dealing with the emotional fallout. She read the latest of Vickerson's articles online. As she did, she tried again to phone Mac as she had several times over the past week. She desperately wanted to know if he was handling the stunning revelations okay. It would have been a hell of a gut punch, learning the truth, just as it had been for her. Still no response. And Martin hadn't been able to raise him either.

The front doorbell rang and a moment later Connie called out, 'Liz, its Martin.'

'Send him through,' she called back from the study she'd now adopted as her own.

Martin walked in. 'Don't know if you've heard…?'

'Heard what?'

'It's just hit the news. Raf's out on bail.'

Liz's muscles tensed. 'How on earth could he get bail? With murder and drug charges like that?'

'As you're aware, the highest-profile criminal defence attorney in the country is in his corner. There are strict conditions. He can't travel or be involved with the company and he must stay at Bruno's place. The bail was set at two million and the family's got the funds to put it up.'

'Bruno put up the bail?'

'Yes.'

'Caterina will love that.'

Liz's phone buzzed. She glanced at the screen and saw it was Bruno.

She picked up the phone and swiped it. 'I just heard,' she said.

'Despite everything, Liz, he's my brother…'

'I understand, Bruno. Family. And if the courts accepted bail, then he's got to be put up somewhere and it sure as all hell can't be here with me.'

'That's part of the reason I agreed to this.'

'How's Caterina?'

'Not happy, but she's going along with it for now. But Raf's going to have to stay out of her way, in the spare room, and use the mini-kitchen at the back of the house, or... well, if he wants to stay here until the trial he's going to have to pull his head in.'

'Do you think he can do that?'

'Time will tell. But, Liz, so far he's... not the same old Raf. He's full of remorse, full of regret. And he's... scared.'

'How does he think Mac must've felt all that time in Jakarta?'

'I know.'

'Has Raf actually admitted anything to you?'

'No. He's barely been speaking... I've got to go but, Liz, I don't want this fallout with Raf to come between me and Caterina and you.'

'It won't.'

'You're important to us. We may not be doing the traditional Vetrani Saturdays anymore, but we'll be over for a visit soon. Promise.'

'Okay.'

Liz had no sooner put the phone down, when Connie appeared in the doorway. 'Liz...'

'What is it, Connie? Is Luke okay?'

'He's great. But you have another visitor. I just saw someone pull into the driveway.'

* * *

Liz sat tensely in her chair.

She could hear Mac's voice at the front of the house, conversing with Martin and Connie who had gone to see who was there. She'd wanted to see him, fantasized about sitting down with him and finding out how he'd been coping. And yet she was on edge. Nervous.

Then there was a light knock on the open door and Mac came through, looking more like his old self, ruggedly handsome, the gauntness gone from his cheeks, his eyes alive with hope instead of despair. 'Hi, Liz.'

'Hi, Mac.' She stood, and they embraced, awkwardly. 'So good to see you, I've been–'

'Calling, I know. I just wasn't ready to talk, so much going on, so much to take in…'

'So, how are you?'

'I'm good. Country air and flying little four-seaters has been a real tonic for me.'

'And now there's a resolution… to everything that happened to you.'

'Yeah.'

Liz cleared her throat. 'I'm so sorry…'

'None of it was your fault.'

'Mac, I'm so… ashamed.'

'Ashamed? Why?'

'For being sucked in by such a… con man. And for not waiting, not being there for you.'

'You thought I'd left you. No way for you to have known otherwise. No reason for you not to have moved on.'

'I fell for a monster.'

'Liz, you've no need to blame yourself. No need to feel shame. And while we're naming and shaming ourselves, I've got a confession of my own.'

'Oh?'

'I should never have gone tearing off like that because of a text, supposedly from Sari. I should've texted back that I couldn't help her. My place was here with you.'

'You couldn't turn your back on someone you knew who asked for your help – that's not you, and I would never want it to be.'

He reached across and held her hand and smiled and she felt the awkwardness fade away.

'I hear you're back on the singles market,' he said.

'I guess I am.' She returned the smile.

'Lucky coincidence. So am I.'

'I come with some baggage.'

'You're not talking about that little bundle of joy of yours, are you? Where is he? I'd love to meet him.'

'I meant my crime kingpin husband. But Luke?' She beamed at the thought of him. 'Afternoon nap. But he'll be up soon.'

'Perfect,' Mac said.

SIXTY-NINE

'I figured,' said Mac, 'that for a first date, after getting back together again, a traditional dinner, movie, walk by the harbour kind of thing wasn't going to cut it. Fine for a second date, but for the first, I think we need something to really blow the cobwebs away, put some distance between now and everything that's happened to us. Make sense?'

Liz linked her arm with his. 'Right now, *anything* you say is the only thing that does make sense.' They'd talked well into the night and now, sharing a bottle of wine, they were still sitting on the deck at the back of the Markham house. 'So, what are we talking?'

'You've been asking me what I've been doing all this time, so for our first reunion date, I figured, why not actually show you?'

'Meaning?'

'That part's a surprise.'

'When?'

'Saturday.'

'Done deal,' she said.

* * *

When Saturday came, they were blessed with great weekend weather. Sunny and breezy, with beach-day temperatures. Mac drove them into the country, west of Sydney, to a small private airfield, a great big multi-acreage of green field, adjacent to a skydiving school. He led Liz from the car and they tramped across the grass.

'There's nothing out here so where are we going?' Liz asked.

'Patience.'

'I'm intrigued,' she said.

She heard the plane before she saw it. At first it was a speck in the far sky, then before she knew it the four-seater Cessna was circling overhead, then swooping in, and coming in to land. A man stepped down from the cockpit and Mac introduced him as Jack Reynolds.

'All yours, lovebirds,' he said with a wide grin.

Liz looked at Mac with an enchanting smile. 'You're taking me flying?'

'Thought I'd show you what Jack's been teaching me.'

'You're in safe hands with this guy,' Reynolds told her. 'But I'd advise you to hang on tight all the same, eh?' He threw back his head and laughed.

Mac handed Reynolds the keys to his car. 'Go for a drive. See you back here in half an hour and you can have your plane back.'

Liz felt the thrill of exhilaration as the plane gained speed and lifted off the ground. The lush green fields fell away, and the switchback curve of roads, creeks and hills spread out below, a panorama that was eternally breathtaking no matter how many times you saw it.

'I've been teaching flying, but I've also been learning stunt flying. And I'm planning to enter myself into the next country air show.'

'Stunts?'

'Like this,' Mac said, eyes sparkling with mischief. He pulled the joystick up and banked the plane slowly to the right before launching into a sweeping arc across the sky. 'A little bit like a rollercoaster—'

'Wow!' said Liz.

'—but without the wheels.'

* * *

Mac had booked the two of them into a room at a nearby inn. They dined al fresco on the spacious terrace to the sounds of romantic instrumentals by a flamenco guitarist. There were several other couples there, enjoying quiet conversation.

'How did you find this place?' Liz asked.

'Would you believe that hard-bitten flying instructor friend of mine told me about it.'

'More to him than meets the eye.'

'I hope today wasn't too over the top, Liz,' Mac said. He raised his glass and touched hers with it. 'Cheers.'

'Are you kidding?' Liz said. 'It was fantastic. And would you believe my heart still seems to be thumping from it?'

'It's a different kind of adrenaline. It can last a while.'

Afterwards, they strolled alongside a river to the chirp of waterbirds. The clean country sky was full of stars and Liz felt a curious blend of calm crossed with the steady flow of excitement from the day's flight. The moment they returned to their room she stretched her arms up and wiggled out of the loose, long emerald dress she'd been wearing, undid the buttons of his shirt and peeled it away, melting into his arms.

'God, I've missed you,' she said. 'I was missing you even when I thought I wasn't missing you—'

He put his fingers to her lips. 'Shush. We agreed we won't talk about or even think about any of that. Not this weekend.'

She kissed him slowly, her fingers tracing the nape of his neck and the contours of his shoulders. 'It's as though none of that ever happened.'

'A bad dream. We got lost. Couldn't find each other.'

Liz felt the beat of her heart as she whispered in his ear. 'But you found me.'

* * *

Liz woke to the first rays of dawn light, which glistened off the billowing drapes of the open window. She eased herself off the bed, pulled a light gown over her naked body and padded into the kitchen. She was making coffee, with Mac stirring on the bed, when her phone rang.

This early? Who?

She answered it and her mood plummeted when she heard the voice on the other end of the line.

'Mrs Vetrani, Detective Inspector Ryan here. I'm afraid I have some bad news about your son.'

SEVENTY

Liz had barely been able to speak since receiving the call that morning.

Her mind had flashed back to the child kidnap attempt she'd witnessed years before, at Sydney Airport. She'd never been able to understand how any man could take a child, causing confusion and fear in his own flesh and blood, and unspeakable grief to a mother. After the call from Ryan, she and Mac had driven immediately back to Sydney and to the Markham house, where a wet-eyed Sally Markham had met them at the door, hugging Liz.

Like Liz, the babysitter, Connie, was barely able to talk. Suffering shock, she'd been sitting on the corner sofa, shivering, a blanket placed over her by Ryan's colleague, Detective Andrea Clifton.

'Connie woke early this morning,' Clifton said, 'and when she checked on Luke, she found his crib empty and the bedroom windows wide open. She went into a state of extreme shock but managed to knock on Sally's door. Sally made the call to report Luke missing.'

'So… so… sorry…' Connie said, teeth chattering.

Sally consoled her. 'It's not your fault, Connie.' She looked to Liz. 'I would've phoned you, but the police wanted to make–'

'You've done what you could, Sal,' Liz said, clearing her throat, finding her voice.

'I came the moment I got your call, Mac,' Martin said. He'd arrived earlier and had been doing his best to console Sally and Connie.

'Given the Federal case against your husband,' Craig Ryan said to Liz, 'when Sally Markham called the police to say your son was missing, she was patched straight through to us. And we immediately made enquiries about Raf to establish whether he was involved.'

'And he's not where he's supposed to be, at his brother's house?' said Mac.

'No. Bruno and Caterina Vetrani haven't seen him since last night. A search of the house and attempts to contact him by phone haven't located him.'

'Do you believe he's responsible for taking Luke?' Martin de Courcey asked.

'We've yet to establish for certain it was Raf Vetrani,' Detective Clifton said, tugging at the blonde bangs of her short haircut.

'It was Raf,' Liz said. 'I went to see him last week, before he was released on bail, and he tried to warn me. He told me, cold as ice, not to serve divorce papers, not to apply for full custody of Luke.'

'I phoned Bruno a short while ago,' Martin told them. 'He and Caterina are in a state of disbelief, they had no idea Raf might pull something like this.'

Sally could barely contain her frustration. 'He should never have been released.'

'I agree,' said Ryan, 'but the placebo pill evidence is circumstantial, and Raf claimed the imported drugs were planted on his boat. His attorney made a strong case for bail.'

Mac shook his head. 'It should never have been granted.'

'Couldn't agree more,' said Ryan.

'What's happening now, Inspector?' Martin asked.

'We have an APD out on Raf and a kidnapped child alert out on Luke. We're cross-referencing their descriptions against all travellers at airports, train stations, and bus terminals and anyone meeting either, or both descriptions, will be detained. And we're questioning Raf's co-conspirators in the drug ring for any clues on his whereabouts.'

'How could he travel out of the country when he's on bail?' Mac asked.

'We've no doubt his Calabrian drug connections could organise disguises and forged passports but we're on full alert for that,' Ryan said.

* * *

After the detectives had left, the time seemed to Liz to be at a standstill. Sally made endless cups of tea and coffee and brandished bottles of water, stubbies of beer and glasses of Scotch. Liz sipped on a Scotch, but her heart wasn't in it. She didn't want her mind impacted by alcohol as she waited for news.

It was late afternoon, the sun beginning its slow descent, when Bruno arrived at the house. He shook hands solemnly with Mac and Martin, nodded to the women, and apologised to Liz.

'I am so sorry Raf has acted like this,' he said. 'As parents, Caterina and I can't even begin to imagine what it's like to have your baby taken. We both feel like absolute fools... not knowing, not suspecting, not imagining anything like this.'

'You can't think like that,' Martin said. 'He fooled a lot of people, Bruno, including me.'

Liz embraced her brother-in-law. 'Thanks for coming over. I know it can't have been easy.'

'I came because I want to help,' Bruno said.

'It's pretty much a waiting game now,' Mac said.

'I don't believe it is,' Bruno replied.

'What do you mean?' Liz asked.

Bruno looked her in the eye. 'I think I know where Raf has taken Luke.'

SEVENTY-ONE

'Our father was a member of the Calabrian Club in Sydney,' Bruno said, 'and he signed up me and Raf once we were of age. I just thought it was a bit of fun, a chance to learn about the old country, and to network with Italian businessmen. I never imagined a few of them were actually involved with the mob or that Raf would become part of that.'

'What's this got to do with where you think Raf has gone?' Liz asked anxiously.

'Before we came to Australia, our father used to take us hunting in the woods, on the Aspromonte mountains, and there was a stone mountain hut, a *rifugio*, where we would stay overnight. One of the Calabrian Club members told us he had inherited one of these stone huts. He too used to be taken on hunting trips there when he was a boy, and a few years ago he took Raf with him for a holiday, just the two of them out in the wilds, hunting like they used to with their fathers. Raf loved it, said it was the one place where you could retreat from the world and make your plans. I couldn't go, Caterina was about to have Chloe, and one of us needed to be here, running the business.'

'And you think that's where he's gone?' said Mac.

'I'm sure of it.'

'Why?' Liz asked.

'It's the perfect hideaway. And no one else knows about it. I've since learned that area of southern Calabria has long been a stronghold of the Calabrian mafioso. They are known there as the *Ndrangheta*.'

'You need to tell the Feds about this,' Martin told Bruno.

'I have, and they'll interview the Calabrian Club member, and because he would never betray a fellow club "brother" he'll give them a decoy location, for another rifugio. That information will be passed on to the local *polizia* there, and they'll conduct a search, find nothing, but the wheels move slowly and that will all take time.'

Liz was holding her head in her hands, visibly shaking, Mac rubbing her shoulders to comfort her. 'So, what can we do?' she asked.

'I'm going over there to find Luke,' Bruno said.

'Bruno, you need to leave this to the police.' Martin had poured a Scotch and he handed it to Bruno.

'I won't be interfering with the police' – Bruno took the glass and cradled it in his hands, his eyes intense – 'but I can move faster than they can, and there's no law against me going into the Aspromonte woods. I will find Raf and Luke, and I will convince my brother to let me bring Luke home.'

'I'm going with you,' Liz said.

'Liz,' said Martin, 'you need to stay here and let the police handle the search.'

'I can't just sit here, waiting for a phone call. I need to be out there, looking for Luke.'

'Then we go together,' Mac said.

SEVENTY-TWO

Liz tilted her head back against the headrest of the seat as the 747 levelled out at forty thousand feet. She forced her mind to close out the memories of that childhood nightmare, of the curlew bird in the woods that sounded like a woman screaming.

It's as though I always knew that, one day, that woman would be me.

Bruno had already booked his flight to Italy when he'd stopped at the Markham house and revealed his thoughts on where he believed Raf had gone. His flight left early the following morning but Liz and Mac had been forced to wait for the first available seats on a flight the day after that. They stepped off the plane at Fiumicino Airport, jet lag descending.

Liz's nervous energy kicked in, spurring her on. 'Rome. I would have liked to see it under different circumstances.'

'One day we'll come back,' Mac said, 'and I'll show you the Rome everyone should see.'

There was a delay of more than a couple of hours before they could board the hour-and-ten-minute flight to Reggio Calabria, the closest airport to the Aspromonte National Park and its surrounding region.

'It's about an hour's drive out to meet Bruno in Taurianova,' Liz said, consulting the map on her iPhone, 'and from there we head off to this stone hut Bruno says is somewhere in the mountains.'

She tapped Bruno's number into her phone and moments later heard his voice.

'Bruno, we're still at least half a day away, where are you?'

'I've been checking out the roads leading into the mountains,' he said. 'I'm certain I've figured out the correct direction to find that rifugio.'

'How long will it take to get there?'

'I'm not sure exactly,' said Bruno. 'I've tried to describe the area to locals and they're guessing four or five hours, maybe more, maybe over a day. It's a remote spot, and it's rough terrain.'

'We don't even know for sure we're on the right track.'

'Some of the locals saw a man and a small child pass through the town.'

Liz felt a ray of hope, but it barely lasted a second. 'It will be dark soon. We won't be able to hire a car and reach Taurianova until tomorrow.'

'I know.'

'We've lost so much time—'

She felt Mac's hand on her arm. 'There might be another way to make sure we can drive out to Taurianova before dark,' he said.

SEVENTY-THREE

'Martin called me,' Mac told her. 'He's spoken with an air charter group here at the airport. We can hire a plane and I can fly us to Reggio Calabria.'

'Right now?'

'Right now. And he's arranging a hire car at the other end so we can drive into Taurianova before dark.'

The air charter manager escorted them from his office at the farthest end of the airport and across the small private tarmac. Mac smiled when he saw Liz's eyes widen as the charter came into view. The Piaggio Avanti II had a sleek design that looked as though it could lift up to the sky on a thought. It was made more striking by the twin turboprops that faced backwards at the rear of the plane.

'You don't need a co-pilot?' Liz asked Mac as he helped her into the seat beside him in the cockpit.

'The Avanti doesn't require a co-pilot or a crew,' Mac said.

The top-of-the-line instrumentation was something a pilot with his broad experience could master quickly. Within half an hour they'd taxied onto the runway. Liz held her breath as the small airplane accelerated rapidly, lifting off and climbing into the heavens.

Her thoughts were so full of her missing child, she was oblivious to the stunning views of crenelated peaks and thick forests of beech and pine that blanketed the valleys and cliffs below.

'It's somewhere out there that Mafia families were known to create strongholds,' Liz said.

Mac nodded. 'A place where anyone from their clans, on the run from the law, could easily disappear.'

'Which is why Raf chose it,' Liz said. 'But he is *not* going to disappear with *my* son.'

* * *

From the Reggio Calabria Airport, they drove for over an hour to the hamlet of Taurianova. It was twilight, the sun's rays filtering like mist through wooded hills of silver fir, black pine, and beech trees that were alive with birds and wildlife.

They met Bruno at a guesthouse where he'd arranged rooms. His face betrayed his tiredness, his eyes uncharacteristically puffy. In the courtyard outside the inn, after Mac had locked the vehicle, Bruno took Liz by the hand and pointed to the mountains.

'You see that peak?' he said.

Liz nodded, looking over the treetops, through the near-dark, at a mountain in the distance.

'That's Montalto, the highest mountain in the Aspromonte wilderness,' Bruno said. 'That's the direction my father took Raf and me when we went hunting. Going that way, I recognised the dirt track we used to turn into.'

'You're sure?' asked Liz.

'As certain as I can be, Liz.'

'Now you've established the area,' said Mac, 'have you told the *polizia*?'

'Yes.' Bruno frowned. 'They're checking out my information, but they're not convinced; not yet anyway.'

'What?' Liz said. 'Why?'

'They've checked the passenger flight records for any small children flying from Sydney to Rome,' Bruno said. 'There are several, always flying with two parents, and none of them have then flown on to Reggio Calabria. They have gone elsewhere. So, the *polizia* are looking into those passengers.'

'But Raf could have had a woman masquerading as Luke's mother, then he could have flown here in a private plane, like we did,' Liz said.

'Exactly. But there was no record of a private charter here.'

'That wouldn't pose a problem for a Calabrian crime family if they were helping Raf,' Mac said.

'It wouldn't faze them in the least,' Bruno said.

Liz had started pacing. 'God, I wish we could head up there now.'

'At first light,' Bruno said. 'I've hired a four-wheel drive and it's stocked and ready to go.'

Liz stopped pacing. She placed both hands on the bonnet of the car and leaned against it, stretching her legs, looking at both Mac and Bruno.

'You've both gone so far out of your way...' she said.

'We'd do anything for you, Liz,' said Bruno.

'We're here to get Luke home safely,' Mac said. 'And besides, as we all know, I've got a pretty strong reason of my own to see Raf brought to justice.' He moved forward, took Liz's hands in his. 'Right now, we have to get some sleep. We need to have our wits about us in the morning.' He looked to Bruno. 'Early start. 5 a.m.?'

'Yes,' Bruno said. 'We still have a long way to go.'

SEVENTY-FOUR

The roads were narrow and winding and overgrown. They'd been driving for four hours when the first powerful gusts of wind swept across the landscape, buffeting the four-wheel drive, and dropping branches and clouds of leaves across the road.

From the front passenger seat, Liz looked out the window in alarm. 'We don't need this.'

'Maybe we can use it to our advantage,' Bruno said. 'We don't know if there are mafioso members at the hut with Raf. We're heading into this blind. They won't necessarily be expecting anyone to find them, but if there's a storm, any protectors watching over Raf are more likely to stay inside, with limited visibility.'

'Enabling us to approach without being spotted,' said Mac.

'Potentially, yes.'

Ten minutes later Bruno turned onto another dirt track that forked from the road they'd been following.

'My father's old rifugio,' Bruno said as the shape of a stone dwelling loomed before them. It was at the end of the track and partially covered with forest growth.

'It looks like it's been deserted for a while,' Mac said.

The three of them stepped from the vehicle.

'Not so unusual,' said Bruno, 'if the current owners have fallen on hard times.'

He tinkered with the faulty lock on the front door and it opened easily. Then he went exploring. Minutes later Bruno came back from the shed at the rear of the rifugio, carrying a ladder.

'What now?' Liz asked.

Bruno scampered up the ladder and perched on the roof. He had binoculars in hand. 'If it's close enough, I'm pretty sure I'll be able to see the Calabrian's rifugio from up here.'

Another gust of wind rocked him, and Bruno held tightly to the side of the tin roof.

'Be careful!' Liz called up to him.

She stood back, tense, watching. She noticed Mac was away to her left, his phone pressed against his ear.

She walked across to him as he pocketed the phone. 'I didn't think there was coverage up here.'

'There isn't. That was a text and a voicemail message left early this morning, before we left the inn; before we were out of reach. I only just realised it was there.'

'Who was it?'

'Vickerson.'

'What did the great roving reporter have to say?'

'He's been snooping around the Feds investigation, he has a good inside contact there,' Mac said. 'Says he found out something unusual, that may be of interest. Wants me to call him.'

'But you can't call him from up here.'

'No.'

SEVENTY-FIVE

Bruno came down the ladder, gesturing east. 'It's closer than I thought. One kilometre.'

'We don't know for certain it's the right hut,' Mac said. 'There could be several scattered around the area.'

'That's true.' Bruno pulled the ladder down and lay it on the ground. 'You two wait inside, let me go and quietly check the place out' – he waved his binoculars – 'I won't get too close. Should be able to ascertain if it's Raf holed up over there. If it is, I'll try to make him see reason. I'm really the only one he's likely to listen to. Best he doesn't know the two of you are waiting back here. Okay?'

'How will we know what's going on?' Liz asked in desperation.

'You won't, not until I turn up back here with Luke. The little fella will be fine once he sees his mum, then we head back to Taurianova and tell the *polizia* where Raf is.'

Liz embraced her brother-in-law. 'You need to be careful, Bruno.'

'We're brothers. I'll talk him round.'

'If there are mafiosi with him…' Mac let the end of the sentence trail off.

'Then I won't approach. We go back and get the *polizia* first.'

They watched as Bruno pulled on wet weather gear he'd stored in the boot, then waved as he headed off into the woods. Liz looked skyward. The thick, dark clouds were rolling in. The wind was wild. She wrapped her arms around herself, shivering.

Mac took her hand. 'Let's get inside.'

Mac closed the old, creaky door behind them. Liz sat on the dusty, moth-eaten two-seater sofa. She was still shivering, but it was with the fear, the uncertainty, not the cold.

She looked at Mac who was standing by the window. 'You're wondering what it is Vickerson's thinking.'

'It's probably nothing,' he said.

SEVENTY-SIX

Liz felt she'd been sitting there, frozen, waiting, for hours when in fact it had only been twenty minutes when she heard the gunshot. The sound boomed from somewhere in the distance.

'Oh my God!' She and Mac raced out the front door.

The rain was beating down now, causing mist to rise off the forest ferns. The woods around them were awash. They looked for any sign of Bruno, listened for any other sounds but the roar of the rain drowned out everything else.

Mac put his hands on her shoulders. 'Liz, I'm going to head up the trail there, see if there's any sign of Bruno—'

'I'm coming with you.'

'No point us both going and getting drenched. I'm not going far, just up the trail to see if I can spot Bruno. In case he's hurt—'

'You think he's been shot?'

'Damned if I know what to think. I hope not. We just don't know who Raf might have with him at the rifugio. But we need to make sure Bruno's not lying hurt out there before we figure our next move.'

'We need to go back and get the *polizia*.'

'Yes.'

'This is all my fault.' Liz was shaking.

'No, Liz–'

'It was my crazy idea to come racing over here to look for Luke. I pushed you and Bruno into it when all the time we should've waited for the *polizia*.'

'Liz, just go inside, keep dry, and wait for me. I'm not going to be long. Okay?'

'Bruno had wet weather gear in the boot.'

They retrieved a parka from the vehicle and Mac pulled it on, the hood covering his head. Liz stood at the door, watching as he marched off, the rainy mist enveloping him.

SEVENTY-SEVEN

The sniper's orders had been clear. Gain a position high up a tree, within binocular range of the other rifugio, and wait. He would see the first man leave the hut and head towards his uncle's place. After twenty minutes, he was to fire a shot into the sky. This would lead the second man to leave the shelter, in search of the first, whilst the woman stayed behind.

It had played out exactly as he'd been told it would.

These past few years he'd taken on more and more of an active role in his uncle's mafioso operations. His uncle praised his nephew's shooting abilities, and had arranged training. This wasn't the first time he'd been enlisted to do a job because of his skill with the rifle.

He knew his uncle was protecting a man who ran the Australian side of their drug distribution business. What he didn't understand was why there was a baby with the man, why the sniper's sister had been ordered to care for the baby, or why he needed to target this second unarmed man who was now heading out from the rifugio. His uncle had made it clear he was a foot soldier. And soldiers follow orders. No need to concern himself with the reasoning. The strategy had already been worked out.

He watched through the telescopic lens of the rifle as the second man approached. He aimed the rifle, at the same time feeling the pressure against his side of the sat phone covered by his jacket. His orders were clear. Take him down.

Then, when the woman also left the shelter and headed towards his uncle's place, he was to use the sat phone and call the man who was giving the orders.

The kill shot requires intense focus and concentration, and for him, it was mingled not just with adrenaline but also an exhilarating sense of excitement.

His target came into focus.

The wooded hillside made this particular shot a challenge, further hampered by the wind and the rain.

The sniper tensed.

The man trudged through an area where the forest wasn't obstructing the sniper's view of him.

The sniper's finger rested on the trigger.

Just a little closer.

Now his target was clearly in frame, while still momentarily clear of the overhanging foliage.

Now.

The sniper's finger pulled back on the rifle's lever, the recoil was powerful, the shot rang out, and he saw his target spin and fall back to the ground then lie, unmoving, sprawled on the forest floor.

SEVENTY-EIGHT

The wind and the rain had stopped but there was a thunderous roar, like a plane flying low, interspersed with continuous booms. Something colliding? But what? This didn't sound like the storm. Luisa Toscano went to the window and her gaze was drawn immediately to the slopes of the mountain that rose above the surrounding forest. Enormous rocks were falling and rolling emitting clouds of debris.

She crossed herself. *Mother of God.* A landslide? It had been a violent storm and she'd grown up hearing stories from her grandfather of landslides, years before, in these mountains.

The roar was deafening. So close. And it wasn't stopping, if anything it was louder. And closer. Her brother was out there somewhere, with his gun. She wished they had not been called into service, on this occasion, by her uncle. She'd been tasked with looking after a child and following orders from the Australian man who was one of her uncle's drug ring connections. She did not want any part of her uncle's criminal activities, unlike her brother, who seemed to revel in becoming involved.

Was she safe here with the *bambino*? She'd been given no instructions on what to do in a situation like this. She'd been left with a satellite phone, for her employer to contact her. This area had no cell phone coverage. The sat phone lay silent on the table. She had no idea how to use it.

She'd been warned it was imperative no harm should come to the *bambino*, Luke. When he was awake the toddler had been a handful, crawling everywhere, constantly getting up on his feet, wobbling, walking then falling, snatching at everything. He'd been asleep but now the deafening roar woke him, and he began to cry.

We must get away from here.

Luisa took the baby in her arms, rocked him, and soothed him as she headed out the front door. She could see the larger, three-bedroom structure, further up the slope. The lights were blazing up there, but she'd been instructed not to approach.

She'd been told to stay hidden until contacted. There was no time now to go seeking further instructions. She could feel the spray of mud and stones and looking to the mountain she saw masses of rock and soil and trees toppling, cracking, and sliding like a flowing river, the ripple effect spreading across the mountain range.

She'd never seen anything like it before.

She placed the child in the passenger seat of the van – there was no child restraint in this vehicle – and she gunned the motor and began to drive up the steep driveway that ran alongside the higher rifugio.

The mountain looked like it was a living thing, groaning, breaking, and plummeting.

We must get away.

In that same moment, a chunk of boulder smashed into the windscreen. She heard both hers and Luke's screams as she lost control of the vehicle, careering off the track and down the slope. The foliage was sparser here and the car crashed through it.

SEVENTY-NINE

It happened in an instant, with no forewarning, a deafening sound that rang in Liz's ears, and then it was raining again, not water but columns of dirt and grassy soil.

Five minutes after Mac had left the rifugio, she'd heard the gunshot and she knew she couldn't wait any longer; no matter the danger, she had to follow. She'd donned one of the parkas but instinctively, she'd decided to go out the back door and into the forest. She then circled, under cover of the tree canopy, around the perimeter of the hut and in the direction Bruno and Mac had taken. If anyone was out there watching, she hoped by taking this action she wouldn't be spotted.

She'd been moving stealthily through the undergrowth for ten minutes, her heartbeat drumming in her ears, when the ground rocked, and a thunder-like roar boomed in the distance.

A ragged chunk of flying rock glanced off the side of her face. She felt the flow of blood and the throbbing pain as her cheek swelled. Liz put her arm up, a useless gesture to shield her from the falling debris. She glanced at the mountainside.

She could scarcely believe her eyes. Treetops flattened out as mounds of earth and forested slopes rolled down and over them like an enormous and unstoppable steamroller.

Not this. Not now. Please.

She ran forward, no attempt now to keep herself hidden from view. The downpour of small rocks lessened but the resounding crash of crumbling cliff echoed louder and louder. She saw the Calabrian's rifugio up ahead. Where was everyone? The rain came again. Biting, stinging, driven by sweeping gusts of wind. It was as though hell itself had rolled into the region on a stopover tour.

Why is this happening?

As she reached the front porch she saw the lights of a vehicle, shining through the dark haze created by the clouds of dirt. The car was coming from the rear of the property, up a steep side access road. A rock hit the windshield and Liz gasped as the car, wheels spinning, ran off the road.

She was about to run after it when she heard shouts from inside the shelter and saw the silhouettes of two men through a side window.

Bruno's voice. 'You didn't anticipate this, did you? Where is Luke?'

Mounds of dirt rained down on the hut and a large rock smashed into the side of the roof.

Liz burst through the front door and took in the scene before her; the two brothers, facing off against each other like two boxers in a ring, ready to throw punches. A section of roof had splintered and sagged under the weight of the fallen rock.

Liz saw the shoulder of Bruno's parka was torn.

Both men glared at Liz.

'He tried to shoot me,' Bruno said. 'And Mac's been gunned down.'

'God no,' Liz gasped, 'not Mac.'

'That's bullshit,' Raf said.

'Where is Luke?' Liz shouted at him. '*Where is my son?*'

Raf gestured to the chaos outside the window. 'We need to get out of here, that mountain is coming down.'

'There's another hut on this property, down the back,' Bruno said, seething. 'Is that where you're keeping Luke, in the care of one of your mafioso helpers?'

Raf exploded. 'I've only been here a few hours, I don't know anything about–'

'Bruno! A car from back there just went over the hillside. If Luke...' Liz's voice trailed off, her unspoken fear left hanging in the air. She raced out the front door, closely followed by Bruno.

Liz was aware, as she ran, that the rainfall was lighter now, and the sounds of the landslide had stopped. She and Bruno tramped down the hillside, through the undergrowth, sidestepping or climbing over chunks of rock.

Liz saw the van just ahead. It was partially covered by heavy branches.

Bruno grabbed her by the arm, pulling her back from racing forward.

'What–?'

'The car is tipping,' Bruno said. 'Something's wrong. We need to approach very carefully.'

They inched forward, just close enough to see there was a sudden, steep cliff; a sheer drop. The van had been halfway over the edge when it had come to a stop. It was teetering back and forth. They could just make out the head of a woman, slumped in the driver's seat.

'She was trying to outrun the landslide, with Luke…' The words trailed as a lump rose in Liz's throat. She swallowed hard. She saw the passenger side door was open. 'I've got to get him out.'

'Too unstable,' Bruno said, looking on in dismay. 'The whole thing will tip–'

'I have to try!'

She cautiously tested the ground with the toe of her right foot but as she did the soil beneath shifted and slid. There was the crack of a branch breaking free.

Once again, she felt Bruno's hand on her arm. 'Any slight movement…' He left the rest unsaid.

'If I can just reach in.'

'Liz, you'll both go over.'

'If Luke goes over, so do I–'

'Liz–'

Before either of them could say another word or make another move, the ground around them began to slide, the trees toppling as they slid with the soil.

Liz screamed out in anguish as the van bucked then disappeared over the side and into the abyss.

EIGHTY

Bruno held Liz tightly and scampered back up the slope, struggling against the moving land mass. He reached the road and as he looked desperately at the ground around them, the movement stopped again.

'Thank God,' he said, groaning, 'but it could start again at any moment, Liz. Totally unpredictable…'

Liz was hysterical, screaming out Luke's name, pulling against Bruno. '*Let me go!*'

'We have to get out of here, Liz, there's another four-wheel drive…'

A figure appeared out of the cloud of dust.

'Mac!' Bruno shouted.

'Raf took the other four-wheel drive that was around the side,' Mac said.

He rushed forward, talking Liz in his arms and for a moment she was still. She stared at him, as though uncomprehending.

Bruno pointed back the way they had originally come, to where the first rifugio stood. 'If we can make it back, on foot, to our own vehicle…'

'Help me with Liz,' Mac said.

'I thought you'd been shot,' said Bruno.

'So did I.' As he spoke, he lessened his grip on Liz and she broke free, pushing herself away, turning back towards the cliff.

'Liz!' Mac shouted after her.

'I need to save Luke,' she shouted as she ran.

'He was in the van that went over the cliff,' Bruno said to Mac as both men launched themselves after Liz.

They each grabbed hold of one of her arms, pulling her back from the edge as the ground beneath them shifted. She fought against them, shrieking.

Mac pulled her in close, held her tightly, his mouth against her ear. 'Liz, *please*, you can't do any more here, we *have* to go.'

'We need to move *now*,' Bruno said. He exchanged a glance with Liz, who had quietened again, her breathing raspy, her body shaking.

The men began moving back up the slope, maintaining their firm hold on Liz.

'You weren't shot?' Bruno asked Mac.

'I guess the heavy rain made things difficult. The shot knocked me off my feet, but it wasn't a direct hit' – Mac lifted his left shoulder where his parka was torn – 'it only grazed me–'

'The shooter's still out there?' Bruno said.

They'd reached the roadway at the top of the slope. The landslide had stopped.

'He's dead,' Mac said. 'I saw him. Debris must have hit him in the head. He fell from a tree.'

The dust drifted like a dark mist, the ground was misshapen, and there was now an eerie quiet across the landscape.

Liz was silent. Bruno noticed there was a glazed expression in her eyes, but he also sensed despite the turmoil that must've been in her mind, she was listening.

'This was the perfect place,' Mac said, breathing heavily from the exertion. 'Remote, with a mafioso network nearby to call on. *Except* – he held up his finger to make a point, sucking in a deep breath to control his anger – 'for the unpredictable.' He opened up the palm of his hand as he motioned to the mountain. 'If it hadn't been for the landslide, the woman watching over Luke wouldn't have fled, and her windshield wouldn't have been hit by that rock.'

'Raf would never have wanted this,' Bruno said, also gasping for breath. 'But, Mac, there'll be time for this later... the landslides could start again at any moment. Let's get back to our car.'

'We'll be safer,' Mac said.

'Yes.' Bruno's voice was a rasp.

'Except I won't be.'

Bruno met Mac's eyes. 'You said the sniper was dead.'

'He is.'

Bruno frowned, cocking his head to the side. 'You think there are others?'

'I went to the sniper's body,' Mac said, 'and found *this*.' He pulled a sat phone out from under his parka.

'Great, we can call for help,' Bruno said.

The ground beneath them rocked again and there was a rumble from the distance. A higher shelf of the mountain began to crumble.

Bruno reached for Liz. 'We're out of time.'

She swatted his hand away, turning back to face the slope from which they'd just come. 'Wait,' she said. 'Listen!'

* * *

Mac took hold of her arm. 'We need to run.'

'*Listen*,' Liz said again. She heard it again, the sound that had stopped her, and she saw the surprise register on Mac's face as he heard it also.

A child's wail.

A cry coming from further down the slope.

Shaking free of Mac, she ran back towards the cliff, oblivious to the danger. In just that instant, as she heard that wail, she was completely re-energised, alive with adrenaline, her motivation and all her hopes flooding back through her. Anything else happening was whisked from her thoughts, all that mattered was her son.

Luke?

Could it be?

Mac ran after her. 'Liz! Stop!'

'The passenger door was open,' Liz shouted back at him. 'If Luke was thrown out *before* the car hit the edge...'

Was it possible? Was she being rational? Or was she delusional, was the shriek something else that simply sounded like it could be a child? Just as the cry of the curlew sounded like the shriek of a woman. She came to a stop, listening intently, hoping against hope. Where was the cry coming from?

Silence.

There was no crying. She'd been mistaken after all.

Her heart sank.

Delusional.

Mac reached her. She stared into his eyes as though there could be some answer there. She was broken, ready to drop to her knees. What the hell did anything matter now?

The cry started up again and her heart leapt.

Mac pushed past. 'This way,' he said.

Then Liz saw her baby boy. Lying on his back on a thick sheaf of leaves, covered in mud and shards of branch, terrified, screaming. Liz snatched him up in her arms. 'Oh, dear God, thank you, *thank you.*'

There was an ear-splitting crash. Liz and Mac looked back up the hill as a wall of earth slammed into the remains of the hut. Like something alien, the fragments of forest and rock sluiced across the road towards them.

There was nowhere to turn, nowhere to run.

EIGHTY-ONE

The sliding ground came to a stop again. Positioning himself behind Liz as she held Luke close, Mac manoeuvred them sideways, across the slope to a point further along where the rise met with the twisting road.

'Give him to me,' Mac said, easing Luke from her grasp. 'Now follow me and run!'

They'd no sooner scampered along the slope, up the rise and back onto the road, when the earth shifted again. The rocks and crushed trees rolled down over the side of the cliff with a deafening roar.

They didn't look back. They ran as fast as they could.

Then the mountain was silent again.

After a while, their run slowed to a brisk walk.

'I think the worst of it's over,' Mac said, in between heavy breaths.

Liz didn't respond at first, her head was spinning, her focus was on the ground beneath to ensure she didn't fall. She was consumed with a newfound strength, beaming inside that both her son and Mac were alive, but fearful at the same time they weren't out of danger. And where was Bruno? Had he managed to run free of the landslide or was he buried somewhere back there? Her pulse pounded in her temples.

In the distance, through the haze, they saw the outline of the rifugio.

'Mac,' Liz said, 'what on earth was all that back there about the sat phone… are there other snipers?'

'Sorry, but I didn't tell you everything in the text message from Vickerson,' Mac said. 'I needed some time to digest.'

She stopped walking, catching her breath, and looked at Mac. 'Digest what?'

He turned to face her. 'The Feds' analysis showed Raf's signature on those documents had been forged, just as *your* signature had been.'

'That's what Vickerson wanted you to call him about?'

'Yes.'

'But they don't know who *did* forge those signatures?'

'Not yet. But it means it wasn't Raf who shipped those drugs or arranged my imprisonment.'

She simply stared back at him, speechless. How could this be even remotely possible? She resumed walking, Mac falling into step beside her.

As they reached the hut, they saw that neither the four-wheel drive Raf had sped away in, nor the vehicle Mac, Liz and Bruno had originally arrived in, were there.

'Someone else's been here ahead of us and taken off,' Mac said. 'Let's get Luke inside and see if we can dry off.' He brandished the sat phone. 'And we can call for help.'

The wind had died but the rain still came in random bursts. They reached the front door and Mac handed a weary Luke over to Liz. He swung the door open then stood aside for Liz to go through first. As he did, he caught a glimpse of movement from the side of the building.

A dishevelled Bruno came limping around. 'Thank God you made it. And with Luke…' He bent over, catching his breath, then straightened. 'I got clear of the rocks but couldn't see where you were…' He stepped toward Mac, reaching for the sat phone. 'We can call for help.'

Mac remained motionless.

He glanced over at Liz. 'When I found the sniper's body, on an impulse I called the last number the sat phone had rung,' he said. 'A voice came on the line and said "Is it done?" so' – he reverted his attention to Bruno – 'I adopted a gruff tone and said "Yes."'

As shaken and distraught as she was, Liz was staring intently at Mac.

'Mac?' she said.

Bruno reached out his hand again. 'Mac, we really need to call for help.'

'It wasn't Raf's voice on the line,' said Mac, his voice rising. 'Just as it wasn't Raf who ordered those pills or forged those signatures.'

Mac stepped forward, pushing Bruno back and grabbing him by the lapel of his parka, simultaneously tearing at the zip. The gap where the zip had been torn revealed another sat phone. '*You* answered that call.'

Bruno pulled free and moved away. 'That's crazy talk…'

There was a rumble in the distance and the ground shook again, a signal from the mountain that it hadn't finished venting its rage.

Bruno turned and ran back around the side of the rifugio.

Liz's eyes were fixed on Mac. 'Bruno wouldn't–'

'Stay right where you are, both of you.' Bruno reappeared from around the side.

Instinctively pulling Luke in tighter to her breast, Liz looked around and froze.

Bruno was aiming a rifle at Mac. 'First mistake was finding that phone and hitting redial,' Bruno said. 'Second mistake was leaving this weapon with the sniper's body.'

Liz stared at him in disbelief. '*Bruno?* What–'

'Throw the sat phone over here,' Bruno said.

'For God's sake, Bruno–' Mac began.

'Throw it,' Bruno said again, focusing the rifle closer on Mac.

Liz felt her heart thumping and an ache drumming in her head. She barely recognised the man facing them. This wasn't the Bruno Vetrani she'd known so well for so long. There was a deep sorrow in his eyes, his expression one of despair.

Mac threw the sat phone towards Bruno and it landed on the ground at his feet. Bruno picked it up and shoved it under his parka.

'The four-wheel drive is hidden around the back,' Bruno said. 'Liz, bring Luke, get in the car. There's a duffel bag with Luke's clothes in the back.'

'No, Bruno.'

Bruno lifted the rifle higher, square with Mac's head. 'Get in the car or I'll fire.'

'You're not a killer, Bruno. You won't shoot.' Even as she spoke Liz watched Bruno's finger tighten on the trigger. She saw tears in the corners of his eyes.

His voice was shaking. 'Don't make me do this.'

Liz held her son tightly against her chest. 'Okay.' She glanced helplessly at Mac as she moved towards the side of the hut.

'Stay,' said Mac. 'He won't fire that thing.'

The expression Liz shot back made it clear she wasn't taking any chances. She no longer knew how to read this. Bruno wasn't acting anything like himself. He was out of control. Raf had fled, leaving them all behind when the landslide had hit. No one else knew exactly where they were. She was going to have to go along with this.

Minutes later Luke was strapped into the baby seat in the back of the vehicle and Bruno was in the front passenger seat, the rifle propped up beside him. Liz was behind the wheel.

'Drive,' he said.

With no sat phone and no vehicle, an exhausted Mac watched as the four-wheel drive pulled out and headed off, down the mountain, on the road back to Taurianova.

EIGHTY-TWO

An inner voice whispered to Liz. Stay calm. For Luke's sake. For all your sakes. Try to make sense of all this.

As she drove, Bruno wiped tears from his eyes, and Liz noted he was jerking his head about, looking at her, glancing out at the landscape as it flashed by, as though unseen terrors were lying in wait.

He's on the edge of desperation.

'What is happening?' she asked him, keeping her voice low.

Stay calm.

'Raf never loved you,' Bruno said. 'You were the latest in a long list of playthings. And now, of course, he's abandoned you again, saved himself, left you and Luke and me to the mercy of the landslide.'

'I know...'

'But I was there for you, as always.'

'Yes, you were. But, Bruno, what's this all about? When Mac found the sniper's phone and redialled, *you* had your own sat phone, *you* answered, and you held a rifle on Mac, *a rifle for God's sake*. Why?'

'Mac's no good for you either. Man-about-town airline pilot, probably has a woman in every city–'

'He's not like that.'

'I may have done a few underhanded things but it's only because I was looking out for you, Liz.'

'Underhanded things?'

'But you were never meant to know.' His voice dripped with anguish. 'It was never meant to be like this.'

'What wasn't I meant to know?'

'The damn storm then the landslide, couldn't have predicted... ruined everything. The babysitter taking off and going over that cliff... Mac finding that phone, redialling...' He was rambling.

'You sent Raf here, on his own, didn't you?' Liz said. 'So he could avoid trial back in Sydney, escape, lay low here while he planned a new life. But he didn't kidnap Luke, did he? You had Luke taken and brought here and looked after by that woman in the adjacent hut.' Realisation dawned on Liz. 'It was you who theorised Raf had come here, to these mountains, but of course you knew all along for certain because you sent him here.'

'I never wanted it to go like this.' Bruno's voice was a croak.

'You brought me here, so I'd believe it was Raf who'd kidnapped Luke and so that... what? You could be seen finding Luke and reuniting us?'

'Just drive,' he said.

'Bruno?' Liz's voice rose as the full impact of Bruno's betrayal slowly unravelled. None of this made sense.

Stay calm, she reminded herself.

'Just drive,' Bruno said again with the tone of a man on the edge.

EIGHTY-THREE

In the early hours of the morning, as they reached Taurianova, Bruno directed Liz to turn off and follow a road that led to a large country house. 'My contacts have made this house available to us for a few days,' Bruno said as Liz pulled up in the wide driveway that circled the house in a loop.

'Your contacts,' Liz said. 'It wasn't Raf with mafioso contacts here in Calabria. It was you?'

Bruno didn't respond as he stepped from the vehicle, motioning for Liz to do the same and to gather up the sleeping Luke. A middle-aged woman, with silver streaks through her dark flowing hair, ushered them into the house. Liz tucked Luke into a single bed in one of the rooms then returned to the main living area. She was aware there was a man outside – a guard? A lookout? The woman brought steaming hot bowls of soup, placed them on the long wooden dining table, then left.

'There's a change of clothes—' Bruno began but she cut across him.

'I don't care, Bruno.'

She was shivering. She sat and spooned up some of the soup, staring at this man whom she no longer knew or understood. She was struggling to believe any of this was real. At the same time, there was a strong inner resolve reminding her no matter how confused or angry or fearful she was, it was essential to remain calm and in control. She had to think of Luke, in the other room. And of Mac, stranded up there on the mountain.

Bruno was standing by the far wall. Awkward, restless, silent.

'Eat some soup,' Liz said.

He went to the table, pulled out a chair and sat.

Liz saw he was shaking. 'Won't Caterina and your daughter be wondering where you are?'

'Caterina thinks I'm away on business.'

'Caterina doesn't know about any of this?' Liz watched him closely as she took intermittent mouthfuls of the soup.

'Caterina and I have been leading separate lives for a long time,' Bruno said. 'The Saturday get-togethers have been to keep up appearances, and to keep in touch with yourself and other friends.'

'So, it's all been a façade?'

'To an extent. There'd been indiscretions, on both our parts.'

Liz thought of the list Monica Leeman had given her. 'Caterina and Raf?'

'You knew?'

'Monica gave me a list of Raf's supposed conquests.'

'Ah, Monica…' Bruno picked up a spoon and toyed with the soup. Liz noticed he seemed calmer. 'I'm asking you to give this a chance,' he said.

Liz fixed him with an unrelenting stare. 'I don't need to give anything a chance, Bruno. I need to know what's been going on, what this is all about. I thought you were my friend.'

'I am.'

'Then how could you be a part of any of this?'

There was a long silence.

Liz waited.

Finally, Bruno said, 'From the moment we had our first meeting – you and I and Raf – I fell in love with you, Liz.'

'You?'

'I did not want this, did not want you to think of me in this way… I'm so sorry.'

'Sorry? Sorry there was a landslide and Mac survived your sniper, so that I've found out the truth.'

'Liz, there's so much you don't understand.'

'Make me understand.' Her voice had risen in anger again. She took a deep breath. *Stay calm.* 'You owe me that.'

Bruno's shoulders slumped, as though in acceptance he had to come clean. 'I've always been the one in Raf's shadow,' he said. 'Raf the perfect son. Yes, he slept with my wife. My own brother.'

He paused, and Liz sensed he was searching his mind for the right words.

'And yes, I knew,' he said. 'Monica sent me the same list, long ago. She was always trying to sabotage Raf, always trying to drive a wedge between us. I pretended I didn't know, for the sake of our daughter, for the sake of the firm. I played the dutiful husband, but I wanted out. I played the reliable business partner, always Raf's second in charge, but I wanted so much more…'

Another long pause. Liz looked at him in disgust, wanting to scream but biting her tongue.

'I fell in love with you the moment we met,' Bruno found his voice again. 'It felt deeper than anything I'd ever known. But of course, you were with the great Captain Mac. Then Raf tells me he's smitten with you and knows in his heart he must be with you. Another one of his fantasies; I've seen them so many times over the years, Liz. And of course, the great golden boy always gets what he wants. I knew he'd find a way to win you away from Mac. He didn't deserve you. Neither of them did.'

'What gives you the right–'

Bruno cut across her, lost now in his own story. 'I decided to test fate. Carl Vickerson's news story gave me the perfect way to see if Mac could be removed from the scene. I sent him the fake text, and if he hadn't gone charging off to this exotic love of his from the past, none of this would have happened. I would've left it at that. But he did. That's how I knew he didn't deserve you, and that I did.'

His mood was changing rapidly. This was the side Liz had never seen. She'd heard of "quiet" borderline personality disorder – not all such conditions were in your face – but this had to be an extreme version of something like that, didn't it? A deluded mind in turmoil, kept hidden from all around. Until now. Going to extreme lengths to pursue an obsession.

'I used all the resources of the drug ring to have him imprisoned, knowing Raf would step in and win you,' he said. 'I didn't have any way to stop that, but I also knew it wouldn't last, so I used it to my advantage, made sure I was the one you could count on as a friend, the one who was always there for you.'

'So, you and I could be together once Raf eventually split from me?'

'Yes.'

Liz thought back. It wasn't Raf who'd been with her when she gave birth to Luke. It was Bruno. When she'd split from Raf, it was Bruno who picked her up from the airport.

How could I not have seen it?

Her spoon dropped with a clatter.

Bruno didn't notice. 'Of course, I couldn't keep Mac detained forever, and I had to make sure you wouldn't get back with him. So, I switched out the birth control pills, so you'd be pregnant when Mac was back–'

'What? Oh my God, Bruno.'

'It sounds awful, I know. But, Liz, please understand, I did this for you and me.'

'There is no *you* and *me*!' Liz sobbed, the enormity of Bruno's warped mind and betrayal engulfing her.

'I didn't anticipate that Raf would've eloped with you anyway,' Bruno said.

'And then you contrived the fake police raid enabling Mac to escape,' Liz said.

'There was never any intent to harm him, Liz. But no, I didn't enable his escape.'

'Then who…?'

'I don't know. He would have been released eventually, of course, but he was freed too soon; that wasn't part of my plan at that point.'

'Do you even hear what you're saying?' She looked down and saw her hands were shaking, the full extent of Bruno's cruelty resonating, her jumble of thoughts so loud in her head she wasn't even sure if she was saying them aloud.

'I didn't want you to know any of this, Liz, but… if you could *just understand–*'

Liz ignored his pitiful plea. 'So, what was ultimately intended? You would fraudulently expose Raf as having been the one who abducted Mac then Luke, so you could save the day and I would fall lovingly into your arms?'

'I know it all seems crazy right now but, Liz–'

'It doesn't *seem* crazy, Bruno, it *is* – it's totally insane.' The time for Rational Liz is over, she thought.

Forget calm.

'I'm taking Luke, *now*, and I'm leaving.' She headed for the bedroom but Bruno's voice, like chilled ice, stopped her.

'I have friends standing watch outside, Liz. You can't leave.'

Liz had witnessed Bruno's anger on display when she'd been at his home and overheard his phone call with Raf. She recalled Caterina's words. "He bottles it all up inside. Puts on a brave face." But it wasn't a brave face. It was a mask.

She whirled towards him. 'Are Luke and I your prisoners now? Like Mac was in Indonesia?'

Bruno gestured frantically as he responded, showing the depth of his anguish. 'It's the last thing I wanted. We should've been returning to Sydney, together–'

'To live happily ever after as you assumed full control of the company?' Liz screamed the words at him, her eyes flashing with rage.

'I can't have you blurting out what's happened here, so it's just for a while, Liz, until you've settled down, until we can get past this together.'

Liz seethed. 'We're not getting past this; do you *get* that?' She marched into the bedroom, nestled Luke in her arms, then headed for the front door. 'And stay out of my way,' she said to Bruno through gritted teeth.

'You're not leaving.'

'What are you going to do? Shoot me? Shoot Luke?'

'The men outside won't let you pass. They'll take Luke from you, and they'll block you from going anywhere. Please, Liz, don't make this harder than it already is. We need time, I'm sure of that, we just need time.'

'Don't you dare try to stop me,' she shouted.

She got to the front door and was reaching for it with her free hand when it was flung open. One of the men, rifle in hand, stood there, every nerve and muscle tensed and primed.

His eyes bore into her as he raised his weapon.

EIGHTY-FOUR

'If I need to use this to wound you then I will,' the man said. There was no emotion in his eyes or his voice. Just a vacant sociopathic stare.

Liz didn't reply.

Does Bruno even have the control over these people he thinks he does?

She returned the sleeping Luke to the bedroom, then stepped back into the main living area.

'Okay,' she said to Bruno. 'You win. At least let me retrieve that bag of Luke's clothes from the car.' She pushed forward, past the armed guard, and Bruno nodded to the man to let her pass.

There were two other men outside. More than she'd realized. As she reached into the back of the car, while the men watched her intently from the doorway, her eye caught a flash of colour between the front passenger seat and the door. She squinted and saw it was one of the sat phones. She realised it must have slipped from underneath Bruno's parka as he got out of the car and he hadn't noticed. As she partly entered the back seat, clutching hold of the duffel bag, she covertly slid her hand along, grabbing hold of the phone, and pushing it into the bag.

I pray that creep didn't see me do that.

Holding the bag innocently by her side, Liz trudged back into the house. She didn't make eye contact with the guard. Walking through the front door, she observed a second man around the right corner of the house.

She threw the bag into the bedroom and turned to face Bruno.

'It's best I go back home,' he said. 'And that we have some distance, so you can take all this in.'

'Running away?'

'No. Just giving you some space, and I'll be back, maybe in a week or so, and we can try to talk through all this.'

Liz couldn't hide her cynicism. 'Sounds great. Bring some wine.'

Bruno stared at her, despair in his eyes. 'I hope in time, Liz—'

'No, never.' She brushed a strand of wet hair away from her face, and then she placed her hands on the back of a chair, to steady herself. She thought her anger had beaten her nerves, but she was shaking again. 'Were you the one who had Monica feed me all that poison on Raf?'

'Anonymously. She never knew the details were being sent to her by me… Monica was easy to manipulate… she hated Raf; his doing, not mine.'

'And her father's death? The pills?'

'When Raf first started seeing Monica, I knew he'd tire of her, but at the same time, I needed him to stay with her, marry her, to give the two of us time to gain a foothold in the Leeman company. I hit on the idea of manufacturing those placebos.'

'But Monica didn't get pregnant.'

'No, but it didn't matter, Raf stayed with her long enough anyway, married her–'

'Long enough to swap fake heart pills so her father died and Raf, as Monica's husband, inherited a half share in the bulk of the company stocks.'

'I'm not proud of any of it, Liz. But Raf was a wild card, a great salesman, yes, but he burned every bridge he crossed. We never would've achieved anything, got hold of any of the companies, without my planning behind the scenes.'

'I've been so blind…' Liz took deep breaths. She needed to keep her wits about her.

'I wish I could hold you, make you see it will all be okay.'

'Don't you come anywhere near me.' Liz gripped the back of the chair tighter. 'You weren't really very successful at all, were you, despite the murder and despite forcibly taking control of Leeman's business? You were funding everything you and Raf did with drug money. And even that hasn't been successful. The Feds have been tracking your activities for years and now they've pounced.'

Bruno spread his hands. 'I know what you're trying to do. Insult me so I'll get angry and hate you. I could never hate you, Liz. I want only the best for you, for us.'

'But you're happy enough to keep me imprisoned here while Raf is on the run for your crimes.'

'I never wanted that to happen, but I had to be prepared for any eventuality.'

'By having everything you ever did, in case it was exposed, set to implicate Raf, not you. You forged his signature on documents, masqueraded as him on phone calls and emails, used his boat and his crew on the Hawkesbury to collect and transfer the shipments.' Liz could see the hurt on his face.

Bruno headed for the door. 'It's best I go for now.'

'You can't leave Mac stranded up there.'

'The emergency services are heading up the mountain, to assess damage from the landslide and check for any injured or stranded locals. They'll find Mac.'

'And he'll tell them everything he knows.'

'What does he know? That I had a sat phone and was in touch with a mafioso sniper? There's no proof it was me and everyone believes Raf was behind all this, even that ace journo Vickerson. And Raf's fled. My friends here have already sent men to remove the sniper's body so there's no proof any of it happened. And they will back me up, suggesting Mac's been mentally affected by the landslide and by losing you, that we all believe you and Luke were in that car that went over the cliff. They'll find its ruins, and the driver, and the open doors will suggest you and the boy were thrown clear.'

'And they'll never find our bodies.'

'If you can find it within yourself to accept me, Liz, and I hope in time, love me, for all I've done for us, then we can start new lives, with new identities, anywhere we wish.'

'And what about your daughter?'

'I'll bring her with us.'

Liz had heard enough. 'Just go, and don't come back,' she said in defiance.

She watched as he walked out. The house guard out front, a large, bearded bear of a man, slammed the door closed.

Then she heard the click as the door locked.

EIGHTY-FIVE

The woman with the silver streaks emerged from the kitchen. She hadn't introduced herself before and she didn't on this occasion either. She held up a small electronic unit that fitted neatly in her palm.

'I've been told to press this panic button if I even suspect you're up to something or if you wander out of bounds. It will send my colleagues rushing in.' She gestured to the kitchen. 'You're free to use the kitchen, bathroom, living room, and the first two bedrooms along the hall. Do not move anywhere else in the house and do not give me reason to get suspicious. The men outside are stationed at the front and the rear, and they will get nervous if they even spy you near one of the windows. Understood?'

'Understood,' Liz said. She looked at the woman with curiosity. 'You know who I am. Who are you?'

'You can call me *La Vipera*.'

'Viper?'

'Trust me, you don't want to find out.'

Liz could tell from the scorn on the woman's face she was never going to reveal her real name.

The woman returned to the breakfast bar in the kitchen, where she remained perched most of the time, browsing magazines.

Liz looked in on Luke who thankfully was still sleeping soundly. The poor child was exhausted. She sat on the edge of the bed, watching him.

Thank God, my boy is safe and unharmed.

Liz didn't know much about satellite phones, but she did remember Mac saying you usually needed to be out in the open, with a clear sky overhead, to send and receive calls.

How am I going to manage that?

Her mind flashed over everything Bruno had said.

He was obsessed with her and she'd never even remotely suspected it. But then neither, apparently, had Raf or Caterina.

He'd said Mac would be found by the emergency services but if the mafioso found Mac before the emergency services reached him, why not correct the first sniper's failure, and finish the job?

Bruno was humouring me.

She went to the window, making certain she was hidden by the heavy drapes, and peered through the gap. The window looked out on the side of the house. She couldn't see the front, but the angle of the side wall was such she could see just a fraction of the front corner. The rear of the four-wheel drive jutted into view there and she could see Bruno standing beside it, talking animatedly on his sat phone, hands gesticulating wildly and pointing back in the direction from which they'd come.

The first faint ray of dawn was filtering down through the top of the woods.

Bruno was issuing commands.

He's going to have Mac killed, Liz thought.

EIGHTY-SIX

She had to get free of the house, so she could use the sat phone before Bruno discovered it was missing. She took the phone from the duffel bag and rammed it in the waistband of her hiking pants. She picked Luke up and as gently as she could she placed him on the floor, under the bed, out of view.

This isn't going to work if he wakes up.

She went back into the first bedroom – her room – drew back the drapes, picked up the chair in the corner of the room, and smashed it with all her might into the windowpane. That would bring the woman and the two men running and it was imperative they believed she and Luke had fled out that side window.

She stepped into the closet, pulling the door closed behind her, and positioned herself behind the hanging clothes. The bedroom door flung open and she heard her three watchers push in.

'Check for the boy,' the woman said.

'He's not in the bed!' one of the men shouted seconds later.

'No one in the other rooms,' called the second guard.

'Get them!' the woman shouted back.

The three of them rushed outside, heading off from the side and spreading out. Liz crept from the cupboard and slipped out the back, running in the opposite direction and into the woods. She'd heard Luke cry as she went, and it broke her heart, but she had to close her mind to her little boy's terror.

She had to raise the alarm.

She wasn't sure what number would get her through to the local authorities or to emergency operators. She knew Martin de Courcey's number, so she punched in the numbers, hoping, praying, he would answer regardless of the time back in Australia.

She felt like yelling out in triumph when his voice came on the line.

'Martin,' she spoke rapidly, 'I'm being held captive and Mac's in danger. You need to get in touch with the Calabrian *polizia* and–'

'Liz, where are you?'

'Somewhere on the outskirts of Taurianova. And Mac's in a hut on the Aspromonte mountains… Bruno's sent gunmen…'

'Bruno?'

'Yes.'

'Liz, leave the line open. I've got the sat phone number showing, I'll see if the *polizia* there can trace your location–'

'Okay,' she said, 'but I've got to go…'

She wedged the phone in a branch of the nearest tree, where it was obscured from view by leaves, and she crept back towards the house. When she saw one of the men she raced out of hiding, waving at him.

I need to be returned to the house without them suspecting what I've done.

'I'm sorry…' she called out. 'I'm coming back.'

She put her hands in the air and walked towards him. The other house guard and the Calabrian woman came running, surrounding her.

'I'm sorry,' Liz said. 'I must've gone mental… running off, without Luke…'

'Where's the boy?' the woman asked.

'Still in the house… under the bed.'

'Bruno told me you're not to be hurt,' the woman said, 'but I don't always follow orders.' Her right hand rose high and she slapped Liz across the face so hard that Liz toppled backwards, losing her footing, and hitting the ground. 'You try a stunt like that again and I'll tear you apart with my bare hands.'

EIGHTY-SEVEN

Luke had crawled out from under the bed and was sitting in the middle of the floor. He'd found his dummy and was contentedly sucking on it.

Liz took him in her arms. 'Good boy,' she whispered in his ear. 'Mummy's going to get us out of here.'

Morning light was flooding the kitchen as she began preparing breakfast, Luke still in her arms. She heard tyres on the gravel outside and a moment later Bruno came in the front door and into the living room, flanked by the two guards. The Calabrian woman was seated there, and she stood, curious, as Bruno entered.

'Why are you back here?' she asked.

Liz went through to the room. 'Bruno?'

'One of the sat phones is missing,' Bruno said. He faced Liz. 'You found the phone in the four-wheel drive.'

'No.'

'I got a message you tried to escape…'

'It was a mistake, Bruno. I… I went a little crazy…'

'Smashed one of the bedroom windows,' the Calabrian said.

'You would never try to run and leave Luke behind, no matter what,' Bruno said to Liz.

'What are you getting at?' one of the guards asked.

Bruno's gaze was still on Liz. 'You ran out there to get a clear signal for the sat phone,' he said. 'There's no other reason…'

'That explains why suddenly she came back, pretending to be sorry,' said the woman.

'I wasn't pretending,' Liz said.

'Where's the phone?' Bruno asked.

'I don't have the phone, Bruno.'

'Good God, if she got a message through and the line's still open…' *La Vipera* didn't need to complete the thought.

'We need to move to another location, just in case.' Bruno turned to the Italian woman. 'Your father has arranged one of your uncle's houses, on the opposite end of the town.'

'I know the house.'

Liz played for time. 'Bruno, I've thought this through and I'm not going to say anything to the authorities.'

'You expect us to believe that.' The Calabrian woman rolled her eyes.

'Bruno,' Liz continued, 'you said yourself there's no proof tying you to any of this. Raf's out there, on the run, believed responsible for everything. Neither Mac nor I have any physical evidence—'

Bruno stared at her. 'That doesn't mean—'

'Hear me out. I don't want to spend the rest of my life looking over my shoulder, fearing retribution from these mafioso families. And I'd never, ever expose Luke to that kind of threat. You know that.'

'So, what would you do?' Bruno asked.

'She's lying,' the mafioso woman said.

'We return to Sydney,' said Liz, 'and resume our lives, just as they were, but without Raf. You run the company. We put this behind us, Bruno, and we go back to the way we were, *friends*, with our Saturday get-togethers with you and Caterina.'

Liz saw the glimmer of hope in his eyes.

If he was so obsessed with her then, like a drowning man, he might clutch at straws. That was what she was counting on. Would he jump at the chance their "friendship" could develop into something more?

'Don't listen to her,' the woman said.

'I want to believe you,' Bruno said to Liz, 'but I need time, we both need time, and we all need to move from this location.' He turned to the other woman. 'You take your cousins in your car and I'll follow in the four-wheel drive, with Liz and Luke—'

The woman cut him off sharply. 'No. She can't be trusted, and our family cannot take the chance she'll run, and contact the *polizia*…'

Damn, thought Liz.

'We play it safe for now,' the woman said. 'You will take Luke and one of my cousins with you.' She glanced at one of the men. 'You go with Bruno, you know the way.'

'Okay,' he said.

'I will take Liz,' the woman said to Bruno. 'This way we ensure she won't try anything. We will meet you at the new house. The cars need to travel separately so we don't attract any undue attention.'

'An added precaution,' one of the cousins said.

Liz had caught the furtive expressions that passed between *La Vipera* and her two cousins. Bruno wasn't in charge of this situation. The woman was. Her family of criminals had agreed to help their Australian drug counterpart. But just as they hadn't addressed one another by their names in front of Liz, neither would they risk exposure to the police through Bruno's actions.

'They're going to kill me,' Liz said to Bruno.

'Just follow my orders,' the woman said to Bruno, 'and everything will be fine, everything will be okay, and once the heat is off, then you and your lady friend can go home safely.'

Bruno stared at her, unsure.

'Trust me,' the woman said. 'Our family knows how to contain troubles like these.'

'Okay...' Bruno said.

'Bruno, *no*.' Liz stepped back, shielding Luke, as the two men moved towards her.

'These people are my colleagues, they've been helping me all along,' Bruno said to her. 'Everything will be fine. And you and Luke and I can go back to Sydney, together.'

Liz froze as one of the men took Luke from her. She didn't want to frighten her son.

'Mama...' he cried out as he was taken by the man.

'It's okay, baby,' Liz called after him, forcing a smile.

Bruno reached across and stroked Luke's cheek. 'Hey, Luke. Uncle Bruno's here.'

The baby boy calmed at the sight of a face he knew.

Minutes after Bruno had driven off, La Vipera and two of her cousins bundled Liz into their sedan. Despairingly, Liz glanced at the woods as the car sped off. Once her rescuers reached the house she would be long gone. At the mercy of this ruthless couple who intended to kill her.

EIGHTY-EIGHT

The car was driven off the road and along a stony track to a secluded patch of forest. The man pushed open the door and shoved Liz out, keeping his grip on her.

'Take her into the woods,' the Calabrian woman said.

'Bruno won't forgive you for this,' Liz shouted at her.

'He will have to live with it. Bruno is a fool who allowed his obsession to cloud his judgement. My father should never have helped him with his ill-conceived kidnap. Now it's exposed our family, and I need to clean this mess up.' The woman shot a glance at her cousin. 'No time for any of your *fun*,' she said to him with contempt. 'Make it quick and make certain she won't be found. Your cousin and I will keep watch.'

'Got it,' he said, pushing Liz ahead of him into the woods.

She stumbled along, the ground rough beneath her feet, her legs wobbly, the fear weighing down on her. 'Please…' she began but she said no more. What was the point? This brute had shown no emotion from the time she'd arrived at the house the night before; if anything she'd only noticed him staring at her with a cold, callous lust.

They reached an area that was partly clear of the trees, littered with bushes and broken stumps and clumps of long grass. He pushed her free of him then he stood back, lifting his rifle.

She turned to face him, trembling.

He leered at her and there was a half-grin on his lips. 'You're a beautiful woman but you're not worth Vetrani's level of obsession.' He waved the rifle, motioning to the large, rounded tree stump in the clearing.

'Strip off and bend over that stump,' he said.

'What?'

'Do it.'

'Your cousin said none of your *fun*,' Liz said.

'She'll be none the wiser.'

'She'll think you're taking too long.'

'We'll be quick.'

He stepped forward and slammed the butt of the rifle into her left shoulder. She toppled back, gripping her shoulder as the pain exploded.

'Next blow will be to the side of that pretty face,' the brute said. 'You can do this in agony or you can make it painless.'

Liz swallowed hard, trying to fight off the pure terror she felt. She sucked in a breath. Her hands shaking, she removed the parka, pulled her blouse up and over her head, then stepped out of her hiking pants and boots.

'Everything,' he said.

Tears in her eyes, breathing heavily, she removed her underwear.

'Bend,' he said.

Liz turned to the tree stump, stumbled forward, and bent herself over its flat surface.

The tears impaired her vision. How had it come to this? A pathetic, degrading death, at the hands of a stranger, in a country far from home. She would never see her baby son again, never see him grow, never know the comfort of Mac's arms embracing her.

She sensed the presence of the man. He'd stepped up right behind her now. She heard his trousers unzipping.

She stared intently at the ground in front. There was a shape there, and squinting through the tears, she saw it was a broken branch limb, with a narrow, spiked end. The tears dried, her vision came sharply into focus, and she felt a sudden surge of adrenaline, of anger, of the will to fight back.

She felt the brute's hands grip her thighs, lifting her from behind.

She reached forward, grabbed hold of one end of the branch and in one rapid movement she swung her body around, raising the branch, and drove its spiked end into the man's throat.

He reared back, a distorted scream escaping his mouth as he dropped onto his back, his body convulsing and blood shooting like a geyser from the wound.

Liz watched in horror.

Is he dying? Have I killed a man?

She pulled herself quickly out of her shock. In its place anger rose, fuelling her will to survive. 'Who's the fool with the obsession now?' she said to the man's twitching body, her voice ragged.

Instinctively she knew she had to act fast. *La Vipera* would have heard the man's scream. Liz heard the rustle of someone tramping hurriedly through the foliage, approaching. Oblivious to the pain in her shoulder, she pulled on her underclothes, and looked around for her boots but couldn't see where they were. Clutching her hiking pants and blouse, and the branch, she ran deeper into the forest.

She'd been given the chance to live. She had to survive. For Luke. For Mac.

I have to outrun that viperous bitch and her cousin.

She could hear the crashing sounds of her pursuers as they trampled through the foliage, hot on her trail. A vulture took wing from a low-hanging branch as she raced into the clearing beneath it. She fell, gouging her knee, but pushed on, disorientated, gasping for every breath, heart pumping.

She fell again, her ankle twisting on a stone, and she lay on the forest floor, the pain in her ankle making her fear she'd sprained it.

The rustle in the woods was much louder now and she caught a fleeting glimpse through the towering pines of the man and woman hunting her. Only minutes now before they were upon her. She wanted to scream in anguish, images of Luke and Mac and a lost life with them filling her vision.

There was a sudden movement behind her. She whipped her head around, startled by the sight of a deer, curious, cautious, watching her. Then, after just a few seconds, it took off, darting away in a different direction.

Still on the ground, Liz crawled into a thick tangle of shrubs, hoping they were deep enough to cover her. If she remained deathly still and the woman and her cousin didn't see her, Liz hoped they'd follow the sounds of the fleeing deer, thinking it was her.

Less than a minute passed and Liz heard them, frantically rushing by, alarmingly close, and then veering off in the direction the deer had taken.

After a while, certain the sounds of her pursuers had faded, she rose unsteadily to her feet. Her ankle was still painful but thankfully, not sprained. She headed off, treading lightly at first, in a different direction, eventually starting to sprint.

She wasn't sure for how long or how far she ran. Time had no meaning. The forest flashing by around her was a blur, with strong rays of the sun shining off the sea of green, the birds in the treetops twittering madly as though to encourage her escape. Eventually she dropped to her knees, wheezing for breath. She wasn't sure when she'd dropped her hiking pants and blouse, but she was still clutching the branch. Her whole body was covered in scratches and welts.

She listened intently but still didn't hear anyone following. She readjusted her bra. She rested for a while, her eyes continually scanning the forest like a hunted animal. Her mouth was dry, she needed water, and focusing her hearing on all the sounds of the forest she heard the trickle of a creek. She moved towards the sound and presently came to a narrow, rippling stream.

She scooped up handfuls of the fresh water and drank greedily, feeling the liquid's invigorating power, then she was on her feet again, refreshed, running. When she broke through the bushes and onto a wide country road she felt as though she'd single-handedly discovered El Dorado.

She had no idea which direction to take, or how long it might be before a car came along. She started walking towards the sun. Every muscle ached, then as she marched tiredly, losing speed, her knees sagging, she heard the mechanical hum in the air, faint at first, then very quickly thunderous and she saw a couple of choppers flying overhead.

The emergency rescue crews, heading to the Aspromonte landslide.

She ran to the middle of the road and began leaping up and down, frantically waving her arms and signalling with the bloodied branch that had saved her life.

EIGHTY-NINE

Of all the moments from the past few days, the one Liz would recall the most, calling it forth so she could make sense of everything, was the moment of her reunion with Luke. Her baby boy squealed with delight when he saw her, wriggling free of the policewoman who was minding him, and running forward with those lovable, uneven steps of his, into the arms of his mother. She held him close, then lifted him up and whirled him around as he giggled. Mac completed the picture, embracing the two of them.

They'd arrived at the police station minutes before, with Liz becoming conscious of the press entourage that milled about on the exterior steps that led to the front foyer. In particular she noticed Carl Vickerson, interviewing police officers, taking notes, shooting photos.

'He's got his big story,' she said to Mac.

'He always does.'

'We're going to be plastered all over the news back home.'

Mac shrugged. 'It will die down when the next big story breaks. You once told me that.'

When the rescue helicopter had picked Liz up earlier that day, she'd babbled her story incoherently.

The rescue team had been on their way to the mountain, and when they landed at the old Vetrani rifugio, Mac had sighted them from his hiding spot in the woods, and come running.

The open sat phone line which led authorities to the house in Taurianova, enabled the *polizia* to be granted warrants to raid all properties owned by members of the same family – the Margoli clan. It was at one of those homes they'd liberated Luke and arrested Bruno along with *La Vipera* and one of her cousins.

The Margoli woman had left her other cousin at the local hospital. He was in a serious condition but would recover from the injury Liz had inflicted.

Liz had breathed a sigh of relief at that news. 'Thank God,' she said to Mac. 'I didn't want to kill the man.'

'Of course you didn't,' Mac said. 'He's alive and now he can pay for attempted murder, behind bars.' It angered him and sent chills through his body when he thought of how close Liz had been to assault and death.

When the helicopter crew delivered Liz and Mac to the police station in Reggio Calabria, the two of them had been interviewed by detectives. This was the law enforcement team who'd been investigating the Margoli family for several years. Now that they'd been able to raid the family's homes, the *polizia* had uncovered incriminating evidence of the drug ring.

'This is a family with its fingers in a network of national and international crimes,' the lead detective had said to Liz and Mac. 'It's all going to come crashing down now.'

Liz and Mac were told that until advised otherwise by the courts, Raf was still in custody. He'd been transferred to Rome, then flown back home. They learned, when Raf had fled the landslide, he'd turned himself in to the *polizia* at Reggio Calabria, declaring his innocence.

His testimony, together with the testimonies of Liz and Mac, confirmed Bruno as the kidnapper.

In their hotel room that evening, Liz's first call was to Martin, back in Sydney. His quick action in contacting the Italian authorities had saved the day.

'If Bruno had fled with Luke before the police raid,' Liz said to Martin, 'I might've lost him forever.' The thought still terrified her.

As always, Martin was the voice of reason and calm. 'That's all in the past now. You and Luke and Mac are together. That's the future and that's all that matters.'

That night, she drifted to sleep in Mac's arms, with Luke sleeping in a rented cot beside their bed.

The comfort and the exhaustion didn't stop her waking with a start in the middle of the night, crying out, sweat on her brow, her mind awash with that terrifying moment in the woods, stripped naked, seconds from rape, minutes from death.

NINETY

The following morning, the hotel's cable TV enabled them to access the BBC. It carried a feed from the Australian news reports.

'In an extraordinary turn of events' – the male newsreader's deep voice was accompanied by footage of Raf, flanked by police, coming through the terminal at Kingsford Smith International – 'flamboyant entrepreneur Raf Vetrani has returned to Australia. All charges against Vetrani are expected to be dropped, while his brother Bruno, arrested in the Calabrian district in Southern Italy, has been charged with those same offences. Joining us now is our financial correspondent...'

An image flashed on the screen of Bruno, hands in cuffs, being led away by police. He looked like a stranger to Liz, a man she didn't know. Another image flashed, this time of Bruno with his wife and daughter. Liz felt a great weight of sadness in her heart for Caterina and Chloe...

'With its assets seized, finances frozen, and shares hitting rock bottom,' the financial reporter said as he appeared on screen, 'Vetrani Investments is unlikely to see out the week while the future of Raf Vetrani remains unclear. Whilst it's believed he'll be cleared on the major charges, Raf Vetrani is also under investigation for a series of lesser fraudulent dealings. The bigger story, behind all this, is that Bruno Vetrani engineered a series of abductions, of his brother's wife and baby son, and of celebrity airline pilot Captain Mac. His various other deceits include the murder of businessman Warren Leeman. To fill us in on those details, we cross now, live, to correspondent Carl Vickerson, in Reggio Calabria.'

* * *

Later that morning, at the Reggio Calabria Airport, Mac took their baggage to the check-in desk. As he stood at the counter, a young man of Indonesian appearance approached. There was a brief exchange, then the young man walked away just as quickly. Mac called after him, but the young man simply waved, with a polite smile, then was gone, his figure disappearing into the crowd.

Liz was nearby, at the cafe, with a restless Luke squirming in her arms. She watched as the young man walked away, Mac looking after him. From her line of sight, she hadn't been able to see everything, then the terminal loudspeaker boomed into life, calling their flight to Rome.

∗ ∗ ∗

Walking back towards Liz and Luke, Mac pulled a letter from the envelope the young Indonesian had given him.

His eyes scanned the handwritten note.

> *Mac,*
>
> *My very good friend,*
>
> *Sometimes I wake up in the middle of the night in a cold sweat. I have pangs of regret for the decision I made so long ago now.*
>
> *I loved you, Callan McKenzie.*
>
> *But I also love my country. I've had a passion, ever since I was a young girl, to fight for the rights of those who are wronged. There are many wrongs here, some because of corruption at high levels.*
>
> *My father and I shared this belief. My father's cargo business and contacts made it possible for him to play a small part in the struggle.*
>
> *As you know, that didn't stop the cold-blooded murder of my father by corrupt forces.*
>
> *I knew I could not honour my father without taking up the cause he believed in. They call us rebels, but it is an important fight. We strive to have the true voice of the poor heard.*
>
> *This cause has its own problems and I needed to help to change that.*
>
> *I could not drag you into this new world. I knew, in my heart, I had to let you go. The only way to do this was to simply vanish.*

* * *

As the plane taxied along the runway, Mac reached
across in his seat, placing his hand over Liz's. 'I've got a
confession to make.'

Liz arched her eyebrow. 'I'm past the point where
anything could surprise me.'

'When we get to Rome, we're not switching to a flight
to Sydney.'

'We're not?'

'Remember I said one day I'd show you Rome?'

'Of course I remember.'

'Now's as good a time as ever.'

'You'll show me and Luke the sights?'

'The Colosseum, the Fountain of Trevi, the Sistine
Chapel.'

'All the usual suspects.'

'And a few that aren't so usual.' He squeezed her hand
and she squeezed back.

'There *is* something we haven't discussed…' she began.

'Which is?'

'Being Luke's father, Raf is going to be in the
picture…'

'I've got a feeling Raf isn't going to be around as much
as you think.'

'Maybe not, but even so…'

'We'll deal with it,' Mac said.

She tingled all over as Mac touched her cheek lightly
then traced his finger gently down to her jawline.

'Who was that young guy at the airport?' she asked.

Mac pulled the envelope from his pocket. 'He'd been
sent to give me a letter. Seems there's a group of people
who've been keeping an eye on me.'

'A group of people?'

'Remember you told me Bruno said he *hadn't* arranged for my escape from the Jakarta house?'

'It was this group of people?'

'An underground network. They knew when I arrived in Jakarta and they knew when I went missing, although they didn't know why I was there nor what had happened to me. It took them a while, but they eventually found out I was imprisoned, and they mounted a raid, impersonating POLRI.'

'And they removed the bodies and cleaned the whole place up as though nothing had ever happened?'

'Seems so.'

'That Indonesian guy told you this?'

'Not in as many words… more of a hint.' Mac handed her the letter.

Liz unfolded the sheet of paper and began to read.

> *…hardest thing I have ever done. It ripped my heart to pieces and I know it caused you great heartache.*
>
> *But I knew, in time, you would find a new life and a new love.*
>
> *As for me, these years have been hard but there has been some good also. I have a partner, a good man, as passionate as I am about our cause.*
>
> *But I still have those moments, in the middle of the night, and I relive the pain of my decision.*
>
> *I pray you are able to forgive me. You are a good soul but we are from very different worlds.*
>
> *When my people told me of your return; that you had come to Jakarta and had disappeared, we searched for you.*
>
> *Because your abductors were not the Indonesian authorities but instead a private criminal group, it took us much longer to find you than I'd hoped.*
>
> *We knew, after our raid, that the criminal group would clean up the mess and that they wouldn't contact the POLRI. We left you to make your own way out – not wanting to risk the government linking*

Liz refolded the letter and handed it back to Mac. Her eyes met his and she smiled. Luke squirmed in the baby seat alongside her and she kissed his forehead.

Then she pulled Mac towards her, hugging him, gripping his hand tightly, embracing his strength, his warmth. The plane began its descent and the two of them gazed out the window as the magnificent city below came into view.

* * *

A week later, on their last night in Rome, Liz woke in fright to the sound of an eerie wail and she sat up, heart pumping. It couldn't be a curlew. Not here. Was it Luke, crying out? She listened intently but there was nothing but silence.

Mac, still asleep, shifted in the bed beside her. Liz slipped out from under the sheet and padded her way into the next room, where Luke was fast asleep. She stood for a moment and watched the peaceful rise and fall of his tiny chest.

She calmed her breathing. She didn't think she would be able to get back to sleep, not right away. She went onto the balcony and leaned against the railing. There was a full moon and its luminescence shimmered across the tops of the trees.

This was the second time this week that she'd had bad dreams and woken to the scream in her head. It was a balmy night and she let the touch of the gentle breeze soothe her. Somewhere, deep in the woods on the other side of the world, she imagined that a lone curlew cried out, heard by no one. There was a part of her that suspected the nightmares would always come when she least expected them. She could only hope that, in time, those horrors would fade deeper into the distance, like the cry of that solitary bird.

THE END

If you enjoyed this book, please let others know by leaving
a quick review on Amazon. Also, if you spot anything
untoward in the paperback, get in touch. We strive for the
best quality and appreciate reader feedback.

editor@thebookfolks.com

www.thebookfolks.com

THE PIPER'S CHILDREN

The first book in an FBI mystery series

A boy is found wandering in the woods, dressed in medieval clothes and speaking a strange language. When another child turns up, it doesn't shed any more light on the mystery for FBI agent Ilona Farris. Only by digging into her own past will she begin to work out what is going on, and who these children are, seemingly lost in time.

FREE with Kindle Unlimited and available in paperback!

THE WHISTLER'S OMEN (Book 2)

Special FBI agent Ilona Farris faces a problem when a man is murdered in Seattle: the victim was meant to have died in a plane crash twenty years previously. Worse, spotted by the scene is a man dressed in a straw hat and long coat who rumour claims is the legendary El Silbón, a lost soul that stalks the living. Finding out the truth will be tough and perilous.

THE STORM KILLINGS (Book 3)

As tornado season gets under way, the FBI's advanced computer system highlights an anomaly in the casualties. It looks like someone is using the chaos caused by the weather as cover to kill unsuspecting women in their homes. Special Agent Ilona Farris heads into the eye of the storm to catch them in the act.

Other titles of interest

LIBERATION DAY by Pippa McCathie

Having become stranded in the English Channel after commandeering her cheating boyfriend's boat, Caro is rescued by a handsome stranger. But when the boat is impounded on suspicion of smuggling, she once again finds herself in deep water.

FREE with Kindle Unlimited and available in paperback!

AN EARLY GRAVE by Robert McCracken

A tough young Detective Inspector encounters a reclusive man who claims he holds the secret to a murder case. But he also has a dangerous agenda. Will DI Tara Grogan take the bait?

FREE with Kindle Unlimited and available in paperback!

Sign up to our mailing list to find out about new releases
and special offers!

www.thebookfolks.com